The
Importance
of Being
Scandalous

A TALE OF
TWO SISTERS

The Importance of Being Scandalous

KIMBERLY BELL

Entangled Publishing, LLC
2614 South Timberline Road
Suite 109
Fort Collins, CO 80525

Entangled Select is an imprint of Entangled Publishing, LLC.

Visit our website at www.entangledpublishing.com.

Edited by Kate Brauning
Cover design by Erin Dameron-Hill
Interior design by Toni Kerr

ISBN: 9781633756793
Ebook ISBN: 9781633756809

Manufactured in the United States of America

First Edition July 2017

10 9 8 7 6 5 4 3 2 1

To the boy next door. And to sisters, both frustrating and irreplaceable.

Chapter One

The long driveway hadn't changed at all. As the carriage rolled toward the towering exterior of Nicholas's parents' country home, the last two years dissolved under its austere presence. The dutiful second son was returning home from time spent abroad, and everything would be exactly as before. Why did the thought irritate him?

The entire household was arrayed to greet him. Nicholas's parents hadn't changed, either, but he hadn't expected them to. Their rigid postures greeted him with timeless familiarity. Lord and Lady Wakefield had dedicated their entire lives to presenting the stolid, dignified air of respectable English nobility. Returning home to find them changed…now, that would have been truly unsettling.

Nicholas waited for the footman to open the door. Haste was for the unmannered and the imprudent.

He stepped down from the carriage, stopping in front of his parents to deliver a formal bow to each in turn. "Lord Wakefield, Lady Wakefield."

"It is lovely to see you again, Nicholas." It was the

equivalent of an emotional outburst, coming from his mother.

He was careful not to let his smile cross into unseemly joy. "And you as well, Mother."

Formalities observed, there wasn't much else to say. Nicholas followed his parents up the steps, through the grand double doors, and into the foyer. Smithson took his hat and gloves with an echoing sameness. No, nothing had changed at all.

Nothing except Nicholas.

At the foot of the grand staircase, his mother stopped. "Tea will be served in the south drawing room, after you are settled."

Nicholas nodded. "Of course. I won't be long."

He didn't take the stairs two at a time. That would have raised eyebrows.

A wash basin was waiting in his room. He used it as an excuse to strip off his morning coat and waistcoat. The starchy cravat landed on top of them on the four-poster bed as he rolled his shirt sleeves up. It was only after he pushed the window up in the casement, letting in the cool Berkshire breeze, and sprawled out in the armchair beside it, that he truly could breathe.

Home. It was supposed to fill one with a sense of comfort and nostalgia, wasn't it? Instead, the cold formality of this house filled Nicholas with a longing to be somewhere else. If anyone asked—not that anyone would—Nicholas could claim he was missing the winding streets of Paris or breathtaking frescos of Rome.

In reality, his longing had only ever led him to one place: the estate hidden behind the tree line that separated Wakefield lands from their nearest neighbor.

France and Italy had been fine distractions, but still,

always, his thoughts returned to the Bishop family home, and to one Bishop in particular. Amelia might have remained in England, but her specter had walked every step of the Avenue des Champs-Élysées at his side. Even a construct of his imagination was better than being without her—even if it was equally incapable of returning his affections.

"Lord Nicholas?"

"Come in, Bertram."

The arrival of his valet, and the accompanying footmen with their luggage, marked the end of his musings. Once Bertram had the first trunk opened, Nick pulled two packages off the top of the neatly folded clothes. The first was a stack of letters.

During school, Nick had developed a habit of writing to Amelia every day. He'd tried to when he was away this time, but the romance of Paris had seeped into his words and he hadn't had the courage to send them to her. He tucked them away in a drawer of the desk that sat in the corner of his room. Better to wait until he could be sure they would be well received. And he would be sure. Being away from Amelia for so long…

He went back to the window, staring at the tree line. In Paris, he'd discovered what was important to him. More than his parents' approval, more than the fear that Amelia wouldn't feel the same for him, he needed to declare himself and find out once and for all if she felt the same.

The second package might help his cause. Nicholas picked up the slim book with its unassuming blue cover. It was a first edition collection of sonnets on love that defied distance and time. The little shop he'd found it in would have made Amelia dizzy with excitement if she had been there.

"Shall I lay out a new shirt, sir?"

"Better make it a full change, Bertie."

Looking his best for his visit to the Bishop household would help quell the nervousness that had taken up residence under his skin at the thought of seeing Amelia again.

Although, he'd have to spend some time with his parents first. They were expecting him for tea and he was once again ensconced in Wakefield Manor, monument of familial responsibility. The freedom he'd found during his absence had made him see things differently. For a time, he wasn't just a second son, subject to the whims of his parents and elder sibling. For a time, he'd been able to live the way he wanted (within reason) without anyone frowning their disapproval over the breakfast table. It had been glorious.

Now he'd been summoned back. After the first year passed with no such request, Nicholas had begun to doubt it would ever come. Perhaps they'd forgotten about him. Perhaps they'd been as relieved to have him go as he was to be gone. While the second thought had come with an unexpected sting, it had quickly dissipated under the joyful possibility that his bohemian holiday might be permanent.

The letter had not explained why he was being asked to return. For all Nicholas knew, they could be commissioning him to the army or commending him to the clergy, though he strongly doubted it. No Wakefield—even a second son Wakefield—need do something as vulgar as taking on a profession.

"Ready, Lord Nicholas?"

"Not in the slightest, but I have every faith I will look impeccable for whatever awaits me." Nicholas slid the book into the inside pocket of his jacket and went down.

He took the grand staircase back to the ground floor and made his way to the south drawing room. It overlooked the large manicured lawn that dominated the southern end of the grounds, which ended at the tree line. The Bishop estate was completely hidden from view—a deliberate work of the last nineteen years, tirelessly undertaken by the grounds crew under the direction of Lady Wakefield.

When his mother saw the direction of his glance, her mouth tightened. His father observed very little except the pages of the periodical his face was hidden behind.

"Markets treating you well, Lord Wakefield?" Nicholas sat down in the wingback chair that matched his father's.

"Fine, fine."

They lapsed into silence, broken only by the clinking of teacups and his mother's politely innocuous commentary. Eventually, though, they had no choice but to come to the point.

"Your father's not well."

At first, he thought he misheard. Nicholas's parents had both always been in the peak of health. A Wakefield would never be so inconsiderate as to be burdensome. "Excuse me?"

His father appeared to agree. Lord Wakefield set down his paper and frowned at his wife. "Lavinia."

"No, Arthur. You agreed to bring him home. It's time to tell him."

Lord Wakefield sighed. "It's nothing, really. I'm not infirm. I just—"

"He forgets things," Lady Wakefield said bluntly. "And he has trouble making decisions."

Nicholas froze, still holding his teacup. Lord Wakefield was a force to be reckoned with. Always certain, always in control. "Surely there is some mistake. Perhaps you're just tired."

Lord Wakefield shook his head. "I don't like it any more than you do, but what your mother says is true."

He couldn't wrap his head around it. "For how long?"

"About a year." Lord Wakefield was unable to meet his

son's eyes. "It's getting worse."

A year. And they hadn't said a word.

"Does Philip know?" His older brother hadn't said anything when Nick had stopped over in London on his way to the estate.

"We didn't want to worry him." Lady Wakefield's spine was as rigid as ever. "He's extremely busy with his work in the House of Lords. His reputation is becoming quite prestigious."

Ah, prestige. Nicholas set his teacup down. The furthering of the Wakefield legacy could not be compromised for something as silly as informing the Marquess's heir that his father was slowly losing his mind.

His own presence at their ancestral seat suddenly acquired extreme clarity. He had not been called back for any sentimental reason. He was to be a replacement. "You mean for me to be Philip's proxy until you're ready to tell him."

"Yes."

The old wounds cracked open. His very existence was a redundancy. An heir and a spare. He had been conceived as a contingency plan in case something happened to his brother. Or, apparently, in case his brother was just busy. But along with the old pain came the corresponding complication. Nicholas cared.

The respect his brother had earned in the House of Lords was a credit to Philip's intelligence and integrity. It was exactly what Philip had hoped for as a boy and he was accomplishing it. Nicholas didn't want to interfere with that. And Nick cared about the estate. Hundreds of tenants relied on them and the Wakefield family had made good on that trust for generations.

He cared about his parents, who sat across from him and calmly prepared for their world to fall apart. If he turned out half as strong someday, he would count himself a success. "Why didn't you call me back sooner?"

It was Lady Wakefield's turn to avoid meeting his eyes. "We thought it would pass, and…"

"And it took a long time for me to admit that it wasn't going to."

Nicholas wanted to comfort his father somehow, but they weren't that kind of family.

Silence descended again until his mother broke it with the conversational equivalent of a cannon volley. "Amelia Bishop is engaged."

Just like that, the same way she'd mention how pleasant the weather had been.

Lord Wakefield scowled at his wife, reverting to the relative peace of *The Morning Post*.

A sharp pain started up in Nicholas's chest. "I hadn't heard." If he had, he wouldn't have spent his entire trip home planning out how to tell her he loved her. Amelia was engaged. Amelia was *engaged*.

Lady Wakefield made a neutral humming sound. "To Lord Montrose. It was quite surprising."

"Not that surprising," Lord Wakefield said from behind the paper. "Lady Amelia's dowry could finance an empire. Some people are swayed by that sort of thing."

"Still."

Still, no one respectable should be associating themselves with the tainted Bishop family. That was the rest of what his mother wanted to say but wouldn't, because it was neither proper nor would it end well. Nicholas had placidly adhered to the expectation that he be agreeable at all times, on all subjects, except one—the ostracizing of the Bishop family from polite society.

The sheer proximity of their estates was enough to send Lady Wakefield into a torrent of sniffs and non-committal humming sounds. If Wakefield Manor hadn't been the ancestral seat of the title, Nicholas had no doubt she would have forced his father to sell it long ago and moved somewhere less controversial. As it was, his mother had never forgiven the Bishops for not having the decency to leave the area when they fell from grace.

"I didn't realize the Bishops were acquainted with the Earl of Montrose." They hadn't been when Nicholas had left. *What the devil had happened while he'd been gone?*

"It was an accident. Quite out of the ordinary," his mother explained. "Something to do with a broken carriage wheel."

"One wonders why Lord Montrose sought assistance from the Bishops instead of coming here." Nicholas's distaste for society's prejudice against the Bishops wasn't shared by many.

Lord Wakefield snorted. "One of the benefits of not having a daughter, especially a pretty daughter, is the remarkable infrequency of accidental visitors at one's door."

"We were quite fortunate to be blessed with sons." Lady Wakefield rushed to move the discussion away from the prettiness of Amelia Bishop. "Did you see Caroline or the boys when you visited Philip?"

"No, but Philip says they're doing well."

"That's nice."

Everything was nice. Anything with the audacity to be something other than nice was promptly ignored or hidden from view. Or shipped off to the continent, where Lord and Lady Wakefield could be certain it wouldn't embarrass the family by having unsuitable feelings for the unsuitable neighbor. It was obvious now why they'd waited to summon him back. They would rather risk the estate to threat of senility than risk having Amelia Bishop as a daughter-in-law.

Amelia was engaged.

Suddenly Nicholas needed to escape the confines of the perfectly ordered sitting room. "I believe I'll go for a ride."

Something akin to panic flitted across his mother's face. Lady Wakefield looked to her husband for guidance, but the periodical still shielded Lord Wakefield from view. "I think your father wanted to discuss something with you."

"Hmm?" *The Morning Post* lowered enough to reveal Lord Wakefield's confusion. "Not that I recall."

"Oh, well then." Her composure slipped again.

If his sense of charity weren't somewhat diminished by their decision to ambush him with the news of Amelia's engagement, Nicholas might have allayed his mother's fears by telling her that the Bishop estate was not his intended destination. However, he was not feeling overly gracious, nor was he in the mood to lie.

The swish of the door dragging across the carpet woke Amelia from her mid-morning half sleep. She pretended not to hear it or the tell-tale rhythm of the intruder's steps as they made slow progress across the room. Amelia expected the weight of the body that landed on top of her, but expecting it didn't make it any less jarring.

"Go away," Amelia complained, pulling the covers over her face. She hid herself in a cocoon of periwinkle satin.

"I will not." Julia bounced to add to Amelia's discomfort. "You've been in bed all morning."

"I am unwell. Most people have the manners to leave the ill in peace."

"Most people are not your sister." Julia wrestled the covers away from her. "And you're not sick. You're hiding."

"Am not."

"Are so." Julia stopped squashing her to death and settled

onto the mattress next to her.

Amelia turned to face her, clutching a pillow to her chest for comfort. "It's our parents."

Julia smiled. "I tried to tell you."

"Honestly, Jules. Where do they find the energy? Do they never get tired?"

"Being the favorite is exhausting."

Amelia tugged on a piece of Julia's perfect gold hair. "I'm sure you're still their favorite."

"I wouldn't be so certain." Julia tugged back on Amelia's brown strands. "You've landed an earl, and a young, handsome one at that. I think you're just going have to get used to it."

"I can't." She truly couldn't. Until she'd feigned sick this morning, Amelia hadn't had a moment to herself all week. It was a never-ending stream of planning parties, making vital introductions, and playing catch-up on a lifetime of social skills Amelia had never expected she'd need to learn.

Julia took their two locks of hair and started weaving her golden strands into Amelia's brown, linking them together. "Of course you can. Meanwhile, I am desperately excited to discover what it's like to be left alone for a while."

"Can't you pretend to have a headache so Mother will rush to your side?"

"Absolutely not. Once you marry, they'll be worse than ever. I'm taking this reprieve while I am able."

Amelia groaned. She rolled over, facing the garden windows instead of her completely unhelpful sister.

"Cheer up. Once you're Lady Montrose, you'll live with Embry and you won't have to see any of us if you don't you wish to."

Lady Montrose. Amelia was going to be a countess. It was too much to fathom. Even her parents had never expected her to marry above a vicar or some lesser merchant.

"Julia," Amelia asked seriously. "Are you certain you're all right?"

"Of course. I'm thrilled."

It sounded sincere, but Amelia knew her sister better than that. "We always said—"

"Don't be silly. We both knew you'd marry someday."

"Not before you."

Julia rolled her eyes. "We're not children anymore. I think we can admit that's never going to happen."

"I will not, and you shouldn't, either." Amelia's sister was beautiful, intelligent, and talented. Julia was superior to Amelia in every way, right down to her impeccable style and lyrical voice.

"No suitable man wants a crippled wife, Mia."

Amelia leaned forward, resting her forehead against Julia's the way they used to when they shared a room and would whisper under the covers until late into the evening. "Then none of them are worthy of you."

"Certainly not," Julia said. "I was obviously meant for Prince Albert, but he's gone and settled for the queen, so now there's nothing for me but spinsterhood."

"If only he'd met you first."

"If only." Julia kissed Amelia's nose. "Enough of this moping. I have a plan for how we can cheer ourselves up."

The gleam in her sister's eye had never meant anything but trouble for Amelia. "Does it involve burying ourselves in blankets and napping through the afternoon?"

"It does not."

"It never does. Your plans are rubbish."

"Fine. If you don't want to know, I won't tell you."

Amelia didn't need to know. She was eighteen years old. Mastery of one's curiosity was surely a requirement for a future countess. She would be perfectly fine, staying in her room, not knowing. "Tell me."

"There's a new maid," Julia said, eyes twinkling.

Amelia groaned. "I knew it. Can't we let well enough alone for once?"

"She called me a 'poor dear' when she brought my chocolate this morning."

Strangers only ever had two reactions to discovering Julia's infirmity. Pity was the lesser of the two evils, and the less common, but it was still not to be borne. Amelia shoved off the bedcovers and went to the wardrobe. "What shall it be, then?"

"Jolly Roger, I think."

"Somehow, none of these plans ever involve *you* carrying heavy objects up and down the hallways."

"When you're born with a life-threatening spinal condition, then we can start taking turns."

"Liar."

"Whiner." Julia swung her legs off the bed, briefly revealing the unusual angling of her left foot before she covered it again with her skirts. "Wear the grey one. Last time I saw Roger, he was extremely dusty."

Amelia traded her nightgown for a chemise and tea-gown, finishing the ties as she heard Julia come up behind her. "And somehow, only my dresses end up ruined in your plans."

"Hardly. Remember the elderberry incident? And a little dust won't ruin anything." Julia made quick work with a brush, tidying Amelia's hair into something close to presentable.

Sooner than she liked, Amelia was ready for mischief. The sisters went their separate ways once they reached the hall, Julia carefully making her way down the stairs while Amelia went in search of the marble bust of their long-forgotten ancestor. She found him in the library, happily collecting dust.

"Good morning, Uncle Roger, how are you today?"

Amelia wrapped her arms around the stone head and lifted it off its shelf. "Oof. You've gotten heavier."

Amelia and the bust lurched their way back down the hallway until they reached the top of the stairs.

Julia's loud whisper sounded from below. "She's almost done dusting the salon. Do you have it?"

"Roger would like to lodge a formal complaint against this undignified treatment of his person," Amelia hissed back.

"Duly noted," Julia said. "Fire at will."

Rolling her eyes, Amelia let go of the bust. It tumbled down the stairs in a series of loud thumps. Amelia chased after it while Julia made corresponding sounds of distress. Her sister finished in a flurry of dramatics, complete with a very convincing wail and billowing of skirts as she threw herself in a heap on the ground. Amelia barely managed to scoop up the head and dart into the dining room before the salon door opened, followed by the new maid's scream.

Chapter Two

Lord Bishop frowned down at the aristocratic brow of his ancestor in its new, slightly more dignified position on the desk. Amelia waited quietly with her sister. This was hardly their first meeting of this nature. The dark wainscoting of the study had witnessed more than its fair share of Bailey daughter lectures over the years.

"Why always this one?" he asked his daughters. "There are a dozen others in the house. What did Sir Roger ever do to you girls?"

"It's the nose," Amelia said. "He has a better bounce than the others."

"He's the heaviest, as well. More noise," Julia added.

A slight smile betrayed Lord Bishop's amusement. "I keep telling your mother you'll grow out of these pranks. You seem determined to make a liar of me."

Julia's smile was sympathetic. "It's a matter of necessity, Papa."

"Oh?"

"Nora called Julia a 'poor dear.'"

Lord Bishop's face darkened. He was as sensitive to the treatment of his eldest daughter as the rest of their family. "You must tell me or your mother immediately when these things happen."

Amelia shook her head. "You'd have let her go."

"Rightly so!"

"Papa," Julia admonished. "If we tossed out everyone who misstepped in their early days with us, we would be making our own beds."

"That's not true."

Amelia interrupted Lord Bishop. "The only people who accept employment with us are those without other options. If you let Nora go, she may not be able to find other work."

"It's better this way," Julia said. "I feel vindicated, and Nora has learned not to underestimate me. No one suffers unduly, and we can go about our lives with better understanding."

"It's quite humane," Amelia said.

Lord Bishop stared at his daughters. "If you had been born sons…"

"We'd be impossible."

"Thoroughly out of control."

"Far better this way." Julia lifted the tumbler of amber liquid from Lord Bishop's desk and up to her nose. She raised a comical eyebrow at their father, who took it away from her and placed it out of sight.

Amelia wasn't fooled by her sister's light-hearted response. If they'd been born sons, their lives would have been much different. Julia might have joined society, gone to school, lived a passably normal life. As a woman, the moral impurity associated with disfigurement excluded Julia from the possibility of marriage—the only respectable future for females of their station.

It wasn't just Julia who bore the cruel consequences of

her misfortune, though she certainly bore the worst of it. By nature of having produced a defective child, the moral purity of their parents—and by extension the entire family line—was called into question. Amelia was content to be ostracized by society. It saved her from having to associate with small-minded fools who couldn't see past Julia's limp to her sister's myriad enviable qualities.

"Just so," Lord Bishop agreed with a smile. He was oblivious to the melancholy undertone. The Bishop sisters had long ago committed themselves to a facade of perpetual frivolousness. Their parents suffered enough regret without being exposed to their daughters' darker moments. "Now go and see your mother. She had quite the fright thinking something had happened to Julia."

"Why does no one ever worry something might happen to me?" Amelia complained as the girls left the study.

"Because you are healthy as a horse."

"Am I?"

"Of course."

"Shall we put it on my engagement announcement? Perhaps my headstone," Amelia said while they went in search of their mother. She pitched her voice upward into a formal tone. "Here lies Amelia Bishop. Her constitution was favorably comparable to livestock."

They were both laughing when they found their mother in the salon, noticeably not riddled with fright or distress. She was also not alone.

"Excellent! I was about to send for you girls."

Lady Bishop's companion turned, the curling edges of his black hair catching a stray beam of sunlight. Nicholas Wakefield. Amelia's heart performed a tiny stutter-step in her chest and she convinced herself she'd mistaken him for her fiancé. His shoulders were broad like Embry's—far broader than they'd been the last time she'd seen him—and the beginnings of a beard shadowed his jaw, giving a slightly disheveled impression. There was something different about the way he carried himself.

How could two years have changed him so? When he'd left, he'd been a boy of nineteen. Now here he was, looking very much like a man.

"Good afternoon, Lady Julia." He rose, giving her sister a warm smile as Julia embraced him.

Amelia felt a pang of jealousy that didn't make any sense. Of course they would be happy to see each other. Julia and Nicholas were friends. Perhaps not as close as Amelia and Nicholas, but very nearly. Amelia had even harbored a not-so-secret hope that Julia and Nicholas might marry someday.

To Amelia, he gave a formal bow. When his eyes met hers, the most peculiar sensation sprang to life in the pit of her stomach. "Good afternoon, Miss Amelia."

Oh dear.

Amelia's laugh froze Nicholas in place. Seeing her with her hazel eyes lit and a smile dimpling her cheeks erased two years in an instant. As he'd suspected, distance had not been playing tricks on him. Everything else in a room still disappeared when Amelia Bishop walked in. Why did she have to go and get herself engaged, just when he'd managed to gather the courage to declare himself?

His foolish emotions didn't care about her engagement. All the distance *had* done was make him forget how to prepare for being around her. Nicholas used to have an entire routine for keeping his breathing and his emotions under control before he visited the Bishop household. He employed those methods now, taking deep breaths in through his nose and reciting the more boring sections of one of his Latin texts from school in his head.

"I hear congratulations are in order," he said, once the ladies had settled themselves into seats.

Amelia's brow furrowed.

"Your engagement." Julia raised an eyebrow at her sister. "You remember your fiancé, Embry?"

"Oh yes!" Amelia laughed, a blush spreading across her cheeks. "Goodness. We haven't even officially announced it yet. How have you heard already?"

"Lady Wakefield has eyes and ears everywhere."

"Isn't that a terrifying thought?" Julia murmured, low enough to keep Lady Bishop from hearing.

Nicholas allowed himself a small smile. Amelia shot her sister a sideways smirk.

"Have you been back long?" Julia asked, this time at full volume.

Nicholas shook his head. "Just in from London this morning."

"And the first thing you did was come to visit us?" Lady Bishop pressed her fingers to her lips, blinking rapidly.

"Oh, for God's sake." Julia shook her head. "You are not going to cry, Mother."

Lady Bishop blinked all the faster. "I'm quite touched."

"You're certainly something," Amelia said under her breath.

Nick coughed to cover his chuckle. Their debate over who had it worse—Nicholas with his mother's imperious interference, or Amelia with Lady Bishop's love of hysterics— had never been properly settled.

Julia took charge. "Mother, is the laudanum still on your dressing table?"

Lady Bishop's waterworks dried up immediately. "Are you all right? Is something the matter?" She rang the bell beside her, calling out. "Mrs. Polk! Mrs. Polk, summon the doctor immediately."

"That won't be necessary, Mrs. Polk," Julia called over her. "I just feel a migraine coming on."

The look Julia sent Amelia said it wasn't actually one of the headaches that could trap her in bed for days at a time. Nick appreciated the sacrifice. Lady Bishop's dramatics weren't quite the backdrop he would have chosen for his reunion with Amelia.

"Still, we should put you to bed immediately. Perhaps a hot bath." Lady Bishop ushered her eldest daughter out of the room as Mrs. Polk arrived to assist her, forgetting about Nicholas and Amelia entirely. "We can't have you sick with Lord Montrose's family visiting."

The swirling chaos of concern moved down the corridor, leaving the salon in silence. Leaving Nicholas and Amelia alone. Together.

Pull yourself together, man. It's hardly the first time you've been alone with her. Nicholas fell back on his old habits, taking deep, steady breaths.

"…nice to know some things never change," Amelia was saying.

"Hmm?" Thankfully, Nicholas's calming ritual went unnoticed.

"Mother. Everything has been so different lately. It's nice to know some things will always stay the same."

Nicholas had known her too long and too well not to hear the things she didn't say. "Are you all right, Amelia?"

She shook off her reverie. "Of course. Everything is wonderful."

"Truly?"

"Truly." She smiled.

It was a lie. He could read it in the way she wouldn't quite meet his eyes and in the tension at the edges of her mouth. Apparently more had changed than Nicholas realized.

Amelia jumped up, breaking the awkward silence. "Would you like to go for a walk? I've been stuck inside this house for days."

Amelia needed space. She needed fresh air to distract herself from the scent of him. Had he always smelled like coffee and oranges and…what was that other smell? Something masculine that made her want to lean over and breathe him in. He couldn't have smelled like that before he'd left. She would certainly have noticed.

When he asked if she was all right, she'd desperately wanted to tell him the truth, but he wasn't the gangly youth who'd left her two years ago. The forelock of his hair might fall across his brow at the same boyish angle, but the tailoring of his jacket now hugged muscle and sinew that were entirely man. This new Nicholas was a stranger, and he inspired strange feelings. The fluttering feeling hadn't gone away, and it was now accompanied by the strangest prickling sensation when he looked at her. Perhaps she was coming down with something.

If he were still the old Nicholas, she would have told him everything in an instant. He'd always been her confidant, her safe harbor in the oftentimes overwhelming chaos of the Bishop house.

Amelia didn't know if she was all right or not. She certainly wasn't as happy as she would expect to be under the current circumstances. A girl in her position should be thanking her lucky stars to have caught the honorable interest of a young, attractive earl. Instead she was exhausted.

Without Nick, all of her misgivings had piled up with no outlet. She couldn't tell her parents she wasn't certain she wanted to be a countess; it was everything they'd never dared to hope for her. And Julia would slap her silly for second-guessing the opportunity. He was her best friend. When he left, so did the afternoon discussions in the hayloft and the moments of crisis when she'd climbed the tree outside his bedroom. He hadn't even written her. He was different now. Would the man who'd come back in Nicholas's place still have time for her girlish insecurities? Would he even care?

She couldn't say any of that. Not to this new Nicholas. So instead she said, "The continent looks to have suited you."

"It did. It was a bit of a revelation, actually." Even his voice was different. He used to sound hesitant, like everything he said was a question. There was no uncertainty in him now.

Amelia tried to make her own voice sound as confident— with dismal results. "How so?"

It was difficult to be confident of anything when one's organs were flipping somersaults inside one's body.

Falling into old habits, they started toward the wooded area that straddled the Bishop and Wakefield estates. Nicholas gestured emphatically with his hands while he spoke. That, at least, was still the same. "At first, I was only touring. It wasn't unpleasant but it wasn't particularly riveting. But then I met Jasper and—"

"Jasper?"

"Viscount Bellamy. I met him in Caen and went with him to Paris."

"On a whim?" Amelia asked. "You went to Paris with a complete stranger?"

"I did." The corner of his mouth tilted up. "I tried to argue, but Jas is extremely persuasive."

He must be. The old Nicholas would have never behaved so recklessly. Amelia left that development for later consideration. "Presumably Paris had more to offer in the way of entertainment?"

"It did."

Amelia waited for him to say more. When he didn't, she realized why and heat flared across her cheeks. A revelation, he'd called it. Well, she should be glad for him. That was how boys became men, wasn't it? It had clearly worked for Nicholas.

"It's not what you're thinking."

"You have no idea what I'm thinking."

"Two years hasn't changed that much, Mia." Nicholas leaned against a tree trunk. "I can still read you like a book."

Of all the nerve! Amelia crossed her arms. "What am I thinking, then?"

He leaned in close. Dangerously close. The coffee and citrus smell surrounded her as his eyes met hers and a jolt of awareness sparked between them. "You think I spent the last two years steeped in debauchery, bedding my way through the French countryside."

The heat in her cheeks tripled. "Hardly."

"…Mastering the sensual arts with voluptuous young women of questionable moral fiber." His voice was pitched low, and it sent shivers rippling across her skin.

Amelia breathed in to steady herself, but it only made it worse. "Did you?"

"Master them?" He leaned closer. There was no room left between them. If either shifted, the front of her dress would brush against the fabric of his jacket.

Amelia nodded, eyes wide.

He was staring at her parted lips. She swayed forward, her own lips parting in response.

"Not really, no." He backed away with a grin. "Mostly I learned about art."

It was the blush. The pink flush had positively begged him to tease her, but Amelia was an innocent. He shouldn't have baited her like that, even if she weren't spoken for. The fact that she was made him the worst sort of cad. Nick forced his feelings back down. It was just friendly teasing. That was all it would ever be.

"Learned about art." There was nothing friendly about the way she was looking at him now. The breathlessness was gone, replaced by a cutting glare. "Apparently you also learned how to behave like a complete bounder."

If only. If he were a complete bounder, he would know what she tasted like right now. "It was meant to be humorous."

"You should stick to art."

He should stick to safer topics.

Nick couldn't think about the romance of a true masterpiece without his feelings for her bubbling out in his words. He couldn't tell her being in Paris had felt like the first time she'd hugged him, setting every nerve ending in his body alight. That had been the plan, but not now. Not when she was engaged to Montrose.

"What?" She watched him, still frowning. "Tell me."

Nick had to find something else to distract her with so he didn't end up baring his soul and making a fool out of himself. "We lived with Bohemians."

Amelia's eyebrows flew up. "Bohemians? For how long?"

"The entire time."

Her glare disappeared entirely. She grabbed his hand, dragging him down to sit on the ground with her. "Tell me immediately. Was it exciting? Oh, of course it was exciting. What were they like?"

Once he got over the rush of her hand on his, Nick laughed. Reliving it for Amelia was like being there all over again. Nick told her about the painters and actors and writers he'd met while he was away. He told her about a man from the Balkans who lived with his tiny dog and wrote the most beautiful poetry Nicholas had ever heard. She laughed and called him a liar when he told her about an Irish woman who sang in a deep baritone that somehow made perfect sense.

Sometime in the middle, between missing the midday meal and the sun disappearing behind some ominous-looking clouds, they became friends again. Nick was glad. He might have lost the chance to marry her, but he couldn't bear to lose her friendship, too. She'd been far too important to him for far too long to be satisfied with polite distance between them.

"How are you not sitting somewhere quiet with a view of the Seine right now, reading modern philosophy or learning to paint?"

"It was lovely. It truly was, but…" Nicholas was beside her, staring at the sky through the tree branches. He couldn't tell her it hadn't been enough without her, now that she was engaged, and he didn't want to talk about what was happening with his father. Not yet. Not until he knew how he felt about it. "It wasn't for me."

"What is for you?" she teased.

You. Nick put a stranglehold on his heart so he didn't say it out loud. "Parts of it were beautiful, but there are so many problems in the world. I'd like to help mend them."

Her teasing was replaced with genuine curiosity. "How?"

"I'd like to study the law." Anathema as the idea might be to his parents, Nicholas couldn't spend his life as *just* a scion of the house of Wakefield. He'd hoped to spend it as Amelia's husband, too, but clearly he'd missed his chance at the one thing he wanted most.

"Like your brother, in the House of Lords?"

Nick shook his head. "God willing, I'll never be a lord. No, I think I'd like to try for barrister."

Amelia's eyes went wide. "Barrister. A profession? Would your parents allow it?"

"I doubt it." There were a lot of things Lord and Lady Wakefield would never allow, but it had never stopped him from wanting them. Or her.

She looked at him with the shy grin that only turned up half her mouth. "Well, I think it's wonderful. If you can find a way to do it, I think you should."

For a moment it was hard for Nicholas to swallow. He saw their whole lives stretched out before them. Him in his barrister's wig. Her welcoming him home after a long day. Tiny children racing around her skirts while he kissed her like he'd longed to for his entire adult life.

It wasn't to be, though. Amelia would welcome Lord Montrose home. The tiny children racing around her skirts would be Lord Montrose's children.

He stood up, putting much-needed distance between them. "Well, I think you should find a way to sit beside the Seine and read modern philosophy while you eat pain à la duchesse."

"I'm not sure Embry would enjoy that sort of thing." The pause before she spoke was a touch too long.

Was Amelia not certain of her fiancé? The beat of Nicholas's heart raced a little. A good friend would want her to be happy, but Nicholas had never just wanted to be her good friend. If there was a chance her engagement would be called off, maybe there was still hope.

"Your fiancé's not one for philosophy? Or perhaps he has an intractable aversion to French desserts."

"Embry seems to have an aversion to most frivolities."

"Don't tell the French he considers their cuisine frivolous. You'll start another war."

She rolled her eyes at him. "You know what I mean."

"He sounds rather serious." Nicholas pulled a thin branch off one of the trees and tested it against his leg. Serious was not what Amelia needed.

"He is, a bit. He's not boorish," she rushed to explain. "He's quite clever. He's just…"

"Serious?"

"Serious." Amelia held out her hand. "It's going to start raining. We should head back."

A rumble of thunder sounded in the distance. Nicholas took her hand, ignoring how suited it felt to his own as he helped her to her feet. When she placed it on the crook of his arm and leaned in close against the chill breeze, he certainly ignored the warmth of her body pressed against him and the softness of her hip against his.

Rain fell in waves, like the ocean had been turned upside down above their heads. Amelia stared out the window of the drawing room at a world washed grey. Her breath frosted the glass in great big puffs of fog.

"Don't," Julia said.

"I'm not."

"Yes, you are."

Yes, she was. Her engagement party was only days away

and Amelia was sitting in the window seat, moping over the wave of change heading her way. Much as she tried, she couldn't see how to stop it from coming. "I can't help it."

"You're announcing your engagement. You're supposed to be thrilled."

"Well, I'm not."

"Is it because of Nick?"

"What? No." Perhaps Nick was a small part of it, but it wasn't *only* him. It was all of it; the engagement, marriage, a title, leaving home, leaving her family, Nick coming back unexpectedly… Suddenly feeling a jolt when he did something he'd done a thousand times before.

Julia raised an eyebrow as she worked her needlepoint. "I thought you gave up your Nicholas nonsense when you were twelve."

"I did." She had, when he'd openly admired the new dairymaid whose raven hair and bright green eyes were as far from Amelia's medium-brown-everything as a person could get. "He does look different now, though. It took me by surprise."

"He's exactly the same."

Amelia paced the room. "Don't tell me you haven't noticed how much broader his shoulders are, or how certain he is when he says things now."

"Fascinating."

"What?"

"You're spoony on Nicholas."

It wasn't like that at all. Yes, she'd had an unexpected reaction to him, but they hadn't seen each other in years. It was completely understandable. Amelia slumped down in her father's favorite overstuffed chair in front of the fire. She pulled her feet up underneath her, watching the flickering flames. "Don't be ridiculous. He's different and I noticed. It's not a crime."

"It is when you're sitting here moping instead of jumping for joy because a handsome earl wants to marry you." Julia tossed her embroidery back into the box. Amelia was surprised she'd lasted so long. Julia excelled at everything a lady was expected to excel at, but she preferred less docile pursuits.

"What do you think is the matter with me, truly? I should be excited. I'm going to be a countess, for God's sake."

"Nerves, most likely."

"Is there anything to be done about it?"

"I doubt it. You'll probably die. I hear conditions like this are fatal."

Amelia flopped onto the settee, sticking her tongue out at her sister. "Very amusing. I wish I could just be left alone for a little while. There has been entirely too much excitement these last few weeks."

"At least men notice you." Julia's soft tone made Amelia immediately regret her wish.

"Jules—"

"Don't worry about it." Julia pushed herself off the couch. "We're lamenting your imminent death right now. We can be sad about my spinsterhood tomorrow."

It was too late for that. "Tomorrow, then."

Julia grinned. "Oh yes. Tomorrow, we'll have a proper bout of pity over it. Hair tearing. Clothes rending. But today, we'll be sad for you and your terrible judgement."

"It's not terrible!"

"An earl asked you to marry him. An earl! And you're frowning into your lap, giving yourself wrinkles."

"I blame the weather."

"I'll show you weather." Julia pulled the bell-cord. "Get up. We're going for a ride."

Amelia groaned. "It's wretched outside."

"It's wretched in here. A race will do us good. Come on."

Protesting any further would be futile. While Julia arranged for the horses to be saddled, Amelia went upstairs to collect their riding boots and jackets. A full change would take too long, and Julia was shorter of patience than usual once the thrill of a race was on her.

Outside, their mounts were waiting for them.

"Good afternoon, Tryphosa." Julia greeted her mount with the utmost formality, in the tradition the sisters had established years ago.

Amelia followed suit. "Good afternoon, Dionysia."

Dionysia flicked her tail and stamped a hoof in response.

Just seeing the stocky little horse improved Amelia's mood. She was a cross-bred Arabian, shipped across the Atlantic when Lord Bishop discovered his daughters had a love for the smaller, American-bred sprinters. Amelia and Julia had named their horses after the oldest and youngest of a trio of ancient Turkish sisters renowned for their sprinting prowess in the Roman arenas.

Of the two, Julia's mount usually proved faster, but Amelia contended that hers possessed more heart and athletic talent. It was only the reckless abandon with which Julia rode that allowed the older sisters to consistently beat the younger pair.

They set off into the rain, letting Dionysia and Tryphosa start out at a moderate walk. Amelia's thoughts drifted to Nicholas while they picked their way through the mud and out of view of the house. She'd wanted him to kiss her under that tree—there was no denying it. When he'd leaned close, saying those wicked things, she'd wanted him to kiss her more than she'd ever wanted anything else. That had never happened before. Even when they were children and she'd spent a brief summer fancying herself in love with him, he'd never had that effect on her. She'd wanted his attention, certainly, but she'd never *needed* his touch.

What was the matter with her? It was Nicholas, for goodness sake. He might cut a more masculine figure now, but he was still just Nicholas. Even his shameless flirting on their walk wasn't anything out of the ordinary. He'd been practicing his charms on her and Julia since he'd come back from Eton with a shameful understanding of exactly how lacking they were. And she was engaged! Embry was widely regarded to be quite handsome. Amelia had no business wanting to be kissed by anyone but her fiancé.

That was another problem. Amelia had never needed Embry's kiss the way she'd needed Nicholas in that moment. She hadn't thought anything of it—hadn't realized there was even anything to think—until her whole body set to tingling at a few wicked, whispered words from Nick. It was still alight and he'd gone hours ago.

Embry was a good man. A good fiancé. He'd brought her books the second time he came to call, for goodness sake. He was perfect. Who was to say these tingles were specific to Nicholas? Perhaps if Embry whispered wicked things to her while smelling like dessert she would react the same way.

Maybe all she needed was for Embry to behave a little less properly. Not that Amelia had the slightest idea how to bring that about. Embry was extremely diligent in his propriety.

Still, she was up for the challenge. She would forget all about Nicholas Wakefield and his wicked whispers, and set her mind to figuring out how to seduce her fiancé. That was the proper course of action. Well, proper enough anyhow. She was a Bishop, after all. She couldn't be expected to behave entirely.

"Well, what shall it be?" Julia asked. "The forest or the meadow?"

"The meadow stream will be swollen over with all this rain," Amelia warned.

"You're right. The meadow it is."

Of course. Julia wasn't happy if she wasn't actively trying to get them both killed—either by genuine catastrophe or parental wrath once they were found out. "Are you certain? You're not immune to consequences anymore now that I'm the favorite."

Julia squinted for a moment, like she was pondering it as they urged the horses into a trot. "What's the worst they might do to me?"

"Ban you from riding."

"They wouldn't dare. They wouldn't be able to stand how morose I'd be."

Amelia was certain her sister was right, but she played the devil's advocate anyway. "You never know. They might."

Julia shrugged. "A lot of things might happen."

"Yes, but those things aren't under our direct contr—"

With a shout, Julia and Tryphosa shot off across the field.

Amelia swore, giving Dionysia her head when the mare lurched forward, unwilling to let her sister have the lead without a fight.

Chapter Three

"How do I look, Bertie?"

"Exceptionally capable, my lord."

Nicholas grinned at him in the gilt-edged mirror over the dressing table. The corner of Bertram's mouth twitched up.

"All right, then. Time to fulfill my glorious destiny."

The meeting with his father and the estate agent would take place in the study. Nicholas had to admit a certain thrill of anticipation. True responsibility would do wonders for keeping his mind off Amelia's impending marriage. Once he knew the extent of what needed to be done, he would find a way to make time for studying as a barrister. He could do both. He could be there for his family and follow his dream.

"Lord Nicholas." Smithson appeared at the bottom of the stairs. "This arrived for you with the morning post."

Nicholas took the folded sheet of paper. He would have left it for later, but the seal promised it would be short. Lord Bellamy despised writing.

Nick,

Paris is dismal without you. Last night I drank <u>alone</u> at Marcelles. Come back at once.

Jas

P.S. Claudette also demands your return. Her claim is obviously inferior to my own, but if lures of the flesh will accomplish what friendship cannot, so be it.

He smiled. Unfortunately, Jasper would have to accept disappointment, as would the talented Claudette. Nick had a job to do. His arrival in the study, however, threw him immediately off balance. A man he'd never seen before was sorting through the papers on the desk. The desk that belonged to Nicholas's father, and his grandfather before that.

He looked up when he heard Nick enter. "Lord Nicholas, I presume?"

He did not appear to be an intruder, but he was still a stranger to Nick. "You presume correctly. Who are you?"

"David Fletcher, my lord. I'm the estate agent."

"What happened to Dickson?"

"He retired about six months ago, my lord. I was hired to replace him."

Six months ago. "Was it because…"

Mr. Fletcher's expression smoothed into one of extreme tact. "I believe it was difficult for him to adjust to the new situation, my lord."

His father's condition. "How bad is it?"

The estate agent spent a moment considering the tips of his shoes. His answer was interrupted by the arrival of Lord Wakefield.

"Nicholas! When did you get back?"

"I've been home all mor—"

Lord Wakefield rang the bell pull. "We must tell your mother. She's been on about bringing you back from the continent for months. I told her you'd come back when you were ready, and here you are."

Surprise struck Nicholas like a blow to the gut. His father didn't remember speaking with him yesterday. It was one thing to have his parents tell him calmly that his father was forgetting things, but quite another to have it so vividly proven.

Mr. Fletcher stepped in. "You did summon him back, Lord Wakefield. He arrived yesterday. You set a meeting for the three of us to discuss Lord Nicholas taking on some of the estate running."

Confusion clouded Lord Wakefield's face. "I did?"

"You did." The estate agent was the soul of patience. "Would you like to reschedule for a different day?"

"No, no. I don't want to…" Lord Wakefield stared around the room, settling on the painting of his favorite hunting dog that hung on the far wall. He smiled. "Of course that's what happened. I remember now."

The emptiness of his smile made it obvious that he did not.

Smithson arrived in answer to the pull. "My lord?"

Lord Wakefield stared at him, struggling with his own mind. "I…"

The butler and the estate agent exchanged looks.

"My lord," Smithson began gently. "Lady Wakefield requested your presence in the garden. It seemed rather urgent."

Mr. Fletcher selected a stack of papers from the desk. "I have the detailed notes you wrote for Lord Nicholas. If you need to leave, we can probably manage and give you an update after, my lord."

"Yes, I think that would be best." Lord Wakefield nodded, taking the offered excuse. "I should go find my wife."

When he'd gone, with Smithson in tow, Nicholas lowered himself into a chair on the visitor's side of the desk. It felt like his legs didn't want to carry him anymore.

His formidable father. One of the leaders of the country and the irrefutable leader of their family.

A tumbler of whiskey appeared in front of him.

"I shouldn't. It's not even midday yet."

"Some days are longer than others," Mr. Fletcher countered.

Nicholas took the glass. "How often does that happen?"

Fletcher sat in the chair next to him, leaving the desk chair empty. "More than it used to. One day in ten now. It used to be once a month, maybe."

One day in ten, and it was getting worse.

"On the good days, we plan. He writes things down, just in case. On the bad days…"

"You and Smithson manage him."

"Lady Wakefield mostly. We have a system. It seems to help him to be outside on the bad days."

It was too much for Nick to try to process all at once. The change in his father. The kindness of this stranger. The sudden, uncharacteristic sympathy he felt for his mother. Lady Wakefield was a hard woman, but he couldn't imagine how it had been for her here, alone. She wouldn't have confided in the staff easily, not his endlessly proper mother, and she had no one else.

Nicholas swallowed a mouthful of whiskey and took a deep breath. "Well, it sounds like we'd better get started, then."

"Mia, did you hear me?"

Amelia held up her hand, blocking out her sister until she could reach the end of her paragraph. Usually the ballroom could be counted on for a quiet place to read uninterrupted—it wasn't like they used it for anything other than storage—but apparently her sanctuary was one more casualty of the impending engagement party. When the derelict furniture had been hauled away and her mother had set the maids to work shining the parquet, peace was no longer an option.

She marked her place and closed the book. "What?"

Julia splayed her hands behind her and leaned back against a column. "I said, he's here."

"Nicholas?"

She rolled her eyes. "Your fiancé, you muttonhead."

Embry was here? "He's not supposed to visit until…"

"Today," Julia interrupted. "And you're not even dressed."

Amelia looked down at her cotton day dress. "I am so."

"Not for a visit from your intended."

"It's daytime. What's wrong with wearing a *day* dress in the *day*time?"

Lady Bishop breezed into the room. "Amelia, Lord Montrose is in the driveway and I—why aren't you dressed?"

"For goodness sake." Amelia set her book down with a thump. "I'm hardly lounging in the nude."

Her mother was not in the mood to be amused. "Go upstairs and put on something appropriate. Julia, help her."

Julia coughed out a surprised sound. It was usually Amelia being ordered to assist Julia.

"Go. Now. And hurry, before he gets to the foyer and sees you on the stairs!"

"Hurrying isn't really my bailiwick, Mother."

"I swear to you both, if this engagement is ruined because

your father has let you run amok like hoydens…"

"Then we'll be pampered and adored for the rest of our lives?" Julia grinned at Amelia as Lady Bishop expelled a sound of extreme frustration and they fled the room.

"Are you ready to be the favorite again?" Amelia asked as they climbed the stairs.

"I doubt I could be. Apparently being unmarriageable has relegated me to the position of your lady's maid."

"You don't have to help. I can manage."

"You can't, actually. You still think that's an acceptable dress to greet your fiancé in."

"It is!"

Julia stumbled as they reached the top step. On reflex, Amelia caught her. The stumble wasn't a bad one, only the usual sort.

"You're hopeless," Julia said as she made the right turn down the hall toward Amelia's bedroom.

"What would you have me wear, then?" Amelia demanded.

"The lavender gown."

"Without a corset? It would look ridiculous."

Julia answered her with silence.

"Truly?" Amelia groaned. She hated corsets. Without visitors or formal occasions, she managed to avoid wearing one most of the time.

"If you go back down there without a corset, regardless of which dress, Mother is going to have an apoplexy on the spot."

They entered Amelia's room. Julia went to the wardrobe and began searching through its contents.

Flopping onto her bed, Amelia suggested, "What if I don't go back down at all?"

"Then Lady Bishop's mortification shall immolate this entire household, us included."

Amelia scowled at the ceiling.

"Also," Julia said, depositing a corset and a pile of petticoats on the bedcover. "Your ridiculously handsome fiancé will assume you don't want to see him, probably throw you over, and destine you to a life of spinsterhood."

Amelia dangled the corset off her index finger. "Do spinsters have to wear corsets?"

"Constantly."

"Liar." With a sigh, Amelia stood up and let Julia undo her day dress. "This whole being engaged business is turning out to be a lot more disruptive than I imagined."

"Oh?" Julia started cinching the corset with unkind force. "I didn't realize you had something planned for today other than reading and daydreaming out of windows."

"Reading and daydreaming are vital activities for my health and happiness."

"As I said: muttonhead."

Amelia grinned, stepping into the petticoats.

The girls sat across from Embry in the parlor. Amelia was dutifully attired in the lavender gown, complete with hated corset, that brought out the chestnut tones in her otherwise mouse-brown hair. She doubted Embry noticed, but at least her mother appeared pleased.

As she sat silently, she couldn't stop herself from comparing him to Nicholas. Embry was older by almost a decade and it showed in little ways on his face. Rougher skin, a line between the eyebrows, deeper grooves around the edge of his mouth. They shared dark hair and a quietness, but Embry's was more serious than the flirtatious teasing of Nicholas's charm.

"It's lovely to see you again, Lord Montrose," Lady Bishop was saying. "Amelia has been anticipating your visit all week."

They were a family of liars. Her father was the only honest one in the lot.

"As have I." Embry's attention was settled firmly on Amelia.

Amelia squirmed, trying to dislodge the corset boning from her spleen.

Lady Bishop continued, oblivious. "What did you have planned for today?"

"I thought your daughters and I could go for a walk down to the meadow. It could be quite nice to take our midday meal by the stream."

"It's quite a long walk. Perhaps we could ride?" After the wince during their stair climb, Amelia doubted Julia would be able to make the distance without pain.

Embry frowned. "If we must. I've been in the saddle all morning and would like to stretch my legs."

"Perhaps once we get there, we could walk."

Julia interrupted him with a chipper expression that didn't match her tone. "My sister is trying to spare my dignity by not telling you the walk is too long for me."

"Oh." Embry frowned. For a moment it looked like disapproval. "Of course, we can ride or stay indoors. I didn't realize."

It must have been disappointment. He seemed to get on well enough with Julia, so it would be silly for him to mind her company.

Lady Bishop put her hand on Embry's forearm. "You need a stroll. Julia doesn't have to go. Unless you'd like to use the bath chair, Julia?"

Both sisters stared at their mother in shock. Julia hated nothing in life more than she hated the wheeled chair and how it made her look and feel like an invalid. Everyone in the household knew it.

"Mother," Amelia warned.

Lady Bishop's expression tightened as she stared at Julia and she made an almost imperceptible gesture with her head between Amelia and Embry.

"I don't have to go." Julia's tense delivery would have been comical under different circumstances.

Embry watched all three Bishop women with growing concern. "We can stay here. I wouldn't want to leave anyone out."

Julia ceased the staring contest with their mother and smiled at Embry. "It's all right. Really. I wasn't feeling well anyway."

"Amelia?" he asked. "What would you like to do?"

Strangle her mother, but that would undoubtedly make the situation even more awkward. It wasn't Embry's fault Lady Bishop was completely ridiculous.

Julia answered for her. "Amelia adores country walks, especially in the meadow."

"Julia."

"Honestly. No matter what you decide to do, I'll be going to my room for a lie down."

"That settles it," Lady Bishop announced, clapping her hands. "I'll have cook prepare a basket."

Walking back to the house with Embry, Amelia was ashamed to admit it had been nice. Too nice. For a moment, she'd forgotten all about her mother's awful behavior and how angry Julia must be, and just enjoyed the peacefulness.

During the stroll, she and Embry hadn't had much to say to each other. Amelia had worried about that, but maybe it was all right. She didn't mind silence, liked it even, especially after a lifetime of her mother's hysterics and Julia's cutting wit.

Maybe she and Embry truly would be happy together.

When they stepped onto the terrace, Amelia stopped him. "Let's not go in yet."

His concern was immediate. "Is something the matter?"

"No," Amelia assured him. "I'm just enjoying your company."

The obvious pleasure he took from her confession made Amelia smile. No one had ever valued her good opinion before, except maybe Nicholas, and he didn't count.

"I have something for you," Embry said abruptly.

"Oh? What sort of something?"

Embry reached into his waistcoat and removed a bundle wrapped in silk. He flattened his hand and unfolded it, revealing an oval pendant with gold filigree. Pink sapphire and pearl dominated the piece, with tiny flashes of diamonds glinting in the sunlight. "It was my mother's."

It was beautiful. It also didn't suit Amelia in the slightest. She pushed the thought down. He'd brought her something that was clearly very important to him. The spirit of the gift was what mattered. "It's lovely."

"The first day we talked after my carriage broke down, I knew I wanted to give it to you." He moved to put it on her. When it settled against her dress, the disparity in styles became apparent, even to Embry. "Doesn't quite suit, does it?"

"Through no fault of your gift, I assure you." Amelia stared at her feet so she didn't have to meet his eyes.

Embry frowned. "I'm sorry. I thought it would—"

"Don't apologize. I have plenty of dresses that will suit it marvelously." She didn't, actually, but she didn't want him to feel bad.

The frown cleared and he nodded. "That's good, then."

"I'll just hide it for now." As she tucked the pendant into her bodice, Amelia's arm brushed his waistcoat. She realized how close they were standing.

Embry's gaze was locked on the shadowed space between her breasts where the pendant had disappeared. It was as good a time as any.

"Embry, may I speak candidly?"

"I hope you will, always."

"Have you ever wanted to kiss me?"

His eyes raised, searching her face before answering. "Yes."

It wasn't quite wicked whispers, but it was a start. The intensity of his attention filled the space between them, making the air feel thicker. Amelia touched her tongue to her lips and his eyes followed it. The faintest of tingles started under her skin.

"Would you like to kiss me now?" she asked.

"Very much." He brought his hand up, running his thumb along the edge of her chin. "But it wouldn't be proper."

Amelia leaned into his touch. It was nice. Her body wasn't humming the way it had been yesterday, but there was certainly something happening. "Could we be a little improper? I've never been kissed and I—"

His lips interrupted her.

It was late afternoon when Nicholas left the study and he was exhausted. There was only one person who would understand all of the feelings he couldn't quite find words for. He promised himself he was only going to talk to his friend. He wouldn't do something foolish, like try to kiss her again. Not that Amelia would notice. She had a remarkable knack for attributing his romantic gestures to playful teasing.

He crossed his property onto the Bishop estate and let himself in. Today, it was a good thing the Bishop household treated him like a member of the family. The staff were rushing around in a frenzy, cleaning and moving things in preparation for the engagement party. If he'd waited for someone to notice and announce him, he might have waited all day.

He found Julia first, in the upstairs library, leaning precariously over the back of an armchair with her head angled to an open window.

"The house is in a flurry. Do you know—"

"Shh!" She nearly tipped herself and the chair over in the process of shushing him. "They'll hear you."

"If only this were the most ridiculous position I'd ever found you in," he answered in a loud whisper. "Who will hear?"

"Amelia and Embry."

The serious fiancé? They were together, down there. Were they affectionate? Did Amelia laugh musically and touch his arm like she did with Nicholas? He crossed to Julia's eavesdropping spot. "When did he get here?"

"This morning."

"What does he want?"

"Amelia, judging by his offer of marriage."

"Low blow, Bishop." A brief moral debate occurred inside Nicholas. He should mind his own business. Amelia's relationship with Embry was private. He didn't have any right to assuage the burning need to see how they were together. "Scoot over."

"You won't fit."

"I will if you scoot over."

She rolled her eyes at him, but she was smiling as she edged to one side of the seat cushion. "Remember that time in the hayloft when we made you—"

"Shh!" Nicholas adjusted until he could see the couple standing on the terrace below. "What are they doing down there?"

"We don't know. Mother's in fits thinking Embry's trying to call off the engagement."

Hope surged inside him. He squashed it down. "Why would he do that?"

"Because we're unmannered wantons."

"Well, obviously." Nicholas grinned as he dodged the elbow she tried to jab into his ribs. "But surely he knew that before today."

Below them, Montrose reached into his waistcoat and pulled out something wrapped in silk. When he uncovered it, Julia let out a soft whistle. "Pretty."

"It doesn't suit her at all." If Nicholas ever brought Amelia jewelry, it would be delicately made with brilliant sapphires, not some heavy antique.

"Maybe you shouldn't be watching this," Julia said. "It's certain to upset you."

Upset him? Like he was still in the nursery and someone had denied him a sweet? "I am a grown man."

"You're in love with my sister. Torturing yourself is perverse."

"And you're not torturing yourself?"

"Of course I am," she said, attention riveted to the scene below. "But we already knew I was perverse. You, we still had hope for."

"I will worry about myself, thank you very much."

"As you wish."

It was possible Nicholas had spoken too soon. As they watched, Montrose reached for Amelia's cheek. He had to turn away when Amelia's face was blocked out by Montrose lowering his head to kiss her.

Julia's gasp was full of degenerate glee.

The curse that left his lips at full volume didn't even register for Nicholas until Julia ducked down and speared him with a glare.

"For God's sake."

"I'm sorry," he whispered. Unless the curse had been loud enough for them to hear on the terrace and had disrupted the kiss by some miracle. Then, he was delighted.

She twisted, sharing the chair with him in an awkward slump. "I knew you couldn't handle it."

"What's he even doing kissing her? It's highly inappropriate."

"Remember the first time you tried to kiss Mia?"

Unfortunately. "No."

"Liar." Julia grinned. "She was so happy with her new dress Papa brought her and she looked quite nice."

"Perfect," Nick corrected. "She looked perfect."

Julia snickered. "How could you not have realized how much mud you'd picked up crossing the property?"

"I was distracted." Nick had been captivated by the sun glinting off Amelia's hair, the way her face lit up making it seem like all the sweetness of her was bursting free—he'd been in a trance. When he'd moved to touch her...

"I honestly never knew she was that strong. With how hard she shoved you, I thought we'd have to call a doctor for sure."

The bruises from his fall over the retaining wall had been nothing compared to the bruise to his pride. And neither of those held a candle to the agony of watching some other man get to be her first kiss. "She can't marry him."

Julia rolled her eyes. "Has something fundamental changed about your circumstances to make it possible for you to honorably pursue my sister?"

Nicholas could not say that it had. His willingness to stand up to his parents on the issue had certainly changed, but his ability to provide for her and his station in life remained the same. He was still a second son. A redundancy. His livelihood relied on the goodwill of his parents, and they would never approve of Amelia.

"I didn't think so. I wish things were different, but they're not. Give it up, Nick."

"I have."

"Obviously not. There's no future for her with you. Leave it alone. Don't ruin what will likely be her only chance at a normal life."

Julia was right. Nicholas couldn't give her what Montrose could. With Nick, there would be no title and no security. It would be a hard life, full of uncertainty.

If he truly loved her, he would let her be happy without him. It didn't matter that he'd written her letters every day. It didn't matter that he'd loved her with every breath in his body since the day they met. That was the past—their past—but the happiest future for her was clearly with Montrose.

After Embry left, Amelia went straight to her room to reflect on the events of the afternoon. However, instead of privacy, she found Julia leafing through the book she'd left on her bedside table.

"Oh, for goodness—"

"Don't even start. After everything I've put up with today, there's no chance you're not telling me every possible detail." Julia patted the bedside in invitation.

Amelia stomped over with as little grace as possible. There

would be no dissuading Julia, and Amelia hardly planned to keep it to herself. She'd just hoped to have little time to consider how she felt on her own first.

Julia smiled. "So. Lord Montrose kissed you."

"Yes."

"How did it happen? Were you expecting it?"

"I should hope so. I asked him to."

"You what?" Julia grabbed her by the shoulders. "Amelia Marie Bishop. I didn't know you had it in you."

"I just wanted to know." Amelia stared down at her lap.

Julia watched her. "It didn't end up how you wanted it to."

Amelia shrugged. She couldn't say if it had or it hadn't. It hadn't been bad, certainly.

"What happened?"

"I thought it would make me…tingly."

Julia raised an eyebrow.

Amelia rushed on to avoid having to explain that particular discovery. "And at first it was nice. His lips were against mine and it was sweet. There was a definite chance for tingles."

"And then?"

"And then he swallowed me? His tongue was in my mouth and it was so strange and I could barely breathe and it was… it was a lot. A lot all at once."

"His tongue—in your mouth?"

"Yes."

"Why?"

"I don't know!" Amelia threw her arms up in a general plea to the universe.

Julia considered the issue with her usual pragmatism. She folded her hands in her lap and pinned Amelia with a focused stare. "Did Embry seem to enjoy it?"

"Yes. Very much. Perhaps too much."

"How do you mean?"

"He was out of breath and afterward, he, erm, apologized for his ardor."

"That's good, then." Julia nodded. "Obviously you were decent enough at it if you inspired him to passion."

Amelia had rather hoped to be inspired to her own ardor. It would have cleared up a few concerns rattling around in her head regarding her new reaction to Nicholas. Instead, it had only confused things even further.

"So tell me about these tingles you were hoping for."

Oh, bother. "It's nothing."

"Clearly, it's not. It's not like you to ask Embry to kiss you, but you did. Because of this tingly notion."

Absolutely nothing was sacred when your sister was a busybody know-it-all. Not a single thing. But why *hadn't* her reaction to Embry been more exciting? "When Nicholas and I walked to the woods—"

"You bloody idiots. Did he kiss you?"

"No!" Amelia fell back on the bed. "But I think he almost did. I was leaning in and he was leaning in, and then suddenly it was all dreadfully intense."

"Oh, I don't doubt it." Julia fell back beside her, shaking her head.

Amelia put her hands over her face. "What do I do, Julia? What if Embry never gives me tingles?"

Julia wasn't listening. She was too busy muttering at the ceiling. "I knew something had happened. When Nicholas came over today and heard Embry was here. I should have known. I should have put a stop to it."

"Nicholas was here? Today?"

"Bloody idiot. I told him he didn't want to watch."

"You were watching us?" Amelia turned on her side. "Julia!"

"Oh please. Don't pretend you're surprised."

"How could you let Nicholas…" Amelia trailed off. She was back in that murky territory. Why shouldn't Nicholas see her kiss her fiancé? Nor was it unusual for Julia to include Nicholas. The three of them had been inseparable since Amelia was six years old. Until Nicholas went away, they were as close as a trio as Amelia and Julia were on their own.

"This is a disaster, Amelia."

"It is."

"Well," Julia said, sitting up with purpose. "You must come to your senses, forget about tingles, and forget about Nicholas Wakefield."

"What? Don't be ridiculous. Nicholas is my friend."

"A friend you have an attraction toward."

Amelia couldn't stop the blush from creeping up her face. "Nicholas is attractive. Don't tell me you don't find him handsome."

"I'm not engaged. I can find whoever I fancy handsome."

"That's not fair."

"Life's not fair," Julia said. She pointed at Amelia, all traces of humor gone. "Forget Nicholas. Marry Embry."

"Obviously I'm going to marry Embry." It wasn't like anyone else was offering.

Julia tipped Amelia's chin toward her, forcing their eyes to meet. "Good."

"Good."

"That's settled, then."

"It is." Only it didn't feel settled. In the place at Amelia's center where the tingles started anytime she thought about Nicholas, it was anything but settled.

Nicholas spooned his soup quietly, lost in thought. Everything was going wrong. Amelia was kissing men—specifically, men who weren't Nicholas. His father was so much worse than his parents had let on. Should he tell Phillip? Could he even do this?

Lady Wakefield had her own concerns. "You visited that girl. Again."

"I did."

Silverware clattered against the Limoges china. She glared across the table at his father. "Arthur."

"Hmm?"

"He's visiting the neighbors."

"That's nice."

"It is not *nice*." Her mouth clamped shut, but she was practically vibrating from the strain.

Nicholas knew he couldn't soothe her without lying, but he tried anyway. "They're my friends, Mother."

She shook her head, refusing to speak to him.

"I've had a letter from Philip," Lord Wakefield announced, oblivious to the discord across the table. "Caroline gave birth to another boy."

Yes, she had. Two years ago. Lord Wakefield was still trapped in the past. Smithson had explained that he could come out of it at any moment, but it hadn't happened yet. Lady Wakefield's anger dissolved in a flash. Her hands shook as she raised her glass to her lips, and she held her napkin a little too tightly.

Why did everything have to become so complicated? He hated his mother's disdain for the Bishops. If he was being honest, he'd almost hated her some days. She was so rigid. But now even that was clouded. She loved his father, and his father was disappearing. If Amelia suddenly couldn't remember... he couldn't even complete the thought. His brain rejected it entirely. Besides, she wasn't his to worry over. By the time that became a concern, she would be decades into her marriage with Montrose and she'd have forgotten all about Nicholas, with or without the help of an ailing mind.

But if she were his to worry about, how would he feel? Nicholas slid his hand across the table, covering his mother's small palm. It was fragile. He could feel every tiny bone under her thin skin. When had his parents become old?

She gripped his fingers back with painful force. "That's lovely, Arthur. Such good news."

The next course came in and she let go abruptly.

"Mother…"

She plastered a smile on her face and addressed the footman. "Please tell Cook the soup was very nice."

They consumed the rest of the courses in dismal silence. If challenged, Nicholas couldn't have told anyone what he was eating. When the last of the plates had been taken away and they retired to the drawing room, his mother stopped him with a hand on his arm.

"Please remember that your real family needs you now."

Nicholas looked up. There were tears pooling on her lower lids, threatening to fall. "I'm not going anywhere."

"That girl—"

He covered her hand again. It was the most physical contact he'd had with his mother since he'd left the nursery. "I'm here. I'll be here as long as I'm needed."

Dragging a finger under her eye, she instantly returned to the formidable Lady Wakefield Nicholas was accustomed to. She nodded and announced, "I think I'll go up early."

Nicholas and his father retired to comfortable chairs in front of the fire with glasses of Burgundy.

"A second son," Lord Wakefield mused. "Well done, Philip."

"I'm sure they're extremely pleased."

"We certainly were when you were born. Such a relief to know the line is secure."

A relief. That's all he was. Something to help them sleep at night in case the worst happened. Nicholas didn't want his value to hinge on something terrible happening to Philip and his nephews. He wanted a purpose of his own.

Smithson had explained that his father wouldn't remember this day out of time. When he came back to the present, it would be like it never happened.

"Father, I've been meaning to ask you something."

"What is it?"

"What would you think about my studying to become a barrister?"

Lord Wakefield's brow rose. "A profession? Surely you're joking."

"No, I'm not."

"No Wakefield has labored in a profession since before the writing of the Domesday Book."

He was well aware. One could not grow up a Wakefield and not be. "But what if I wanted to?"

"Nicholas," his father admonished. "It's high time you abandoned these odd notions. First your fascination with those bohemians, now this barrister business. You're a man now. It's time to grow up. Your place is here, helping me and Philip maintain the Wakefield legacy. Your duty is to your family, not some pack of criminal strangers."

Well. So much for the delusion that his father might somehow understand. At least before he'd been able to pretend the conversation could have gone favorably. Now he knew with complete certainty that Lord Wakefield would never approve of what Nicholas wanted for his own life. It was what he had expected, really, but losing that little shred of hope hurt more than he'd realized it would.

Chapter Four

When Embry came to call the next day, it was not Amelia's fault for not being ready. This time she was certain he hadn't told her he was visiting. After being brushed and poked and stuffed into *another* damned corset, she was rushed downstairs where her fiancé was waiting in the foyer.

"Embry. What a delightful surprise."

"I apologize for the lack of notice."

Her mother, ever-present, chimed in. "Nonsense. You're practically one of the family now. Come whenever you like."

Amelia ignored her. "Was there a reason you wanted to see me?"

"Ah. Yes. Would you be terribly averse to taking another walk with me? I have something I need to speak with you about." His glance slid toward Lady Bishop, who was tilted forward with interest. "Privately."

Horror welled up inside her. He was going to call off their engagement. She'd been much too forward, and after having time to think on it, he'd decided she would not make a suitable countess after all. She squashed it all down, along with the extremely inappropriate hopefulness, which she chalked up to mental instability. She answered with perhaps a little too much cheer. "Not at all. Would you like to go now?"

He nodded.

A short cape was procured for Amelia and they set out across the lawn. He wasn't speaking and Amelia wasn't certain of what to say, so she followed her mother's advice; when in doubt, comment on the weather. "The clouds look frightful. I think we might get more rain."

Apparently, that was all he needed to find his tongue. "Amelia. About yesterday, on the terrace."

Oh goodness. She'd been right. Amelia's cheeks flushed with embarrassment.

"I enjoyed our kiss a great deal, but I realize I might have frightened you with my enthusiasm, and if I did I apologize."

Oh. Well, that was a relief. Wasn't it? "It's quite all right."

"It isn't, though. Since our first walk the day my carriage broke down, you've always seemed so intelligent and certain of yourself, but you are an innocent. More so than most, even, and I forgot myself."

"Nonsense. I asked you to, and it was…" She couldn't say quite all right again, so she trailed off and said nothing. It hadn't been awful, but it certainly hadn't been what she'd imagined it would be.

"I haven't felt this way about anyone since Lily. I know you had other reasons for accepting my proposal, but when you asked me to kiss you…" His hands clasped hers under the branches of a birch tree. "It gave me hope that you could feel the same."

Amelia tried to sort through everything she'd just heard. Embry had deep feelings for her. He knew she didn't return them. "Who is Lily?"

"Surely you heard. It was all anyone in town could talk

about for what felt like an eternity."

Amelia held her tongue, waiting.

When enlightenment came, his face filled with chagrin. "Ah. No, I suppose you wouldn't have. Who would have told you?"

"Who, indeed."

"Lily was my fiancée."

Oh. He'd been engaged before. It made sense, certainly. He was extremely eligible and much older than her. She'd just never bothered to wonder. "You clearly still care for her. May I ask how it ended?"

"She died."

Oh no. Amelia stopped them with a hand on his bicep. "Embry, I'm so sorry."

"As am I. She was so guileless and impossibly kind." He looked away, wiping at the corner of his eye. "You remind me of her a great deal."

Amelia wasn't certain she would have chosen those as her most apparent attributes, but he clearly meant to flatter her and it was hardly the time to correct him. He'd lost someone he loved to cruel circumstances, and he still felt it keenly. "May I ask how she died?"

"Consumption. She was taken far too soon."

And he'd never loved anyone since.

Embry finally noticed her hand on his arm and stepped closer. Tipping her chin up, he looked into her eyes. "You mustn't think it means I don't have the whole of my affection to give you. My feelings for you have been a delightful surprise, breathing life back into a heart I thought otherwise barren."

She didn't know what to say. Amelia opened her mouth, hoping some manner of divine inspiration would take over. Instead, the descent of Embry's lips did.

It was much like before. The sensation was interesting and there was nothing in it that Amelia minded, per se, but it lacked the invigorating, distracting quality of Nicholas's attention. Still, Embry was her fiancé and he clearly cared a great deal for her.

Leaning in, she pressed her lips to his. Embry's arm wrapped around her waist and pulled her closer. That wasn't half bad. When his hand rested against her jaw and the tips of his fingers brushed against the nape of her neck, there was a definite stirring of interest. It wasn't the culmination of all Amelia's hopes, but it was marked progress.

Just as she was starting to get a feel for it, Embry set her away from him. He looked around, flustered, but they were alone. "Amelia, I must apologize again. I—"

"Please don't. I enjoyed it."

She thought he might grab her again then and there. Instead, he placed her hand on his arm and started them back toward the house. Every once in a while he cast a sidelong glance in her direction. It looked to Amelia as if he was well pleased with himself.

"Lord Nicholas. A Lord Bellamy has arrived, asking for you. He's brought luggage." The last part was uttered with all the starch Smithson could bring to bear.

Lady Wakefield set down her teacup with a rattle. "You invited a guest and didn't inform anyone?"

He hadn't, actually, but protocol had never been an area of interest for Jas. Nicholas rose, preparing to intervene. "My apologies, Mother. Smithson. It must have slipped my mind."

"This is not a good time for visitors. Your father…" She stopped herself. "You've never mentioned Lord Bellamy at all. Why not?"

"Our friendship is fairly recent. Jas is a bit unusual."

At *unusual*, his mother's brows lowered ominously. "Is he from a good family?"

"The best, actually."

It didn't take long. "You don't mean Viscount Bellamy, the Duke of Albemarle's grandson."

"The very same."

Her eyebrows flew the other direction. "The rumors about him are quite alarming."

"Would you like me to send him away?"

She couldn't see his smile when she gasped. "Send away a duke's heir? What has gotten into you, Nicholas? You'll have to make sure he only sees your father when he's well, but we can't send him away. Honestly, first you run wild with that girl—"

"I'd best not keep him waiting." Nicholas left his mother to ponder his utter downfall alone.

In the entry hall, a well-dressed but dreadfully disheveled man was sending the household into an uproar waving his arms and ordering the servants about with an air of impossible superiority. "Thank God. Nick, tell them I'm not here to steal the silver."

"I'll tell them no such thing. What the devil happened to you?"

"First the ship was late, then the train." Jasper embraced him with a clasped hand and a pat on the back. "I sacked that fellow I picked up in Cologne. He still can't tie a cravat to save his life. I am, for the moment, living rough."

"You could have at least written. You've sent my mother into an apoplexy."

Smithson cleared his throat conspicuously.

"I have that effect on mothers." Jas followed him to the billiard room. "Besides, I did write."

"To order me to come back to France."

"You should have listened. Then I wouldn't have had to dash across the ocean like some refugee."

"Refugees don't travel first class." It was too early, but Nicholas poured them both a drink anyway. No matter the timing, it was good to see Jasper and good reunions required whiskey. "How long did it take you to miss me, a day? You'd have to have left right after I did."

"Don't be ridiculous. It was two days."

Nick leaned against the billiard table, leaving Jasper to lounge rakishly in the wing-back leather chair. "So what are you doing here?"

"Bringing you back, obviously."

"Not a chance, Jas."

"Do my feelings mean nothing? I'm the heir to a dukedom. Aren't you supposed to see to my every whim?"

Nicholas sketched a bow, laden with extra flourishes. "My apologies, Your Grace. I can't imagine what I was thinking, Your Grace. Whatever pleases you, Your Grace."

Jasper laughed. "Excellent. Pack your bags. We leave within the hour."

"I can't."

"Damn it, Nick." Jas glared at him. "It's that girl, isn't it?"

"No, actually. It's my father." He explained the situation that had greeted him when he'd come home.

"So it is about the girl."

Nicholas shook his head. Being next door to Amelia again was a benefit, when it wasn't an unholy torture, but he was here to help his family. "My father—"

"If you wrote to your brother, he'd rush in to save the day and you'd be free to go study at the Inns of Court. But instead, you get to be a hero and a martyr, all the while staying close to your blessed Amelia."

"I have a responsibility to my family," Nicholas said. "I don't expect you to understand."

"Don't I? How often do I have to rush back here to England because my bloody sister has broken some new heart, and I must make sure everyone remembers how cross the future Duke of Albemarle will be if anyone is unkind to her?"

"That's different."

"Why?"

"Because you adore Lady Ruby, and you love to rub it in her face when you come to her rescue."

"Irrelevant." Jasper propped his boots up on the table, looking every inch of the entitled aristocrat that he was, minus the dishabille.

"You're the heir to a duke. Your grandfather is how old? And you cavort around the globe, avoiding your responsibilities like they're a plague."

"They are."

"Not to everyone," Nick said. Responsibility wasn't just a whim he could take or leave, any more than his feelings for Amelia were. If Jasper understood that, he wouldn't keep asking him to abandon either of them.

"Stop pretending like this is anything but cowardice. You're afraid to take charge of your own life. When did you become so boring?"

Nick was tired of fighting. He was tired in general. The situation with his father was exhausting. He rubbed at the space between his eyebrows, trying to stave off the ache that was inevitably on its way. "It's my nature, I suppose."

Jas's tumbler hit the walnut surface of the side table with a *clunk*. "Your nature, my backside. I saw you in Paris. There's renegade blood in your veins."

"Be that as it may."

"This is a tragedy that cannot be borne. I am going to stay

here and help you reclaim your manhood."

Nicholas laughed. "Sorry, Jas. You're not quite my type."

"Don't be ridiculous. I'm everyone's type."

He laughed again and some of the strain drained out of him. "It's good to see you, Jas."

"That's the first sensible thing you've said since I arrived."

Amelia was on a mission to rid herself of the corset when she heard the unmistakable sound of crying coming from Julia's room. It stopped Amelia in her tracks. Julia never cried. She made cutting comments and plotted elaborate revenge, but she didn't cry. Amelia slid off her shoes and quietly opened the door. Sneakiness was warranted when the goal was taking care of one's sister. Tiptoeing across the room commonly known within the house as the palace, she almost made it.

"I can't believe you bungled it on carpet this thick," Julia said from the chaise in the corner, wiping her eyes. Papier-mâché cranes hung above her in a rainbow of colors.

The skirts must have given her away. "Your carpet *is* much nicer than mine. Papa clearly loves you more."

"Jealous?"

"Dreadfully." It was difficult to keep her tone light when she could see the tear streaks on Julia's face. It hurt Amelia more than if she'd been crying herself.

Julia smiled, but it held no joy. "How was your walk with Embry?"

"You first. What's the matter?" Amelia moved Julia's violin off the bed. It was her preferred seat when she visited the palace. The giant gold canopy made her feel like royalty, which was how the room had earned its moniker.

"Nothing."

"Jules. Is it the pain? Do you need a doctor?"

Julia sighed. "It's nothing like that. It's just Mother. You don't need to worry about it."

Relief flooded through Amelia. Julia was very good at hiding when her condition became too painful to bear—usually with disastrous consequences. Ordinary mother tears they could handle.

"What did she do?" Amelia gestured for Julia to join her under the canopy.

Julia shook her head.

"You're going to tell me eventually. It's obviously your choice if you want to force me to sit on you and tickle you into submission."

The laugh was a good sign, but it died off much too soon. Julia joined her on the bed, curling herself into a ball among the piles of gold and ivory silk pillows.

"Please, Julia, just tell me."

Her sister sighed. "Mother asked me not to go to your engagement party."

"What?" Of course Julia was coming to her engagement party. Of all the people invited, she was the one Amelia most needed there.

"She said it would be better for you, for your future, if we didn't remind everyone about..." She tried to smile through it, but the tears started running down Julia's face again. "And the worst part is she's right. I can't go. You're getting married and I can't go to your engagement party."

Amelia would deal with her mother's overstepping later. For now, she needed to put an end to this nonsense. There could be no party without Julia. "Of course you're going."

"No, I'm not."

"Julia, don't." The unbelievable frustration of it all overwhelmed her. She let it out in an irritated growl. "I will not lose you to have Embry."

"Yes, you will."

"No, that's ridiculous."

The tears dried up and Julia reverted to her usual stoic self. "What did you think would happen after you married? Did you think you would stay here with us?"

"No, but—"

"That's how it goes. Even if your sister wasn't a social pariah, you leave our family and join his."

"That isn't what's going to happen with us."

"Yes, it is, and you're going to let it, Mia."

"I will not." It was ludicrous of anyone to think she would. She and Julia had been inseparable for as long as Amelia could remember. Since the very first. When Amelia started walking and then running, their parents decided to keep the girls separate so Julia wouldn't be upset by it. But they'd snuck in to see each other at night, practicing together until Julia could manage a steady pace on her own.

"You have to. One of us has to be happy, Mia. One of us has to live a full life." She tugged on a lock of Amelia's hair, emphasizing which one of them she thought it should be.

Amelia refused to accept it. "We live full lives. We're happy."

"You don't honestly believe that."

"I do," Amelia exclaimed. "We have each other, and loads of books, and a beautiful garden. Papa buys us anything we want. Look at this room!"

Julia threw her hands up, displacing pillows over the side of the bed. "Unbelievable. I think you actually mean it."

"I do."

"It should have been me!" Julia shouted. "You have this

amazing, handsome fiancé and you don't even want him. You're talking about books and gardens like it could ever compare."

Amelia felt instantly guilty. "Julia."

Her sister shook her head, tears returning. "Get out, Amelia."

"I didn't…it's not…"

"Please, just go."

Amelia didn't know what to say, how to take it back, so she went. The curtains of the canopy swished closed behind her.

Nicholas was lying on his bed, surrounded by papers on soil quality and weather conditions, when a thump sounded on the other side of his wall.

The exterior wall, twenty feet off the ground.

Nick knew that sound. She wouldn't, not in broad daylight. Not hours after she'd ripped his heart out, kissing Montrose on the Bishops' terrace.

Sure enough, a few moments later his window slammed up in the casing. A trouser-clad Amelia tumbled through it, landing hard on the jacket and cravat he'd discarded on the floor when he settled in to spend the rest of the day reading.

"What are you doing here?" It was one thing for her to sneak in his window when she was eight, but it was quite another at eighteen. She had no business in his bedroom.

Amelia didn't answer him. Instead, she moved his papers from the bed to the oak desk in the corner. When they were cleared, she climbed onto his bed, curling up in a ball.

Oh no. Absolutely not. They were not children anymore, and Nicholas could tell himself all day and night that they were only friends, but there was nothing innocent or friendly about the way his body responded to seeing her in his bed. "Amelia, you can't be here. You have to go, for your own good."

Her head lifted. Her eyes were red from crying. "Everyone thinks they know what's good for me today. Don't you do it, too."

Nick's will to remove her evaporated, along with his less honorable thoughts. Amelia never cried. He sat on the coverlet next to her, and she wiggled herself into the space beneath his arm. When her head was safely against his chest, he asked, "Is it Julia?"

Mia nodded.

His chest constricted. He'd hoped it had been something to do with Montrose—and not only for his own interests. The first time Amelia had ever climbed up the tree to his room, Julia had developed an infection after one of her surgeries. It had been terrifying. Every time was terrifying, waiting for news if Julia would get better.

"Is she…"

"We had a fight," Amelia said, sniffling again. "And I don't know how to mend it."

Terror drained away. Just a fight. "About?"

"I like Embry, but not enough to give up my family."

Like, not love. "Is he asking you to?"

So far, nothing Amelia had said about her fiancé since Nick had come back led him to believe they were a good match. If Montrose was trying to take her away from the Bishop clan, surely that would be the end of it. Amelia would never stand for that, no matter how eligible the bachelor.

Amelia told him about her fight with Julia, including Julia's outburst over Amelia having a fiancé at all. When she finished, he was at as much of a loss as she was. He couldn't mend Julia's loneliness, much as he wanted to. Instead of offering her empty platitudes, Nick told Amelia about his own troubles. "My father is losing his mind."

"What?" She lifted her head. Her brow instantly furrowed with concern.

"It's why they brought me home. He forgets what day it is, what year, and my parents have forbidden me from telling Philip because then he'll come home and give up everything he's working toward."

"Oh, Nick." Her hand was on his chest, right below his last undone button. She looked up at him, their faces inches apart.

If only she weren't someone else's.

If only he'd spoken up before she met Montrose.

If only she'd come over to tell him Montrose was all wrong for her and declare her love for Nick. But that wasn't why she was here. She needed him to be her friend.

Much to his shame, Nicholas needed something altogether different, and now that he knew she would be all right, his body was becoming embarrassingly insistent about it.

It was the sharp, honeysuckle scent of her hair. He wanted to bury his face in it and pull her onto his chest so he could feel every inch of her pressed against him. Something must have given his thoughts away, because her lips parted. With their faces so close, he could see her eyes widen and watch the pink flush creep up her neck. Did she even realize the way she responded to him? Did she know how it drove him mad?

"Nick?" She sighed it like a question.

He couldn't. He shouldn't. He lowered his head, their mouths only a breath apart.

The door to his room swished open, revealing Jasper. "Nicholas, what are the chances you—"

Amelia flew off his bed like a scalded cat. He almost took a boot heel to the chin as her exceptional backside disappeared over the edge of his bed and underneath it. It would have been welcome, compared to the stroke he'd nearly had at the sound of the door.

When he regained control of his senses, Nick called down. "Amelia, it's just Jasper. It's all right."

Jasper raised an eyebrow. "Is it now?"

It was finally going to happen. Amelia was going to die of mortification, just as she'd always suspected was possible.

A handsome face topped with curling sable hair lowered itself into her view.

"Good evening," he said, getting comfortable on his stomach. "You must be Amelia Bishop."

She pressed her face into the carpet beneath Nick's bed. "Unfortunately."

"There's nothing unfortunate about it. My name is Jasper and I expect we will become the best of friends."

The man was ridiculous, and it must be catching, because Amelia couldn't stop herself from asking, "Will we?"

"Oh yes. In my experience, it is extremely difficult to get our Nicholas to misbehave. And yet, here you are."

It was exactly as bad as she thought. Lord Bellamy knew what she'd wanted to do, even though Nick didn't feel that way about her. She couldn't let his friend think the worst of him or put any ideas in his head about her having feelings for him, all because she couldn't get this sudden attraction under control. Nicholas was her friend. He didn't deserve to suffer for being kind to her.

"We were only talking," Amelia insisted.

"Were you?" Lord Bellamy was completely unconvinced.

Nicholas's weight shifted on the bed above her. "Jas, leave her alone."

"I ought to be saying that to you, you scoundrel."

Amelia felt a hand close around her ankle. Jasper's face grew smaller and disappeared from view as Nick pulled her out from under the bed. He offered his hand. Reluctantly, she took it and stood up.

"Amelia Bishop, meet Viscount Bellamy. Don't let him intimidate you. He enjoys being aggravating."

"Almost as much as I enjoy your trousers," Jasper said with an appreciative sweep of his eyes.

Nick cleared his throat, taking Amelia's arm and guiding her to the chair farthest from Jasper. "That'll be enough of that."

The embarrassment slowly dissipated as a smile tugged at the corners of her lips. If Amelia wasn't careful, she would develop a fancy for Lord Bellamy, and she was flirting with one too many inappropriate fancies already. "Thank you. It's nice to meet you."

"You as well."

There really wasn't any way she could feel more ridiculous, so Amelia decided to ask, "Did you mean it about us becoming friends?"

"Absolutely, if you'll have me." Jasper seated himself in the armchair by Nicholas's window, clearly not planning to leave anytime soon.

"I should like to have another friend. I'm afraid the only one I've got is Nicholas."

"Marvelous. Now that we're friends, tell me: how is it that you only have one friend? Don't you have a fiancé stashed away somewhere?"

At the mention of Embry, Amelia felt awful all over again. She'd almost kissed Nicholas. What had she been thinking? "He's…"

"He's what?" Jasper prodded.

She couldn't claim she and Embry were friends. They barely knew each other.

Jasper took pity on her, waving his hand. "Say no more. It's quite unfashionable to be friends with your intended. I don't blame you for deciding against it."

"Jasper is an expert on the fashionable," Nick said, settling back on his bed.

"Now that we're friends, you're going to be instantly fashionable," Jasper told her.

Amelia couldn't keep her mouth from lifting at the corners. "Am I?"

"Quite. But first you have to tell me how you and Wakefield came to know each other. I'm dreadfully jealous, you see. It can't be a better story than ours."

She couldn't help it; she laughed. Lord Bellamy exuded a carefree feeling that was contagious. With everything going on, she should be desolate, but talking to him was the most fun she'd had in weeks.

Amelia settled against the chair back, determined to enjoy herself while she could. "Well, we're neighbors and we came across each other one day and he was quite rude."

"You were trespassing," Nick contributed.

"I was six. The intricacies of our property lines were not as clear to me as they were to your advanced nine-year-old mind."

"And you two became fast friends?"

"Hardly," Nick said. "She hit me."

Amelia stuck her tongue out at him to make him laugh.

"Truly?" Jasper asked.

"Square in the mouth. She's quite vicious."

"Not without provocation!" Amelia swung a pillow in his direction, jeopardizing her point. "He said something horrible about my sister."

"The plot thickens." Jasper looked between the two of them. "So you trespassed and he slandered your relative. And then what?"

"And then I spent the rest of the summer begging her forgiveness."

"Which involved a great deal of trespassing onto *our* property."

"Nicholas, you hypocrite." Jasper brought his hand up to his cravat in mock dismay.

"He is, isn't he?" Amelia settled farther back into the pillows in triumph.

"And all this time, you two remained purely friends? Nicholas never declared his affection and asked for your hand?"

Amelia sputtered, nearly choking on her surprise. "God, no. He's a shameless flirt, but he doesn't mean it."

Nick cleared his throat, finding something on his sleeve deeply interesting.

The viscount's eyebrows rose impossibly high. "Nicholas? A shameless flirt?"

This time, Nick coughed, sending a pointed look Jasper's way.

"Of course. He's forever teasing me and saying inappropriate things. He always has. It's quite rude." She followed the looks being exchanged between the two men. "He wasn't that way in France?"

Jasper returned his attention to her with a dazzling smile. "Of course he was; I must have forgotten."

"Jasper often forgets things that aren't expressly about him."

"Quite so," the viscount agreed.

"I'm afraid," Amelia said with a dramatic sigh, "I've never been the sort of girl Nicholas prefers."

Lord Bellamy looked between her and Nick, smirking. "Oh?"

"Since when?" Nick said at the same time.

How ridiculous. He should know better than anyone that she wasn't his type. "Since your parents hired that Welsh dairymaid when you were fourteen and you spent the entire spring extolling her virtues and trailing after her."

"That doesn't... I didn't..." It was Nicholas's turn to blush, and Amelia found herself enjoying it immensely.

"A Welsh dairymaid. How risqué." Lord Bellamy grinned.

"That's it." Nicholas stood up, holding out his hand to her. "You're clearly feeling better, so it's time for me to take you back before someone finds you in here."

Amelia didn't want to go. She wanted to stay here, laughing and forgetting about her troubles, but Nicholas was right. It wouldn't do for anyone else to discover her in his room. She'd been as lucky as she was going to get with Jasper. "It was lovely to meet you, Lord Bellamy."

Nick pulled her toward the door. "Watch out. If you're not careful he'll follow you home."

"Maybe I'd like that," Amelia joked.

"I guarantee you would," Lord Bellamy told her.

They shared a grin that was cut off when Nicholas closed the thick door of his bedroom behind them. There were no more jokes as they snuck silently through the long hall of the gallery and down the backstairs, but the smile never left Amelia's face.

Chapter Five

They were sitting at breakfast when Jasper leaned surreptitiously across the table.

"I think there's something amiss with your mother," he said under his breath, using his glass to shield his lips.

Nicholas looked over. Sure enough, his mother was rigid as a board at the far end of the table, staring at the post like it had turned into a viper ready to strike. It was nice having Jasper there to sit across from him in Philip's old chair. Without him, it had just been the three of them, sitting what felt like miles apart in total silence.

Jasper kicked him under the table.

Sneaking another sideways glance, Nick saw she still hadn't moved. "Is something the matter, Mother?"

She continued to stare at the card sitting in front of her, oblivious to the question.

Lord Wakefield stuck his head over the paper from the opposite end. "Lavinia."

Lady Wakefield shook herself, looking up at them all as if they'd only just arrived.

"Is something amiss?" Lord Wakefield called, actually going to the trouble of setting his paper down. It was one of the good days and he was back to being himself. For the moment.

"The Bishops," she explained, spitting the word, "have invited us to their daughter's engagement party."

"That's a bit short notice, isn't it?" Since there was no imminent national or familial crisis, Lord Wakefield returned to his periodical.

"As if that was the most offensive thing about it!"

"If you don't want to go, refuse."

In all his life, Nicholas had only seen his mother lose her refinement when the Bishops were involved. It was part of the reason he'd sought them out. As he watched her sputter and glare at his father now, it was everything Nicholas could do not to smile. It didn't last long, though. Nicholas realized his mother now had more reason than spite to refuse. Had they entertained any invitations since his father became ill? They certainly hadn't since he'd been home. Soon the Wakefields would find themselves as isolated as the Bishops.

"Of course I shall refuse. Honestly, Arthur." She sifted through the stack, her face growing even more pinched. "Lord Bellamy, I believe you've received one as well."

"Excellent! I do love a good party."

Lady Wakefield recovered her decorum and handed a piece of ivory cardstock to one of the footmen, who set down the pitcher he was holding to transfer it to Jasper. "I didn't realize you and Amelia Bishop were acquainted."

"Oh yes, we're the best of friends."

And that was the nicest thing Jasper could possibly have done for Amelia—and by extension, Nick. Regardless of how much Nicholas's mother hated the Bishops, she would not deliberately offend a duke's heir.

"Nicholas, will you accompany me? I believe the invitation is for both of us."

He took a page from Jasper's earlier method and kicked him. His mother might not be looking quite so murderous, but it was still an exceptionally sore subject.

Jasper raised an eyebrow.

"I don't think so, no. I suspect I'll be too busy." One was always too busy to celebrate the engagement of the love of one's life to another man.

"Certainly you can make time. You do wish her all happiness in her marriage, don't you, Nick?" Jasper's expression was wickedly calculated.

Suddenly, both of Nick's parents were paying keen attention to their exchange.

"You're her oldest friend," Jasper insisted. "It would appear quite strange if you didn't go and give your blessing. What might Lord Montrose think? Or the rest of the guests?"

"Jas," Nick warned.

"Don't you think that could give the wrong impression, Lady Wakefield?" Jasper turned his most charming smile on her.

His mother was immune to Jasper's charm but not, apparently, to his implications. "Obviously, you must go, Nicholas. Even though it would be ludicrous, we mustn't give the gossipmongers any reason to start up."

It was far from ludicrous and everyone at the table—never mind most of the county—knew it.

After his parents had left to pursue their separate interests for the day, Nicholas threw down his napkin. "What the bloody hell was that?"

"Hmm?"

"You know why I can't go, but now you've trapped me into it." Going to that party would be about as enjoyable as attending his own execution. Every time Montrose spoke to her, touched her, every time someone congratulated them and wished them many happy, healthy children…

"Yes, I do know why you don't want to go." Jasper sipped his coffee. "And it's why I think you should. You might be willing to push down your feelings and commit yourself to a life of misery, but I want better for you, Nicholas Wakefield."

"Nothing will come of me going to the party. It won't change anything."

"Then you have nothing to worry about."

He had everything to worry about, not the least of which being that he might end up tossing Amelia over his shoulder and running off with her like some cave-dwelling barbarian.

"If it makes you feel better, I didn't do it solely to torture you. You said yourself her sister won't be there. She needs you."

Nicholas spent the rest of his morning damning Jasper De Vere to hell and back, because he was right.

Bravery wasn't Amelia's strong suit. Julia was the one who begged her into doing things she couldn't bear to do. Julia was the one who made her stand up to her fears. But Julia couldn't help her with this. It had been three days and they still hadn't spoken to each other.

She went to the keepsakes box on her dressing table, digging through the dried flowers and scraps of ribbon until she found a small piece of paper with a wax seal on it. The raised parts of the seal were worn down from years of her thumb brushing across their edges, but it didn't matter. She knew what it was; the seal of the Marquess of Wakefield.

One summer day when she was ten, all three of them had gone to town together—Amelia, Julia, and Nicholas. It had started as such a wonderful outing. But then one of the ladies of the county had seen them buying ribbons. She was horrible. She'd insisted the shop owner refuse Amelia and Julia service, that they were disgraceful, and he'd done as she asked. It was the single most mortifying experience of Amelia's life. They'd done nothing to deserve it. Nothing beyond existing. They were only children.

The next day Nicholas had come to visit, and he'd brought her a small piece of paper, stamped with the Marquess's seal on one side and writing on the other. It read:

Lady Amelia Bishop is the bravest, most honorable woman in England.

The house of Wakefield is eternally devoted to her happiness and welfare.

It was in Nicholas's handwriting, of course. Julia had received one as well. He must have snuck in and used his father's seal when no one was looking. He'd told Amelia she couldn't possibly be disgraceful. That the Lords of Wakefield were pillars of respectability, and if she ever had difficulty holding her head high, to remember that she carried their seal of approval.

She re-rolled the paper, like she'd done a hundred times, and wrapped a section of hair around it until it was hidden at the base of her neck. There would be a number of people at the engagement party who didn't think she was good enough for Embry. Amelia could use all the encouragement she could get.

All the help she could get. *Damn.* She left her room,

making the short trip down the hallway to Julia's room. Taking a deep breath, she knocked on the door.

"Come in."

The skirt of her gown swished against the doorframe as she moved past it.

"Oh," Julia said, looking up from the easel where she was painting a scene of the garden below. "It's you."

"It's me." Amelia stood still by the end of the bed, studying the exotic animals embroidered in sweeping scenes across the canopy fabric. Julia hadn't insisted she leave, but any sudden movement might break the fragile peace.

Her sister looked her dress over with a frown. "You don't like pink, or that style."

"It's the only one I have that doesn't look awful with Embry's necklace."

The corner of Julia's mouth twitched. "It's a beautiful necklace."

"For someone."

Damn. Awkward silence filled the space between them. It made Amelia sick to her stomach. She shouldn't have said anything about the necklace not suiting her, but they had never not been able to be honest with each other. A tear built up and escaped down her cheek.

Julia sighed, setting down her brush and moving to sit on the end of the bed. "It's all right, Mia."

"No, it's not."

"Fine, it's not all right. But that's all right."

Amelia sniffled. "That doesn't make any sense."

"Yes, it does." Julia sighed. "Do I wish I was the one with the handsome suitor, getting ready to announce my engagement to all and sundry? Of course. But I'm not, and since I can't be, I'd rather it be you than anyone else."

"What if I don't want it to be me?"

Embry was a stranger. All she truly knew was that he wanted to marry her and he liked to read. She didn't know how many children he hoped to have, whether he preferred life in the country to life in London, how his family felt about his engagement to one of the scandalous Bishops. So much could change once they married. He would be her husband. Her whole future would be in his hands. Amelia didn't even know what type of books he liked.

Julia's eyes narrowed, but she didn't yell. "Don't be a coward, Mia."

"I'm not."

"You are. Stop waiting for life to happen. It's here and it's happening. To you. Enjoy it."

Enjoy it, like it was that simple. And it was, for Julia, but it had never been that way for Amelia. She'd never wanted anything beyond life in the Berkshires with her family.

"What if I can't?"

"Learn. This time next year, if we're both still here placidly marching toward spinsterhood, I will never forgive you."

She wouldn't, either. Julia could hold a grudge for eternity if she set her mind to it. Amelia wiped her eyes with the back of her gloves and sighed. "I wish you'd come down."

Julia shook her head. "I won't be far, and you know I'm happy for you. You don't need me there."

Amelia disagreed, but even if she didn't need Julia, she wanted her. No one else mattered nearly as much. "Will you wait up for me?"

"Of course." Julia tugged on one of her curls, careful not to dislodge the pins. "Who else am I going to get every last detail from?"

Amelia groaned. "I'm being punished. Twice."

"Mm-hmm." Julia leaned forward and kissed her cheek. "I'm far too spoiled to be unhappy by myself."

"Tyrant."

Julia nudged her with a slippered foot. "Go on. You have a party to host."

Amelia left feeling better, but she still couldn't muster up anything close to excitement. There was something fundamentally wrong with her. She was announcing her engagement. She should be happy, but all she wanted was for it to be over.

Seeing the house filled with guests was an unsettling experience for Nicholas. Every time a belled skirt or the tails of a gentleman's coat brushed some piece of furniture he'd played on as a child, he had to stop himself from yelling at them all that they didn't belong there. And that was before he ever saw Amelia.

She looked lovely. She also looked extremely uncomfortable. As he sipped his punch, yet another stranger touched her elbow and she flinched, covering it with a smile. His fingers tightened on the glass.

"Steady, now." Jasper peered around the room as if nothing was amiss.

Nicholas said under his breath, "It's no good, Jas. I can't do it."

"You can and you will."

Nick's argument was disrupted by a hush falling over the half of the room closest to the door. The last two people he'd have ever expected appeared at the entrance of the ballroom. Lord and Lady Wakefield stood there, looking every bit as uncomfortable as Amelia had.

"What the devil?" Jasper whispered.

Lord Bishop was the first to recover. "Lord Wakefield. Lady Wakefield. So good of you to come."

"Thank you for inviting us," Lady Wakefield said with perfect formality.

"Why—"

"They're here to check up on me," Nicholas told Jasper. "They must not have trusted I wouldn't do something rash."

"Well, that's not very sporting of them."

His parents made their way toward him, exchanging greetings with their acquaintances on the way. "Nicholas."

"Lord Wakefield. Lady Wakefield. I hadn't expected to see you here."

"Your father and I thought it would be nice to get out of the house for a change."

They were there to make sure Nicholas behaved himself; anything else they said was a blatant lie. Nicholas could only assume they hadn't told him they were coming sooner because his mother couldn't be certain Lord Wakefield would be in his right mind when the time came.

"Lord and Lady Wakefield." Lord Montrose joined their group, bowing over Lady Wakefield's offered hand. "I don't think I've had the pleasure since Duke Atherton's dinner party two seasons ago. We never got to finish our discussion on foreign relations with the Americans."

There was no reason the sound of the man's voice should make Nicholas furious. No reason at all, except that he was stealing the love of Nicholas's life. *Keep it together, Wakefield.*

"I'm not much for the social whirl these days," Lord Wakefield admitted. "Getting stagnant in my old age, but we conservatives have to stick together else the Whigs will have us all firmly to hell in a hand basket."

Montrose laughed. "Quite so."

Lord Wakefield clapped Nick on the shoulder in an

uncharacteristic gesture of affection. "Are you acquainted with my youngest son?"

"By reputation only." Lord Montrose nodded to Nick. "Although I feel as if I've known you for years. Amelia speaks highly of you."

"And you," Nicholas managed.

"Nicholas couldn't be happier Lady Amelia has made such a wonderful match," Lady Wakefield offered on Nick's behalf.

Beside him, Jasper started choking on his punch. "Please excuse me. I appear to be having some difficulty."

Nicholas imagined a thousand tortures as Jasper made his escape.

"So Montrose," Lord Wakefield asked. "Where will you and your bride be staying once you're married?"

While his parents were suitably distracted discussing how far away they could ship Amelia once she married, Nicholas made his escape as well. Everyone was focused on the happy couple, so no one batted an eye when he snuck out and up the stairs to find the one person besides Amelia he could count on to understand his misery.

When Lord Bellamy appeared beside her with two glasses in hand, Amelia had never been so happy to see someone in all her life. "Thank goodness."

"How are you holding up?" Jasper asked her.

"Not well. There are so many people here, and I don't know any of them."

"Bold maneuver, inviting Lord and Lady Wakefield."

"They're here, too?" Amelia scowled. "It must have been Mother's doing. She invited all sorts of people I've never even heard of. She's desperate to rub everyone's noses in my excellent match."

To be honest, Amelia didn't mind rubbing Lady Wakefield's nose in the match a little. Nicholas's mother had only ever come to the Bishop residence once, right after Nick had finished at Eton. She'd declared in no uncertain terms that her son would not be entertaining any romantic notions with a Bishop while she was alive. Not that it had been necessary to declare such a thing, but Nicholas's mother had always been a little high strung.

"Apparently, Lord and Lady Wakefield are old friends with your fiancé."

"Of course they are." As far as Amelia could tell, Embry was friends with everyone in the British empire. The rest of her life flashed in front of her eyes; surrounded by strangers and bored to tears. For a second, the room wobbled as faintness stole the strength from her knees.

Two young women were standing a few feet away and scrutinizing her with an appalling lack of subtlety as they whispered behind their hands. At first, she thought they'd seen her falter, but then she heard what sounded like "horribly disfigured."

Amelia would put up with a great deal, but not that. Never that. "Can I help you with something?"

They leaned together whispering before the older girl looked her over. She drew her fan through her hand—what had Julia said that meant? Something that wasn't nice, but Amelia couldn't remember exactly what.

"It's a shame your sister couldn't make it, though I can see why you hid her away. It must be so embarrassing."

Amelia froze. By the time she shook herself out of it, Lord Bellamy had steered her away and over to the other side of the room.

"Did she...I—"

"Shh. Don't make a scene for that vicious twit. Are you all right?"

She took a deep breath, brushing her fingers against the tightly rolled cylinder at her hairline. "Do you know who those women are?"

"Unfortunately. Olivia and Charlotte Chisholm, your fiancé's cousins."

Unbelievable. Relatives of Embry's. Not only could she not go back and tell them how horrible they were, she would be stuck with those pit vipers for the rest of her life.

Starting right then. Embry had moved on from the Wakefields and was motioning for her to join him with his cousins. Amelia could think of nothing she wanted to do less.

"Another bold move, and this one you cannot blame on your mother."

"Hmm?" Amelia was too busy glaring at the Chisholms.

"Blatantly ignoring the summons of one's fiancée at one's own engagement party. People are definitely starting to notice."

Amelia looked around. *Damn.* He was right. Embry was frowning and the guests around him were definitely looking at her.

"Don't make me go."

"I would never. I love a good scene."

Amelia swore under her breath. She excused herself to the sound of Jasper chuckling behind her.

"Lady Olivia. Miss Charlotte. May I introduce my fiancé, Miss Amelia Bishop?"

"We've met." Amelia might not be able to avoid them, but she would be damned if she'd pretend to be cordial.

"Oh?"

Lady Olivia's smile was pure ice. "We were asking her where her sister was. We were so looking forward to an introduction."

"She's not feeling well," he lied.

Did he know, or was that just what her mother had told him?

Miss Charlotte joined the fray. "Isn't she sick all the time? What difference does that make?"

Miss Olivia shuddered. "Can you imagine? What a burden."

Embry frowned. "She's a nice enough girl, if a bit limited."

Limited? Amelia stared at Embry in disbelief.

"What a shame she couldn't be here," Charlotte said with transparent glee. "Although, can you imagine being overshadowed at your own engagement party by a cripple? Poor cousin Embry wouldn't have a moment's peace. It's probably a relief."

He stared down at his glass. "It is, a little."

The sounds of the party went hazy in Amelia's ears. "Embry?"

He had the decency to look uncomfortable. "I only mean, it's easier. Not having to explain to everyone."

Amelia felt the flush rising over her face. The giggles of Olivia and Charlotte drifted to her like they were coming through water. It was hard to breathe. Embry might have tried to say something, but she was already excusing herself, pushing her way through the throng and out into the hall.

✦————◦⟨❈⟩◦————✦

Nick made his way to the room he knew was Julia's. He'd had his own tree-climbing adventures, although—unlike Amelia—sense had prevailed and he'd restricted himself to the front doors by the time he turned twelve. He knocked quietly.

"Go away."

It was definitely Julia's voice. He ignored the sentiment and stepped inside. "I'd almost forgotten what the palace looked like. When did you get the elephants?" Nick brushed his hand across the backs of the waist-high gold sculptures as he crossed the room.

She turned in surprise, but then turned back to staring out at the garden below from the window seat. "Papa had them sent from India last year."

"Another continent conquered by Lady Julia's collection." He sat opposite her, his back against the wall. She refused to look at him, so there was nothing stopping him from looking at her in detail.

If he was being objective, she was prettier than her sister. Julia's features were perfectly classical, where Amelia's were softer and slightly out of proportion. Not that it had ever mattered. From the first day he'd met Amelia Bishop, Nick hadn't been able to see anyone else. Her lips might not make a perfect pout, but there was a genuineness to her smiles that spoke to Nick's soul. Amelia took a quiet joy in the world that echoed his own. Julia was never content to sit still, never able to settle happily into silent contemplation. As a friend, Nick had a deep respect for Julia's intelligence and sharp wit, but it was Amelia's gentleness that had stolen his heart.

"I'm sorry," he said.

"For what?"

"That you and I never fell in love with each other. We'd both be weathering today much better if we had."

Julia laughed, but there was no joy in it. "Fat lot of good it would have done. Amelia was born perfect and you still can't face your parents for her. Your spine's even worse off than mine."

He couldn't argue with her there. They settled for looking

out the window in silence together.

"How's the party?" she asked after a while.

"Awful."

This time, her laugh had warmth. "Do the guests that aren't you think that?"

"Probably not. Dolts."

Her skirts rustled as she shifted over to his side of the platform. Nick lifted his arm, and she settled under it. This was how he knew. When Amelia leaned against him for comfort, every nerve in his body cried out in elation. In rightness. When Julia leaned against him, it only felt vaguely pleasant.

"I'm sorry my sister is marrying the wrong man."

"No, you're not." He waited for her to say something else cutting, but it didn't come.

Instead, she wiggled closer. "If it were a fair fight, I'd be on your side."

"Thanks."

"Thank you, for saying what you said. We'd be awful together, but thank you."

"We wouldn't be so bad."

"Do you really want to spend the rest of your life losing at chess and horse races to your wife?"

Nicholas grinned. "How is that any different than me marrying Amelia?"

"She's rubbish at chess."

"Excellent rider, though."

"Not better than me," Julia said, sounding more like herself.

It was a subject of much debate between the sisters, but now wasn't the time to argue Amelia's side. Nick pressed a brotherly kiss to Julia's forehead. "Not better than you."

A shudder went through her, followed by a sniffle. Nick squeezed his arm around her shoulder tighter. There was nothing he could say. Nothing either of them could say.

When it passed, she inhaled a deep breath. "I'm not ready to lose her."

"Neither am I."

They sat there, taking comfort in each other's presence as the garden lights flickered.

Eventually, Julia nudged him with her elbow. "You should go back down. People will notice you're gone."

"Wouldn't that be the scandal of the century?" he said with a grin as he stood up, stretching the stiffness out of his limbs.

"Oh, to be at the center of a torrid scandal," Julia said dreamily.

"Someday."

She rolled her eyes. "Get out of my room, Wakefield."

He left with a grin on his face and a much lighter step than he'd entered with—until he came down the stairs to find Amelia in the hallway, bent at the waist, taking deep, heaving breaths of panic.

"Mia? What's the matter? What's happened?"

She looked up, tears streaming down her face. "E-e-e-mbry…he said…awful things," she choked out, before dissolving into more sobs.

Nicholas would kill the bastard. It was one thing to sit nobly by while she married a man who had a chance at making her happy, but Amelia was clearly not happy.

"It's all right. Everything will be fine." Nicholas's arms wrapped around her by reflex. He didn't know what else to do. He felt helpless.

"You two had better not be getting all calf-eyed again." Jasper came around the corner. "Bloody hell. What's happened?"

"You were there, you tell me. Apparently, Montrose is responsible. Will you stay with her? There's something I have to do." Specifically, beat the man to a pulp.

Amelia grabbed his sleeve. "You can't. Your p-parents. You know what people will say."

"I don't care about that."

"Yes, you do."

Jasper looked between the two of them. "Well?"

If he rushed back into the ballroom and called Montrose out, it would be the talk of the county. The talk of London as well. Nicholas swore. "She's right. I can't."

"Right. It's to me, then." He turned on his heel and went back the way he came.

It wasn't long before a collection of screams and shocked gasps rang out. Nicholas raced down the hallway with Amelia in tow. They arrived in time to see Montrose being helped up off the floor, holding his jaw. One of the men Nicholas didn't know was restraining Jasper by his shoulders.

"What the devil?" Lord Bishop shouted.

"Tapped him on the shoulder and decked him," someone said from behind him.

"A lodestone for scandal, that Lord Bellamy. You'd think a duke's heir would behave better," someone else said.

"Shall I expect a call from your second?" Jasper asked, not caring who heard.

Montrose finally caught sight of Amelia, taking in her red complexion and puffy eyes. His face fell. "No. I was in the wrong. I thank you for pointing it out to me."

That set off a tidal wave of speculation that filled the entire room with murmuring.

Beside him, Amelia was finally coming back to herself. She pulled her hand from his. "I think you'd better take Lord Bellamy and go."

They couldn't be seen holding hands, but he couldn't help reaching for her. "Are you certain?"

"Yes. I'll be fine now." Amelia stepped away from him,

speaking up over the crowd. "In fact, I think you should all take your leave. There's been quite enough excitement for one party."

Lady Bishop rushed forward. "Amelia."

"I mean it, Mother. The party is over. Thank you, everyone, for coming."

There was nothing else to do but collect Jasper from his captor and head for the door.

"I can't believe you hit him," Nicholas said as they collected their hats.

"I can't believe you didn't." Jasper slung his coat over his shoulder and sauntered out to the drive.

Amelia closed the door to the drawing room. The last of the guests were having their carriages brought around, and it was just her and Embry in the one room that hadn't been taken over by the engagement madness. She picked up a book with almost every page corner folded over, one of her favorites. Even Julia enjoyed it. They read it aloud when there was nothing better to do.

Embry was watching her, but she didn't know what to say to him. Someone had found him a cold compress for his face. A terrible part of her hoped they hadn't found it soon enough. She wouldn't mind watching him try to explain a bruise.

"I'm sorry, Amelia. I shouldn't have agreed with my cousins when they were being cruel about your sister."

She nodded. He certainly shouldn't have.

"You're perfectly right to be upset. She'll be my sister, too, once we're wed, and it's my duty to—"

Amelia set the book down. "I don't think we should get married."

The words fell out of her mouth before she realized what she intended to say, but once they were out there she didn't want to take them back. They felt right. She didn't want to marry Embry.

"Amelia, don't be rash. I behaved badly, but I am sorry." Embry reached for her.

She moved out of his reach. "I'm not being rash. I don't think we suit each other."

"Don't be ridiculous. It was one mistake! It's not reason enough to break off an engagement."

"I disagree." Here in this room, surrounded by the little pieces of history from the life she loved with her family, Amelia didn't feel ridiculous at all. "And it's not my only reason. It's just the most recent one."

Confusion washed over his face, followed by a dawning realization. "Wakefield. You have feelings for him."

"What?"

He couldn't possibly know about her tingle dilemma, so he had no business making that sort of accusation. Friendship and a general sort of curiosity about what kissing him might be like were no grounds for that.

"Your mother warned me there was likely more to it than childhood affection."

Her mother. Could that woman not leave well enough alone? "Nicholas and I are just friends."

Embry shook his head. "Not anymore. I saw him holding your hand when you came into the ballroom. His intentions can't be honorable, given his behavior, and it is my duty as your future husband to save you from these sorts of grievous errors in judgement."

"You're not going to be my husband. I'm calling off our engagement."

His face stiffened with resolve. "No. I won't accept it."

"You don't have a choice!" Thank goodness she was finding out about this high-handed behavior now, and not after she'd made the mistake of marrying him. To think she'd almost left her family for this.

"I think I do. If you break off our engagement, I shall sue you for breach of promise."

Amelia stepped back, shock taking over her face. "You wouldn't dare."

"I would, to save you from yourself."

Of all the pompous, asinine sentiments. She didn't need saving. "Fine. Do it. Papa has plenty of money."

Embry sighed. "He won't when I'm finished with him. Public opinion is not in your favor. I will take your parents for everything they're worth, and once you've experienced the cold reality of poverty and what it means for your family, especially for your sister, you'll see sense."

Amelia couldn't be hearing him correctly. "You're threatening to hold my family hostage?"

"Please, Amelia. I don't want to do it, but you're clearly not thinking rationally."

She couldn't breathe. It didn't take much imagination to envision how awful things would be for Julia without the insulating benefits of wealth. They would not be able to hide away from the cruel and malicious opinions of general society. The specialists Papa hired would be impossible to afford. Any and all hope of someday discovering a progressive solution would be gone.

Amelia sucked in a deep breath, shaking her head. "You don't want to do this, Embry. You deserve someone who wants to marry you."

"You're young. This is cold feet and it will pass." He put his hands on her shoulders and this time she was too shocked to move away. "I know you're angry with me, but in time you'll see that I'm doing the right thing."

The words hummed around her in her ears, distorted.

"You'll see. Once you've spent some time away from your sister, you won't even miss her anymore."

She stared at the painting Julia had made of Dionysia for Amelia two birthdays ago. The colors blurred as tears pooled in her eyes, threatening to fall. It was a nightmare. She was in a nightmare, and any minute she would wake up.

By the time Amelia made it back upstairs, Julia was practically climbing the wainscoting. She was frantically checking the windows on both walls when Amelia came into her room.

"What happened? Why did everyone leave early? I heard a scream earlier."

"Lord Bellamy hit Embry."

Julia's eyes flew wide. "Why?"

Why, indeed. "Embry is not the man we thought he was."

If anything, her sister's eyes managed to get even wider. "What on earth happened?"

Amelia collapsed on the chaise in a puff of silk. "Embry's cousins are awful."

"Awful how?"

"If they worked for us, we *would* let Papa fire them and we wouldn't feel at all badly about it."

It was all the explanation Julia needed. "But that's not Embry. So his family is horrid. That's not the end of the world."

"He just stood there," Amelia shouted. "And he agreed with them!"

The frown on her sister's face was difficult to read. Julia couldn't want Amelia to marry so badly that she would accept his complicity in his cousin's behavior, could she? Years of helping Julia hold mock-debuts, imaginary introductions to the royal family, and playing the role of a handsome duke during make-believe piled up in Amelia's throat, making it difficult to breathe. That was what Julia wanted, but she wouldn't force it on Amelia. They knew each other better than that.

"I told Embry I couldn't marry him."

"Oh, Mia." Disapproval dragged down the corners of Julia's mouth.

"But he wouldn't accept it. He said he's going to sue Papa into poverty if I don't marry him." Amelia waited for Julia's enraged outburst.

It didn't come. Instead, her sister took a deep breath and nodded. "Maybe it's for the best."

"What?" Certainly she hadn't heard her right.

"Now there's no way to back out. You can stop second-guessing yourself. You're going to be Lady Montrose. It's time to start taking it seriously."

Julia was actually taking Embry's side.

For the first time in Amelia's life, she felt completely, truly alone. Everything they'd shared, the impenetrable partnership their father joked about, was a lie. Her life was all about what everyone else wanted. Amelia could accept it from their mother, from Embry, but Julia? A nauseating ache took up residence in her gut.

"Mother will be thrilled. She can stop sending herself into hysterics, worrying he's going to call it off. It's obvious that's not going to happen if he's willing to take Papa to court to keep you."

The last bit broke through Amelia's despair. She was on her own, but that didn't mean she had to give up and accept her fate.

What *would* she have to do to make herself undesirable to Embry?

It wouldn't be easy. She needed to think it through, alone. Amelia didn't need Julia figuring out what she was up to and trying to sabotage her plan. "I'm going to bed."

"Mia. Please don't be mad. I only meant—"

"It's all right," Amelia said, rushing to the door in a flurry of silk. "It's been a long day. Good night."

If Julia responded, Amelia didn't hear it. She was already down the hall with a half-formed plan in mind. Without Julia's help, she was going to need all of her concentration to pull it off.

Because it had to work.

She wasn't going to marry Embry, or anyone else for that matter. Amelia liked her life exactly the way it had always been, and she wasn't going to let anyone change it.

Chapter Six

Nicholas and Jasper chose to brave the late winter chill rather than share the tense confines of his parents' carriage. Lady Wakefield was in fits—*of course* that Bishop girl would find a way to foul things up—and Nick was afraid of what he'd say if he had to listen to it for even the short distance home.

In contrast, Jasper was in glorious spirits. "I've never been on the honorable end of a challenge. I feel like we should celebrate."

"Do you think she means to break it off?" She couldn't possibly want to go through with it after tonight—Amelia had been more upset than he'd ever seen her. If only he knew what had actually happened between them.

"You know her better than I do."

He would never want Amelia to be unhappy but, since the catastrophe had already occurred, if she happened to end up unattached he couldn't claim he would be disappointed. Amelia deserved a husband who adored and understood her, not some clod who made her cry at her own engagement party.

"Will you declare yourself if she does?"

He wanted to, desperately, but it might not be that simple. She obviously had no idea how he felt, and she had pulled away when he'd reached for her. "I—"

"Because if you don't, you deserve the life of misery that will inevitably follow."

"Tell me how you truly feel," Nicholas choked out around his surprise.

"Always."

When they reached the house, Lord Wakefield was waiting for him in the foyer. Nick's laughter died out.

"Nicholas, I need to speak with you."

Jasper raised and lowered his eyebrows before heading upstairs, leaving them alone.

"Of course." Nick studied his father's face, trying to gauge which version he was dealing with. He'd been lucid at the party, but Nick was learning the changes could happen with disturbing quickness.

"Nicholas," Lord Wakefield began. "I'm certain you're aware that the Wakefield name has never been touched by scandal."

"I am." That didn't help. The myriad lectures on the subject from his childhood meant they could be in any time in his father's mind. His expression while delivering them hadn't changed since Nicholas was a boy of five.

"And I'm certain you're also aware that any interference in the Bishop girl's engagement would result in scandal of more than one variety."

The present then. For the first time, Nicholas wished his father would fall into a different time.

Lord Wakefield pinned his youngest son with a stare honed by generations of Marquesses. "I hold our family's reputation to the highest standard. Your mother has relentlessly protected the Wakefield name while I have been unwell. You will not be the first to bring shame upon us."

Nicholas squared his shoulders. "Do you feel I tarnished our reputation this evening?"

The Marquess took in his son's stance and lifted chin. "Do not think I didn't notice with whom Lady Amelia returned to the ballroom."

"Amelia and I are friends." Saying it was starting to taste like ashes in his mouth.

"Lord Montrose and his intended were happily on their way to the altar, and now there is discord. My mind might not be what it used to, but it has not become so derelict that I cannot see what is in front of my face."

"The falling out tonight wasn't about me." Nicholas wished it had been, but Amelia had no idea how he felt. Even his overt attempts at flirting with her were brushed aside as teasing.

"Do you pretend to claim you do not harbor feelings for Amelia Bishop?"

There it was, in the open. For years they had existed in a silent understanding—his parents did not ask and he did not impose upon them a confession of his affections—but no longer.

"I do not."

Lord Wakefield sighed. "Your feelings may not be under your control, but your actions are. You will not involve yourself in the Bishop girl's engagement."

Nicholas didn't have an immediate response. Fortunately, none was required.

The Marquess of Wakefield had made his declaration; the only possible outcome was for his son to abide by it. Lord Wakefield nodded his head—obligation satisfied—and took himself off to the library.

It didn't take long for Jasper to find him after Nick returned to his room. The Viscount of Bellamy's understanding of the human need for privacy was almost nonexistent.

"What did he want?"

Nick untied his neckcloth and tossed it on the dressing table. "You know, in mannered circles, one knocks before entering a room."

"Mannered circles are boring, populated with boring people who have sticks lodged firmly up their backsides. And not in the exciting way."

"There's an exciting way to have a stick in your backside?"

Jasper's grin was wicked. "You left Paris too soon. There is a great deal of the world that you still don't know about, Master Wakefield."

"If it involves being sodomized, I left just in time."

"Matter of opinion. With a properly deviant partner, it can be quite..." Jasper sprawled out across Nicholas's bed. "No. I'll not be distracted. What did your father want?"

"To declare that I will not be involving myself in Amelia's engagement."

"He must have been pleased to discover that you have been grossly passive."

"I haven't been—"

Jasper waved his arm in Nicholas's direction. "Tell me one thing you've done to secure your future happiness with Amelia Bishop."

"That's not..." Nicholas couldn't think of anything, because he wasn't supposed to be securing anything with Amelia. "Our future happiness will be as friends."

"You're in love with her."

He very much was, and always had been. "But she doesn't love me."

"You wrote her every day we were in France." Jasper threw his hands in the air. "You look like you're about to tear her clothes off every time you see her."

"That is decidedly none of your concern."

Jasper arched an eyebrow. "Wakefield, what did you say to me when we first met?"

"Get out of my train car, you drunken nuisance."

"After that."

Nicholas sighed. "I wish there was more to my life than being a dutiful son."

"That's right, and I swore to make sure you live a life full of misbehavior—"

"At the time you said adventure."

"—and die exhausted, well pleased with the memories you had collected."

"But that was before."

"Before what?"

"Before I was called back home. Before my father became ill."

Jasper squared his shoulders, full of affront. "Do you think a duke's promise is so lightly discarded?"

"You're not a duke yet."

"And won't be for many years to come, God willing, but it will happen and I'll still have promised." Jasper stood up, pacing and riffling through Nicholas's belongings. The pocket watch Philip had given Nicholas when he finished at Oxford landed with a clatter. "Well pleased, I said, and you are obviously not pleased. You're more dismally dutiful than ever."

"My family needs me."

"Only so they can avoid inconveniencing your brother."

It was pointless to try to explain. Jasper was a creature

devoted to seeking his own pleasure. In Jas's mind, the title existed to serve the holder, not the other way around.

"We have to stay out of it, Jas."

Jasper's eyebrows leaped upward as a pair. "*We* don't have to anything. I make my own decisions."

"Fine, but I—"

"Amelia needed you tonight and you did nothing," Jasper interrupted. "The man she is promised to spend the rest of her life with threw her to wolves. Hell, he invited the wolves. Hide your feelings behind friendship if you insist, but a friend would have stood up for her. A friend did."

The words sank into Nicholas and settled like rocks in the pit of his stomach. Jasper had only known Amelia for a few days, and he had come to her aid. In typical, dramatic Jasper fashion, but he'd acted. Nick had wanted to act. It had been his first instinct, and he'd intended to follow it through. He shouldn't have let himself be dissuaded. Jasper was right. He'd been a coward.

After everything he'd learned being away, was he truly allowing himself to settle back into old behavior? Worse behavior, even. He'd never let his parents stop him from being a true friend to Amelia before.

"You're right," Nicholas admitted.

"Obviously."

"But what do I do? How do I make it up to her?"

"First," Jasper announced, in jolly spirits again now that he was getting what he wanted, "we find out how things stand. A great deal hinges on the current status of her engagement. Once we know, we can make a plan."

The hope that crackled to life inside him made him wonder why he'd waited this long.

The candles burned low as Amelia stared into space with the end of the pen between her teeth. Her writing desk was covered in wax and she wasn't much further than she had been in Julia's room. She was trying to organize her thoughts onto paper, but the problem in front of her was daunting. Masterminding was Julia's bailiwick. Amelia's talents leaned more toward assisting.

Something cracked against the window. Amelia looked up. A second crack sounded. *What the devil?* A rock. Someone was throwing rocks at her bedroom window.

There was only one person it could be.

Barely illuminated by the light coming from the ground floor windows, Nicholas stood on the side of the house with a handful of stones. Amelia pushed the window up in its casement—quietly. It wouldn't do to have anyone coming to investigate.

"What are you doing?" she whispered, shivering. She wrapped her arms around herself to block the cold from cutting through her nightgown. How could he stand to be out there at this hour?

"I need to talk to you," he whispered back. "May I come up?"

Could he come up? Of course not. It was…well, fair play after what she'd done the other day, but that was beside the point. "It's very late."

"It's important."

Nicholas might be able to help with her present difficulty. She *was* at her wits' end. Whispering out into the darkness while they both froze to death was less than ideal. Amelia inspected the wall outside her bedroom. There was no way he would manage to climb the tightly fitted bricks without breaking his neck. "Use the back stairs."

Nick disappeared around the corner of the house.

Grabbing a wrapper, Amelia tiptoed to her bedroom door and peeked out. *So far so good.* She sent up a silent prayer of thanks that she didn't have to pass Julia's room on her way to the back stairs.

At the end of the corridor, she slowly pushed the servant's door inward. Nothing. No sound, no Nicholas. Amelia's heartbeat raced. No one had sounded any kind of alarm, so he hadn't been discovered. Unless he had, and he was trying to talk his way out of it. Would Mrs. Polk keep his secret if she came across him below-stairs? She wouldn't let him come up, that much Amelia was certain of. How long should she wait?

Muffled scuffing sounds came from the steps just below where Amelia was waiting. "Ni—"

The new maid's head came around the corner.

"—ora. Haven't you gone to bed yet?"

"Just finishing cleaning up the party. Did you need something, my lady?"

"No, no. Just thought I heard something. Must have been the wind."

Nora mumbled something Amelia didn't catch as she was closing the door. She leaned against the wall. She would count to one hundred. If it took Nick longer than that, that was too bad. Her nerves couldn't take it.

One. Two. Three. … Thirty-four. Thirty-five. Thirty-six. Was that a creak? She didn't dare open the door to check. If it was Nora again, she'd have a devil of a time explaining herself.

The door slid inward a crack. "Mia?"

"Nick." Amelia let out a huge sigh of relief—and sucked it back in. They still had to make it back to her room. *Oh God.* What if her mother—what if her *father* came down the hall? "Hurry. And be quiet!"

"I know how to sneak."

"Shh!"

They were halfway back to her room when the latch on Julia's door at the far end of the hall clicked. It was too much. Amelia abandoned stealth and ran for it. Nicholas was right behind her. They darted inside and Amelia locked the door behind them. She tried to listen for her sister coming after them, but she couldn't hear over her own labored breathing.

"She didn't see us."

Amelia wasn't prepared to take his word for it. She waited a little longer, but there was no inquiring knock on her door. "Let's never go through that again."

"I've gone through that every time you've climbed into my room."

"In the daylight! It's much less illicit during the day."

"I beg to differ," Nicholas said. "I've lost entire years off my life with the sun still high in the sky. If either of our parents discovered us—being discovered by your father at our age—"

"Don't." Amelia pressed a hand to her chest to try to slow down her heart. "Don't even think it. We still have to get you back out."

Nick groaned.

Amelia couldn't agree more. Worried that her knees would buckle any minute, she sat on the end of her bed. She motioned for Nick to take the chair that was still pulled out at her desk. "So, what was so important it couldn't wait for morning?"

"Are you still engaged to Montrose?"

Even hearing his name made her furious. "Yes."

"Oh." Nick's face fell.

"But I'm not going to marry him."

"What?"

"I tried to break it off, but he won't let me."

"That doesn't make any sense."

It truly didn't. In a rational world she would have declared the engagement over, and that would have been that. But there was nothing rational about the situation she found herself in. Amelia stood up. Anger drove away her nerves and made pacing preferable. "He won't accept my termination of our engagement. He threatened to sue my father for breach of contract."

"That's—"

"Villainous, but!" Amelia announced. "I have a plan. I'm going to make myself thoroughly undesirable so that *he* throws *me* over."

"Amelia."

"It's brilliant," she declared.

"It's certainly something," Nick said, rubbing a hand over his eyes. "What's your first move?"

"That's the part I need your help with." Amelia flashed him her biggest, most charming grin. "Also, all the other moves."

"So the whole plan."

"Basically."

Amelia wasn't marrying Montrose. There was still hope. He could weather all manner of nonsense—making herself undesirable? Nick doubted that was even possible. But it would all be all right. She wasn't going to marry Montrose.

"Mia, if you're not—"

"I can't believe how blind I was. He's absolutely beastly and I had no idea."

"I need to tell you—"

"I told Julia and she sided with him! Can you believe that?" She was still pacing, nightgown billowing behind her as she strode back and forth. "Well, the joke is on her. I'm never getting married, so she can find her own adventures. I'm not letting her live through mine anymore."

Never getting married? "You don't mean that."

"I absolutely do."

Don't panic. "You might feel that way right now, but eventually—"

"No. Never. Look at how badly I did this time around. Who's to say I won't be completely deceived again?" She sat on the bed in a frustrated puff of linen. "Not that there will be a next time, but if there was—it's clear I am a terrible judge of character."

This was a train of thought Nicholas could work with. "I certainly agree that you shouldn't get engaged to someone you just met. Or even someone you haven't known for quite some time."

Amelia was shaking her head. "I don't think you can ever truly know someone. I thought I knew my mother, and look what she's turned into in all this engagement nonsense."

He needed a compelling argument, but none came to mind. Fortunately, Nicholas didn't need all the answers right away. He could hang onto his new hope. It was enough that she didn't want to marry Montrose. Once she was free, he could spend every day convincing her they were right for each other. He could spend the rest of their lives convincing her, if he had his way. For now, all they had to do was get rid of Montrose.

"So this plan."

"I need to make myself thoroughly undesirable." Amelia popped up again and resumed her pacing. "It should be fairly simple."

It would be impossible, but it wasn't the right time for Nick to tell her that. "Do you know what he values?"

"Ruining my life," she grumbled.

Nick laughed. "Beyond that."

She sighed. "I have no idea what he values, other than vexing me and idolizing his beloved Lily. How can I be engaged to a man I know so little about?"

Lily. Lily? Nicholas wracked his brain. "Lily Valentine? She was engaged to Montrose, wasn't she?"

"He adored her. She might as well have walked on water." Amelia spun, halting her pacing. "Did you know her?"

It didn't happen often, but every once in a while Amelia would get like this—bursting with energy, pacing and chattering away. Nick loved being near her in these moments. All the time, really, but especially these moments. It was like holding a comet. It was made all the better because he knew he was one of an extremely select group of people who got to see her this way.

"Nick?"

Right. Lily Valentine. "No, not well, but I might know someone who did. Her cousin and Philip are members of the same club in London."

Amelia lit up like a sunrise. "Could you ask him about her? If I could become the opposite of Lily, Montrose would despise me for certain."

"I'd need to go to London." He'd promised his mother he would stay at Wakefield Manor.

"That's perfect!" Amelia threw herself at him, wrapping her arms around his neck. "As Embry's fiancé, I'm expected to suffer through the season. We can endure it together!"

Nick closed his eyes. He was all too aware of how few layers Amelia was wearing. In the name of solving her crisis, he'd managed to block out the way the light from the fireplace silhouetted her legs each time she changed the direction of her pacing, but having her practically in his lap was too much.

"We should do something for you, too."

He could think of a few things.

"While we're in London, you should apply to the Inns of Court!" Amelia grabbed his face with his hands, forcing him to look at her. "You said you wanted to be a barrister. Let's do it. Let's both take control of our lives. While we can both support each other. If you don't do it now, you never will."

His parents were going to disown him, but there was nothing he could do about it. That fact kept proving itself over and over, every day he spent near Amelia. Nicholas couldn't say no to her any more than he could stop the earth from turning. Not when her brown eyes were sparkling and she smiled at him like that. He was utterly lost. "All right. Let's go to London."

When the knock sounded on her bedroom door moments after Nicholas disappeared into the servant's corridor, Amelia was certain he'd been caught.

"Who is it?" She cringed. She never said that. *Pull yourself together.*

"It's me," her father said from the other side of the door.

Amelia almost fainted. After fighting down the urge to hide, she took a calming breath and opened the door. "Papa? What are you doing here?"

"Can't I visit my own daughter?"

Smaller smile. The smile was too big. *He'll know!* "It's very late."

"Some discussions are best held during the witching hour."

Oh no. "I'm quite tired."

He frowned at her, stepping inside. "Mia. Tell me what happened."

This was it. This was where she got accused of every wicked thing she'd thought about doing with Nicholas lately. Touching his face. Feeling the heat of his legs through the thin fabric of her nightgown. This was God punishing her for impure thoughts. She hadn't even gotten to do any of the truly shameful things she'd thought of. "Nothing. Nothing happened!"

"You were crying. Lord Bellamy struck your betrothed. That's not nothing."

Embry! He wanted to know what happened with Embry. Her knees actually did buckle this time—from relief. She caught the edge of the door to keep herself upright. He hadn't found Nick sneaking down the back stairs, but she couldn't tell him about what happened at the party, either. What if he ran off and confronted Embry?

Much as Amelia hated to admit it, taking care of difficult situations was not Papa's specialty. He had an excellent eye for investments, but when it came to the rest of life he often found himself adrift. What if there was nothing he could do and he had to sit by in full knowledge and watch his daughter be given into the hands of a villainous cad? It would kill him. "We had a disagreement. It was nothing."

"You called off your engagement party."

"I overreacted."

Lord Bishop sat down next to her on the bed. "Is this about Julia, Mia?"

Amelia held her tongue. Let him draw whatever conclusions he liked, as long as he didn't find out the truth.

"I know you're used to doing everything with your sister, but you're setting off on your own now. You can't be cruel with Montrose's emotions just because you're scared of living outside each other's pockets."

The sense of betrayal from earlier bubbled up. "Julia's

not at all afraid of living without me. She's more than happy to see me go."

"I'm certain that's not true."

"I'm certain it is. She doesn't even care that he—" Sense shut her mouth before she could stick her foot into it.

"Mia." He tipped her chin up like he used to do when she was small. "Don't fight with your sister. She loves you and she's terrified to lose you."

You mean she's terrified she won't be able to live vicariously through me if I call off the engagement. Amelia stared at the carpet. How could she suddenly have so many secrets? Yesterday, she'd had none.

"I think the distance might do you two some good."

Et tu, Papa? But it suited the plan she and Nick had come up with to agree with him. "I think maybe you're right."

Lord Bishop sighed. "When we came back from India and realized Julia's spine couldn't be mended… I'm not entirely sure we've been fair to you. You deserve to be thought of first by someone."

"I never needed—"

"I wish we'd done better, but Montrose can give you that. He adores you. It's obvious he doesn't see anyone else when you walk into a room. I want that for you."

Amelia wanted it, too. Just not with Embry. She hated not being honest with her father. "Papa, I —"

"We're so proud of you. I know you're frightened of leaving us. Of leaving Julia. But we're so proud of the match you've made. I can't remember being this happy in a long time."

Her father was proud of her. Amelia tried to remember if he'd ever said it before.

He'd been proud of Julia. Proud when she took her first steps without help. Proud the first time she beat him at chess. Proud of her courage after each and every painful surgery that failed to yield improvements. If he'd been proud of Amelia, it had never been out loud. Her father loved her, but she hadn't realized before now how much she needed his approval.

"Thank you, Papa."

What else could she say?

There was light showing under the door of the drawing room when Nicholas crept back in to Wakefield Manor. It was somewhat embarrassing sneaking in at his age. More embarrassing still because for once he'd been doing something he actually ought to be ashamed of. He'd spent the evening in Amelia's bedroom. The rush of it would keep him up all night.

He found Lady Wakefield in the library alone, staring into the fire that had drawn his notice. "Mother? Is something wrong?"

"No. I couldn't sleep." She frowned at him. "Are you just getting in?"

Nicholas sat down across from her. Now was as good a time as any. He'd made his decision—he was committed to Amelia. If he could continue to help his family he would, but if he had to choose, he was choosing her. Even if that meant offering her nothing but himself. He had to do something, for once. "I need to go to London."

"Will you be gone long?" she asked, not really hearing him.

"I need to tell Philip."

That certainly claimed her attention. "You can't."

Nick had come to another decision on the walk back from Amelia's. He was tired of keeping things from people. His feelings for Amelia. His father's illness. If he'd been honest with Amelia from the beginning, instead of pretending to fancy green-eyed dairy maids, maybe this whole mess could have been avoided. He didn't want to look back years from now and wish he'd told his brother sooner. "Philip deserves to know."

"But his work—"

"I'm not giving up the job, but I think he deserves to know. I can run everything from London. Father does it every season. But it's not right not to involve Philip." Nicholas reached out for his mother's hand. "He deserves better than to be blindsided by this."

"When will you go?" Her mouth was tight. She didn't approve, but she wouldn't stop him.

"Tomorrow. I think it's best to tell him as soon as possible."

Lady Wakefield shook her head, resting her face in her hand. "It wasn't supposed to turn out this way."

"Everything will be all right."

"And Arthur? Will he be all right?" She shook her head again. "No, everything will not be all right. It will never be all right again."

"Mother."

"Go. Tell your brother and take that friend of yours with you. I don't care anymore."

Nicholas lifted his hand—to do what? To say what? He couldn't give her husband back. Couldn't bring his father back. There was nothing he could do that would ease the rigid line of her shoulders or stop her from staring blindly into the fire. If they'd had a different relationship in the past perhaps he could have, but this was what they had.

He stood up to leave. "Good night, Mother."

She didn't say anything at all.

Nick went to the study and left a note for Mr. Fletcher before going upstairs to Jasper's room. He didn't bother knocking.

"Is that the unmannered urgency of a man bursting with

good news?" Jasper asked.

Possibly. Hopefully. "Pack your bags. We're going to London first thing."

When Amelia told her parents she wanted to go to London early, they practically tripped over themselves ordering the carriage. They believed she was finally embracing her new role as a countess. Amelia felt awful lying to them, but desperate times called for desperate measures. Julia wasn't as easy to fool. She stopped Amelia in the hall outside of the dining room after breakfast.

"What is going on, Amelia?"

"Nothing is going on."

"Rubbish."

Amelia took a deep breath and recited what she and Nicholas had come up with. "I want to immerse myself in the season."

Julia stared at her. "You're lying."

"I'm not."

Julia's scrutiny almost caused Amelia to buckle, but she focused on her anger. Julia had betrayed her. Amelia didn't owe her the truth. She stared at the standing clock in the hallway and recited, "As the future Countess of Montrose, it's important that I socialize and dispel the rumors from the engagement party."

"You hate social maneuvering. Who are you pretending to be right now?"

God, she was failing this miserably. "I'm sorry. There's a great deal to do before I leave. I have to go."

Amelia fled, desperate to get away before her sister read everything from her face. It was hard enough lying to her parents; she didn't have the heart to get into another argument with Julia. She couldn't be honest with Julia, so the easiest thing was to avoid her, even if it hurt to do it.

When she returned to her own room, two notes were waiting for her. The first note, and accompanying arrangement of deep pink roses and honeysuckle, was from Embry.

Dearest Amelia,

Please accept these flowers as a sign of my admiration, and proof that I harbor no resentment regarding our discussion. Your sweet and innocent nature allowed you to be led astray, and I cannot fault you for such admirable qualities, vulnerable though they might make you to the less scrupulous. I look forward to cherishing and protecting your generous heart as your husband.

Yrs truly,

Embry

Amelia glared at the page. He might not harbor any resentment, but she certainly did. Crumpling it, she moved on to the next note.

Mia,

I've arranged what I can here, so I am going ahead to London. If you have need of me, reach me at Philip's house in town.

Chin up,

N.

Just like that, her spine straightened. She had a plan and an ally. She wasn't alone. Everything would be all right. All she had to do was stay focused and everything would come out all right in the end. Just stay focused. She repeated the mantra over and over in her head.

"Just because you walk faster doesn't mean you can run from me." Julia's breath was labored as she stood in the doorway. "If I'd hurt myself chasing after you, you'd be feeling dreadfully sorry right now."

"Would I?" She absolutely would, but damn it, it was Amelia's turn to be angry. Just this once, she would feel the way she felt and not worry about how it might affect Julia.

"Don't be like this, Mia. I know you think I'm being disloyal, but Lord Montrose is—"

"Lord Montrose is what?" Lady Bishop asked, coming up behind her daughter in the doorway. "Are we gossiping? Extolling the virtues of Amelia's brilliant match?"

"Not quite," Julia said, locking eyes with Amelia.

"Don't be jealous," Lady Bishop admonished. "It puts ugly lines on your face."

"I'll keep that in mind." Julia's tone was like iron striking iron.

Lady Bishop looked between her daughters. "What's the matter? What's going on with you two?"

Julia pushed her hair over her shoulder. "Nothing serious. Everything is fine. It'll sort itself out."

"Good, then. Anyhow, I've loads of packing to do!" Oblivious, Lady Bishop flitted off down the hallway.

Amelia waited until she was certain their mother was out of earshot. "Just to be clear, it will not sort itself out. Everything is not fine, and I do not forgive you. You're my sister. You're supposed to be on my side."

"Mia."

"I needed you, but I don't anymore. So please get out of my room."

Chapter Seven

It had been less than a week since Nicholas last saw Philip. It felt like half a lifetime. Declaring that his brother deserved to know was all well and good, but it was only now sinking in that Nicholas had to be the one to tell him.

As the heir, Philip had always been closer with their father. They'd spent hours together on the estate while Philip learned the business of eventually becoming Marquess of Wakefield. For the first time in his life, Nicholas wished his brother had turned out as rigid and impervious as their parents. It would make it easier, knowing nothing could phase him. Instead, Philip approached the position with more warmth than any of his predecessors. Philip cared. It was part of what made him such an effective member of the House of Lords.

It was also why Nicholas was still standing in the hallway, afraid to go into the study of his brother's London house. Even the house was warm, inviting. Doors were left open to spread the light from the windows throughout. The laughter of the next generation of Wakefields could be heard drifting down from the upper floors.

"Your nephews look exactly like that when they have something difficult to tell their father." Caroline, future Marchioness of Wakefield, stood at the foot of the stairs smiling sympathetically.

"Any advice?" At two and five years of age, Nicholas doubted his nephews had ever had to deal with a confession of this magnitude, but he would take all the help he could get.

"Avoid prevaricating. Try not to cry."

Sound counsel. Nicholas resolved to at least achieve the standard set for the nursery. "I'd better go in, then."

"Godspeed." Caro grinned as she passed him.

Nick knocked on the door.

"Come in."

Too late to turn back. Nick left the hallway behind and stepped inside.

"Nicholas! Glad you made it." Philip put his pen down and stepped around the desk to shake Nick's hand. "How was the train?"

"On time."

"That's a bloody miracle. Perhaps someday they'll even be predictable."

Nick chuckled. "That's not very patriotic of you."

Philip grinned. "If they manage this network of theirs across England and it works, I'll be the first to congratulate them."

"But you still prefer canals."

"I can't help it. There's no soul in locomotives; they're so violent. Canal transport has poetry."

"Don't let Mother hear you waxing lyrical about poetry." Nick chuckled.

"Or Father." Philip smiled back.

It was time. Nick couldn't pretend everything was right in the world when it wasn't. "Were you in the middle of something?"

"Nothing too important. Is there something to discuss?"

"There is." Nick went to the decanter. "Whiskey?"

Philips eyebrows rose. "It's the middle of the afternoon."

"It's about Father."

A seriousness took over Philip's face. "And it requires whiskey."

Nick recalled the fortifying comfort of having a glass in his hand while he discussed the situation with the estate agent. "It does."

"All right, then."

Sitting across from his brother, Nick told him what he knew. He told him what he'd seen, and what their mother and Mr. Fletcher had confessed to him.

The whiskey remained in Philip's hand, untouched, while he leaned back in his chair and studied the lines of the hardwood floor. "So."

"So."

Nick studied the reflection of the light off the cut crystal tumbler, casting patterns onto the dark leather of the sofa, while he waited for Philip to process the situation.

"You never think…you never consider your parents getting old, until it's upon you."

"I thought you should know."

Philip nodded slowly, brow furrowed. "I'll have to make arrangements. It will take a few days, but we can—"

"No," Nicholas said. "They didn't want to tell you because they didn't want you to give up your life in London."

"That's ridiculous."

"It's not. You're doing good work here. The children are happy. Caro is happy."

"He's my father."

"He's my father, too. I can do this until you're ready. I can fill in for you." Nicholas's grin was lopsided. "After all, that's what I'm for."

"Nick, you know that's not how I feel."

It wasn't, and Nick was grateful for it. All through childhood, Philip had gone out of his way to support Nicholas as an individual, not just a failsafe. But it didn't change the facts. "Last year was a hard year for the country, and you don't know what's ahead of us. England needs you where you are."

Philip shook his head. "England will manage."

"Then finish out the session at least. Mother will never forgive me if I told you and then you did exactly what I promised not to let happen."

The whiskey glass finally found its way to Philip's lips. "The session, then. It will give me time to find suitable replacements for my committee seats."

Nick nodded. That would be enough time, and he couldn't pretend he'd be sad to start his life with Amelia earlier. "I also wanted to ask your help with something. I intend to seek a profession."

"A profession?" From Philip's raised eyebrows and incredulous grin, one would think Nick had asked for help stripping naked in the middle of Westminster Church. "You don't need a profession."

"But I'd like one. I'd like to have a purpose."

"What brought this on?"

The plan had been to lie. To say working on the estate had given him a taste for feeling useful, but Nicholas wanted fewer secrets, not more. And he was done with pretending. "Amelia Bishop."

"I don't know why I even bothered to ask." Philip's face creased with frown lines. "I don't condone stealing another man's fiancé, Nicholas."

"I'm not stealing her. It's complicated, but she doesn't want to marry Montrose."

"Does she want to marry you?" Philip asked.

"I—" He hoped she would, eventually. "I haven't asked her."

"Thank God for small blessings."

"I mean to marry her, Philip."

"Well, I can't pretend to be surprised. I think we all suspected it would go that way someday." His brother sighed. "Did you have something particular in mind?"

"I want to try for barrister."

This time Philip's surprise was pleasant. "Barrister? Really."

"Yes. I thought, maybe someday, I'd run for a seat in Commons. There are a great number of wrongs that need righting in the world, but I need to know what I'm doing first."

"House of Commons." Philip frowned, tapping a finger on his glass. "It's not a bad idea. Respectable and worthwhile. All right, I'll help you, but leave me out of your complications. Lord Montrose is a good man and he's been through a great deal."

Nicholas wasn't certain about that, but he nodded. "Nothing to do with Amelia. Just help me find a way to support myself."

And Amelia, when the time came. It would come. She couldn't mean what she'd said about not wanting to marry ever. Eventually, this experience with Montrose would fade and she would start thinking about the future again. When she did, Nicholas would be ready.

———————— ❦ ————————

"Where are we?" The carriage had pulled up to a house in Charing Cross Amelia wasn't familiar with.

Lady Bishop beamed from ear to ear. "Home, darling."

"What happened to the house in Covent Garden?"

"The neighborhood was unsuitable for a future countess," Lady Bishop said, waving her hand as if she could wave away the fact that they had lived there.

"We love that house," Amelia said through clenched teeth. She and Julia would sit for hours, watching the theatre-goers on the pavements. "You got rid of it?"

"No, more's the pity. Your father went on about some sentimental nonsense, so now we have two."

"I want to go to our house."

"This is our house."

Amelia's fist clenched. "I want to go to our real house."

"Nonsense. Stop being childish. You can't live two blocks down from *actresses* if you're going to be Lady Montrose. Besides, the change will do you good."

More change. Why was everyone so enamored of change all of a sudden? Why couldn't anyone leave well enough alone? She wasn't going to be the future Lady Montrose, and she didn't give a damn about her proximity to stage players. She just wanted two seconds where something wasn't shifting underneath her feet. "Julia's going to hate it."

"Well, Julia's not here."

"But she will be." There was something about her mother's tone. Amelia liked this new attitude less than she liked the new house. "She's coming with Papa later this week."

Lady Bishop avoided her eyes. "Perhaps. We'll cross that bridge when we get to it."

They would do no such thing. Amelia and Julia might be fighting—would likely be fighting for quite some time—but eventually they would make up. Lady Bishop was behaving strangely and Amelia wasn't about to let it pass unacknowledged. "Why wouldn't Julia be coming?"

Her mother let loose an all-suffering sigh. "She might not,

that's all. We need to be focusing all of our attention on you, and your sister can be…"

Amelia could not believe it. She was going to strangle her own mother. "Did you tell her not to come?"

"Honestly, darling. We'll discuss it later. The footmen will think—"

"Did you tell her not to come?" Amelia shouted. They were only on opposite benches in the carriage, but she had to do *something* to break through this madness.

"Amelia! Lower your voice!"

"I will not. You will write to Julia immediately and apologize. You will tell her you don't know what you were thinking. And you will stop this nonsense of trying to exclude her."

Lady Bishop lifted her chin, dismissing Amelia's demands. "Julia understands this is what's best for you."

"You will do it, or I will call off my engagement."

All the color leached from Lady Bishop's cheeks. "You wouldn't."

"I would. You know I'd rather stay in my room and read than be paraded around like some broodmare. Refusing Embry won't cost me a moment's unhappiness."

"You say that, but—"

"Are you writing a letter, or am I?" Amelia interrupted without sympathy.

Her mother drew in a tense breath through her nostrils. "Fine, but you're not doing yourself or Julia any favors. If you think people will be kind to either of you, you're wrong."

Amelia got out of the carriage. She climbed up the unfamiliar steps to the unfamiliar door, leaving her mother's words behind. A butler whose name she didn't know greeted her.

"Could someone show me which room is mine?" she asked.

"Of course, Lady Amelia."

"I'm so glad Lord Montrose is escorting you to his aunt's salon. I knew you'd like the Chisholms if you gave them a chance. After that mess at the engagement party…"

Amelia let her mother's chatter fade into the background. She didn't want to hear about the virtues of the Chisholms or how narrowly Amelia had escaped scandal after Lord Bellamy had come to her rescue. She needed to focus on the task at hand—convincing Embry she wouldn't make him a suitable wife.

He'd sent more flowers this morning, these ones representing gentleness, kindness, and innocence. The qualities he had spoken so highly of in his late fiancée. While Amelia had no quarrel with her predecessor or any of those virtues, they were not the sum total of her parts.

"Lady Bishop. Lady Amelia. Lord Montrose has arrived."

Amelia plastered a smile on her face, pretending she was a besotted bride-to-be and not an unwilling captive. As soon as Embry had exchanged pleasantries with her mother and handed Amelia up into the carriage, she let it drop.

"Your cousins are awful, mean-spirited witches. I want you to do something about them." Amelia would bet quite a bit that the angelic Lily had not been in the habit of making demands.

"Amelia, please."

"You told Lord Bellamy and everyone else at the party that you were in the wrong. You told me you were sorry. Was that a lie?"

Embry sighed. "No, it wasn't."

"Then do something about it. How can you expect me to call them family when even you don't condone their behavior?"

"I have had the opportunity to get to know your sister and what a lovely person she is. I'm sure my cousins would feel the same if they met her."

"You claim to care for me, but you won't even stand by your own convictions?" Amelia let her voice escalate steadily toward hysterics. "Is that how little your word is worth? Was it fear that made you tell Viscount Bellamy you were in the wrong?"

Embry tried to defend himself, but Amelia refused to listen to his arguments.

"I can't see how you can claim to care for me, to know what's best for me, and care so little for my feelings." An affected sniffle insinuated that tears would be soon to follow. Amelia was both impressed and unsettled by how easily she'd adopted the persona of a spoiled debutante.

She turned her face to the carriage wall and refused to look at him. They spent the rest of the ride in uncomfortable silence. She stayed that way through their arrival, only taking his hand for the minimum amount of time necessary to step down from the carriage. As she hoped, once inside he abandoned her and her sullen behavior in favor of less dramatic company.

As soon as he was out of sight, Nicholas found his way to her side.

"I see you managed an invitation." She tried not to let her joy at seeing him be too obvious. Without Julia, she felt more alone than ever. Nicholas's familiar, friendly face was a comfort.

"The wonders of the Wakefield name."

"What about the other thing?" she asked as they strolled past knotted groups of party goers.

"Ahh. Well, the late Miss Valentine was a paragon of womanly virtues, especially noted for her agreeableness."

As Amelia had suspected. "Anything else?"

"She was a woman after Lady Wakefield's heart. Never spoke out of turn, didn't hold any unpopular views. Perfectly behaved." Nicholas touched her elbow, directing their stroll through the library.

"It's a wonder your parents didn't try to secure her for you."

"Wouldn't have worked. Aside from her weak constitution, which would have made her unsuitable to Lord and Lady Wakefield, all accounts have her firmly and ridiculously in love with Montrose. They were quite besotted with each other."

Amelia felt a pang of regret. "It's a shame she died. I suspect they would have been quite happy together."

"It is a shame," Nicholas agreed. "But it's no excuse for holding your family ransom."

Right. Focus on the task at hand. "Well, I've already begun. I made demands and had an emotional outburst in the carriage ride over. What else would you suggest?"

"Strong political views."

Amelia pondered. "I don't think I have any."

"Sure you do. You're favorable toward women's rights and labor reform."

"Well, yes, but not enough to make a fuss about it."

"Might I suggest," Nicholas said, as they looped back around to the parlor, "that you consider making a fuss. I hear Lady Chisholm takes exceptional offense to independently-minded women."

Amelia followed his eye line to the woman holding court on a settee, dressed in a mountain of peach bombazine. There were easily fifteen men and women in her immediate vicinity.

"So many people." Amelia had never liked being the center of attention. Even the holiday pageants she and Julia threw, attended only by Nicholas and her parents, caused her deep waves of panic. The only way she'd ever been able to do it was with Julia by her side.

Nicholas squeezed her arm. "What can I do to help?"

The panic was churning in her stomach. Amelia searched for something—anything—that would calm it. "Make me someone else?"

His face immediately lit up with a smile. "Easy. You are Dionysia of Tralles, a woman of exceptional strength and perseverance."

"You only know her story because I told it to you."

"Then it should be easy for you to remember. Channel Dionysia."

Dionysia of Tralles. Legendary sprinter. Fearless competitor. Amelia could do this. Dionysia and her sisters would never let themselves be blackmailed into an unwanted marriage. They would be all for women's rights. "I'm Dionysia."

"You're Dionysia."

"Oh God. Please don't let me be sick in front of all these people."

Nicholas tried to stay close to Amelia when they insinuated themselves into the crowd around Lady Chisholm, but Amelia kept insisting they should stand apart. He strongly suspected she was trying to insulate him from the scandal she was about to cause. He had no one but himself to blame for her thinking that way. Their whole lives, he'd let his family name hold too much sway. Somehow, he would have to convince her things were different now.

"I rather like the new styles from the continent," some young miss made the mistake of saying.

"Nonsense," Lady Chisholm barked. "They stray much

too far from tradition."

From the other side of the group, Amelia spoke up. "I don't think they stray nearly far enough."

"Excuse me?" Lady Chisholm gasped.

"I said I don't think they stray nearly far enough."

"I heard you, Lady Amelia. I only hoped I was mistaken."

Amelia frowned. Nicholas thought she might give up, but then her shoulders straightened and she lifted her chin. "Are you mistaken often?"

"Rarely." Montrose's aunt peered at Amelia. "And what do you imagine might be appropriate attire for a young lady?"

"Trousers," Amelia announced.

A murmur went up through the crowd. It was everything Nicholas could do to hold in a laugh. All the more so because he knew Amelia was being honest. In this regard, he was on Lady Chisholm's side. He'd seen Amelia in trousers a number of times and he knew how distracting it was. Were it to become a popular trend in women's fashion, the entire country would devolve into anarchy inside a week.

Lady Chisholm narrowed her eyes. "Young lady, I see that you think you're being amusing, but I assure you, you are not."

"There's nothing amusing about it," Amelia soldiered on. "By restricting women to clothing that lacks functional practicality, you confine them to lives that amount to little more than being showpieces."

"What's wrong with that," mumbled a young man near Nicholas.

Lady Chisholm turned positively purple. "That is quite enough, young lady. Hold your tongue."

"Begging your pardon, but no. I will not."

It was time for Nicholas to lend a helping hand. "Are you saying you think women would be a match to men if they dressed the same?"

Fifteen sets of eyes swiveled his direction, but they immediately returned to Amelia when she tendered her response. "I do. Take riding, for instance. Many women are exceptional riders, but the restrictions of a side saddle and skirts limit their ability to compete in sport."

"Compete!" Lady Chisholm's shrill tones had drawn the attention of the rest of the party goers, including Lord Montrose. He was on the verge of turning purple and trying to make his way to Amelia's side, but the crowd around her had grown too thick.

"You can't honestly think a woman could outrace a man on a horse," another man said. Nicholas recognized him as Mr. Bradley Preston, third son to Sir Walter Preston and a renowned gambler.

"I can and I do," Amelia said earnestly.

Lady Chisholm wasn't the only one to take offense to that, although she was certainly the loudest. Montrose had finally waded his way through to Amelia. Before anyone could say anything else, he dragged her off by the elbow.

Mr. Preston sneered.

Nicholas wanted to grind his face in the dirt. "I'll wager a hundred pounds she can beat you in a matched race, Preston."

"Do you mean that, or are you causing trouble?"

"I'm a Wakefield. We don't cause trouble."

Preston sized him up. "A hundred pounds?"

"One hundred pounds."

"She'd never do it, though." Preston's covetous expression contradicted his words. He wanted that money.

"I can guarantee she would. If she doesn't, I'll consider the money forfeit."

"Wakefield, you've got yourself a wager."

A silent carriage ride later and Amelia was back at the townhouse, but when the wheels rolled to a stop Embry didn't move to let her out.

"Embry?"

"I blame myself," he said to the tops of his boots. "You were distraught and I neglected you. It's only natural that you should seek to gain my attention other ways."

For heaven's sake. "I stand by the things I said, Embry."

He waved it off like so much noise. "You're hardly a bluestocking, Amelia. No, I drove you to this behavior and that villain Wakefield egged you on."

Amelia was speechless. He was actually blaming himself—and now Nicholas as well. It was beyond comprehension.

After a moment, Embry nodded. "I will think of how to make this right. In the meantime, get some rest. You're not yourself today, but I'm sure you'll feel much better in the morning."

He stepped out of the carriage and reached up to hand her down. There was nothing for her to do but take his offered hand. She could hardly live in the carriage, and she was too baffled by his thought process to trust herself to make a counter argument.

"Please make my excuses to your mother. I'll come around for a visit tomorrow afternoon."

Amelia nodded and made her way inside. How had her plan managed to go so far awry? She'd behaved abominably. She'd been difficult from the first moment, deliberately offended his family member, and caused a public spectacle. He should be livid, but instead he was making excuses and blaming himself. Was he truly that incapable of seeing her for herself?

"Amelia Marie Bishop!" Her mother shouted from the drawing room. "Get in here this instant."

Apparently news traveled fast. "Yes, Mother?"

Lady Bishop put her pen down with a clatter, splattering ink across the lap desk. "Lydia Chisholm sent a rush message over with an appalling story about your behavior. I'm writing her an apology right now."

"I don't think that's necessary. She's going to be my aunt, after all. I think she just has to learn to live with me."

"What on earth is the matter with you?"

"Not nearly enough, apparently." She couldn't even scare off a fiancé properly.

"Excuse me?"

"Oh," Amelia added. "Embry sends his excuses."

"I should think so."

"But he says he'll call tomorrow."

"You'd better pray he's not calling to end your engagement."

Amelia sighed. "He's not. He assured me in the carriage that he doesn't blame me for my opinions."

"Well, if that isn't a blessing I don't know what is."

The words faded as Amelia left and went upstairs again. She wished Julia was on her side. Julia would know how to get her out of this. Instead, Amelia had to face it alone. Being outrageous was exactly as awful as she'd always imagined it would be.

Chapter Eight

"I'm sorry, Lord Nicholas. She's not at home."

Nicholas stood in the parlor of the Bishops' London house as Lady Bishop gave him an excessively polite brush off. "Do you know where she went?"

"I'm not certain."

Because she was absolutely at home. Nicholas had watched her get out of Embry's carriage.

Lady Bishop's smile was stiff and did not reach her eyes—the picture of formality.

"Do you know when she'll be back?"

"I'm certain I don't know."

"Lady Bishop, I know she's here. If there's something I've done to offend you—"

"I'm sure I don't know what you mean. She's not at home." Lady Bishop led him to the door. "Probably out trying to apologize for her behavior at the garden party, but I'm certain you know all about that. I hear you were involved."

Ahh. "Lady Bishop."

"I'm afraid that's all the time I have today. You're welcome to leave your card, though."

You're welcome to leave your card. So. Nick had managed to make himself *persona non grata* with Lady Bishop. He cringed to think what Lady Wakefield would say when she found out. "Thank you, Lady Bishop."

In the meantime, however, he needed to update Amelia on her impending horse race. If he wasn't allowed to see her, he doubted a letter would get through unscathed.

It was time to take advantage of rank.

Nicholas took a hired carriage—this time to Jasper's townhouse. He was not asked to leave his card, and instead was led directly up to Jasper's bedroom where the man in question was undergoing a shave. The dubious benefits of friendship.

"Nicholas! To what do I owe the pleasure?"

"I could have waited downstairs."

"Nonsense. It's not like you never saw me shave in France." Jasper lifted his neck so his valet could get the area under his chin. "Are you here for something in particular or purely the pleasure of my company?"

"I need your name."

"You're going to have to be more specific."

"Lady Bishop is attempting to give me the cut. She wouldn't dare do it to a duke's heir," Nicholas said. "I need your name."

There was a distinct twinkle in Jas's eyes when he responded. "It is useful sometimes, isn't it?"

"I need you to tell Amelia about the wager I put on her beating Bradley Preston in a horse race."

"Amelia is racing Bradley Preston?"

"Yes, but she doesn't know it yet."

Jasper stood up, waving his valet off as he wiped the last of the cream from his neck. "What have you two been getting up to?"

"We went to Lady Chisholm's salon. Amelia got into an argument over women's rights, and I entered her into a horse race."

For a moment, Jasper only stared at him. "At a salon."

"Yes."

"One of those boring parlor functions where some old battle-axe holds court over young people too insipid to challenge her?"

"Yes."

"From now on, I am attending everything you attend," Jasper announced.

"That's not really—"

"I insist. London is going to be much more interesting with you two running around stirring things up. Where you go, I go."

"Fine," Nicholas said. "As long as you're also going to Amelia's—right now."

"Winslow, lay out something for visiting a respectable young lady and have the carriage brought around."

"Yes, m'lord," Winslow said before disappearing.

Nicholas knew from experience that getting dressed would take Jasper far longer than common sense dictated. He found a seat in a chair by the fireplace. "So. Tell her about the race, and I also need to know which room she's staying in at the new townhouse."

Jasper paused again, turning to him incredulously. "Why?"

"In case I need to speak with her."

"I find this bedroom window precedent you two have going on most intriguing."

"It's not like that."

"You realize you're not fooling anyone, don't you?"

Nicholas sighed. Being Jasper's friend was exhausting. "It doesn't matter. Her mother won't let me past the front door, so I need to know which room is hers. In case something urgent arises."

The smirk on Jasper's face was not helping. "Oh, indeed."

"Will you shut up and get dressed already?"

"As you wish," Jasper said, still smirking.

Amelia was pleasantly surprised when the maid came to tell her Lord Bellamy had come to call. She'd expected to hear from Nicholas, but Jasper was an equally welcome boon to her spirits.

"Lord Bellamy!" She greeted him with a kiss on the cheek. "It's lovely to see you again."

"I don't think your mother feels the same way," Jasper said, with a tip of his head toward Lady Bishop's rigid posture.

Her lips pursed visibly. "Lord Bellamy, I'm certain I don't know what you mean."

Amelia was still feeling reckless in the wake of the Chisholm salon and there was something thrilling about Jasper's candor. "She's still angry with you for hitting Embry. My mother adores Lord Montrose, more than she likes me, I'm beginning to suspect."

"Amelia!"

"We're going to keep on like this, Mother. It might be kinder on your nerves if you let us speak in private."

"Despite my derelict manners, I promise not to ravish your daughter senseless." The way he said it was not convincing in the slightest.

Lady Bishop was the picture of indignation as she huffed and rose from her chair. "I'm leaving the door open."

Amelia nodded, watching her go. "Goodness. I enjoyed

that a little too much. She's been so awful lately."

Before Embry's carriage axle had broken in front of their drive, her mother had been devoted to Julia. They had so many more shared interests—Amelia had often been happily left to her own devices with a book while the two of them poured over fashion plates and the latest dance steps. That her own mother could abandon Julia so abruptly, and over a ridiculous wedding, was appalling.

Jasper smiled. "I'm afraid it was contrived on my part. I needed to speak with you privately."

"Oh?"

"I've been sent as a messenger from Nicholas."

"Why didn't he come himself?"

"He did. Your mother told him you weren't at home."

For a moment, all Amelia could do was gape.

"It appears his role in your salon scandal has removed him from your mother's good graces."

"She has no right!"

Jasper patted her hand. "There, there. Is it so awful having to use me as a middle man?"

"Not at all, I just can't believe it." Amelia shook her head. "Did you know she banned my sister from my engagement party?"

"I did."

"She's gone completely addled over this engagement. It's like she's an entirely different person."

"Well, hopefully when you manage to get yourself un-engaged, she'll go back to normal."

"Hopefully, though I'm not sure I'll be able to forgive her for what she's done." Amelia rubbed her temple. "Or that I'll be able to get thrown over. Embry blamed himself for the argument with his aunt."

Jasper's eyebrow raised as he grinned. "How saintly of him."

"It's ludicrous. What am I supposed to do now?"

"Race Bradley Preston on Rotten Row."

"Excuse me?" She couldn't have heard him right.

"Apparently, our Nick signed you up for it already." Jasper settled himself into an armchair, crossing a boot over his knee.

A race on Rotten Row? Was he mad? She clutched a settee pillow to her stomach, shaking her head. "I couldn't possibly."

"He's on the hook for one hundred pounds if you lose or back out."

"One hundred pounds!"

"Nicholas has great faith in your horsemanship."

Amelia appreciated Nicholas's confidence in her, but it was a lot of money to come up with if she lost, which she might very well do. She didn't know a thing about Bradley Preston. He could be an exceptional rider. "Surely he must be joking. Rotten Row, in front of all those people?"

Jasper leaned back against the cushions. "Think of it as an excellent opportunity to commission a new pair of trousers."

Amelia's worried her lower lip with her teeth. "With a matching jacket?"

"Of course," Jasper promised. "You'll be impeccably fashionable."

"While I engage in a scandalous public spectacle."

"The best way to occupy one's time when one is fashionable."

Amelia grinned. It was impossible to be worried in Jasper's company. "All right."

He avoided looking at her, choosing instead to inspect the weave of his own cobalt trousers, when he said, "Nicholas also asked me to find out which room you're staying in here."

The barest of tingles started up under her skin. "Did he say why?"

"In case something urgent comes up."

"I see." Of course. If her mother wouldn't let him in the house, he would need to reach her some other way. Jasper wouldn't always be available to play messenger. "It's on the first floor. Third from the back of the house."

The sound of Lady Bishop coming back down the hall put an end to the discussion. "Amelia. You'd better go up and change soon if you don't want to be late for dinner."

"I won't keep you," Jasper said, rising to leave. "May I call on you again at the end of the week?"

"I don't think—" Lady Bishop began.

"That would be lovely. I'll make sure I'm available."

Jasper bowed formally to her mother. "Lady Bishop, always a pleasure."

Lady Bishop acknowledged him with a slight inclining of her head as he left. Then it was only her and her mother.

"What were you two discussing?"

"The usual," Amelia answered. "Fashion. Horses. The new house."

It wasn't even technically a lie.

On his return—after an inconsiderate number of detours— Jasper announced that Nicholas would be responsible for the costume since it would be difficult for Amelia to procure men's clothing without a great deal of questions being asked. In typical Jasper fashion, he had not collected any of the required information to accomplish that task, requiring Nick to go to great lengths to fulfill the promise. He went to his dressing room and dug through Bertram's kit until he found a measuring cord. Stuffing it in his pocket, he went downstairs to call for the carriage.

There was still a great deal left to be weathered in the task of getting Amelia free of her fiancé. While he hoped to avoid bringing any shame to his family in helping her, he would see it through no matter the cost. Explaining that would take more than a few moments though, so he was glad when the carriage was announced.

Nicholas had the driver let him out around the corner from Amelia's house and made his way through darkened alleys into the yard behind their townhouse. He found the window Jasper had described and started his assault with one of a handful of stones.

"You ought to fight giants," Amelia's voice drifted down.

"What?" he whispered back.

"David and Goliath. You ought to fight giants, the way you're always throwing little stones."

"Can we discuss the Bible at another time? Is it safe to come up?"

There was an agonizing pause as she went to check. "Yes. Be careful, though."

As if he could be anything else, sneaking into a woman's bedroom. He made his way up the back stairs and down the hall without incident, but he could practically feel his hair turning grey. When he closed the bedroom door she'd left cracked, Amelia laughed. "You look petrified."

"You would, too, if you'd had to sneak around below stairs. This is why I have a tree by my window in the countryside."

"Oh? You coordinated with the groundskeeper to make it easier for me to sneak into your bedroom?"

He would have, if he'd thought of it. "How can you be so calm? You're usually at least as much of a wreck as I am."

"Mother went off to the opera with a friend after dinner, and most of the staff have the night off." She stretched out her arms. "I am blissfully alone. Anyhow, what was so urgent?"

"I need your measurements."

Her eyebrows disappeared into her hairline. "For?"

"Your riding costume. I need to have it made at my tailor, and I can't exactly bring you in." He held out Bertram's measuring cord. "So I need measurements."

Amelia blushed, studying the carpet for a moment before nodding. She moved to the middle of the room, arms still outstretched.

Nicholas tried. When they asked him at the gates of heaven, right before they refused him entry, he wanted it on record that he'd tried. He attempted to get an accurate measurement—first without touching her at all, and then without asking what he knew he needed to ask.

"What's the matter?" Amelia asked. "Does it usually take this long?"

"No." This was some sort of cosmic retribution.

"Well, what's the trouble?"

"Your dress. The skirts are all in the way and it has inconvenient poofs in places and I—"

"You need me to take it off."

In more ways than she would ever fathom. He was a complete cad. Still, there was hope to be had in her ready agreement. She wasn't averse to being undressed in his company. Considering that he'd like to spend the rest of his life with her company—preferably undressed—it was a pleasing realization.

He needed her to take off her dress. He was in her room, she was going to undress, and he was going to touch her. It wasn't as if he'd never touched her before. But this was different. It shouldn't be—it was only Nicholas—but the tingles were even worse than when he'd almost kissed her. Part of it was feeling his fingertips flirting against her stockings. Tickling the edge of her waist. Brushing lightly across her shoulders. But the rest—he was going to *see* her.

"I'll need your help."

"H-h—how?" He coughed, like he had something stuck in his throat.

"The buttons down the back."

He stood up behind her. She felt his breath on the back of her neck. The warmth of his hands hovered just out of reach. "Nicholas?"

He coughed again. She felt his fingers make contact with the first button. It slipped loose, and even though she'd been expecting it, it startled her.

"Are you all right? Should I stop?"

"I'm fine. It's fine." Amelia took a deep breath. "You've seen women in their underclothes before. Even if I haven't… been seen. It's fine."

He didn't respond, just went to work on the next button. She wished she could see his face. When he had the buttons undone halfway down her back, she tilted her head back to glean some sort of calm from the ceiling. The flutter of his breath sent a shiver across her skin.

"Mia?"

"Hmm?" She took it back. She didn't wish she could see his face, because then he'd be able to see hers.

"Are… I…"

Amelia took a deep, steadying breath. Her response to Nick was all-consuming and there was no reining it back in.

And if she was completely honest, she didn't want to reign it in. Not with his mouth next to her ear. The way Nick was making her feel was exhilarating. She leaned back, relishing the feel of his hands pressed against the small of her back between their bodies.

"I think that's it," he said as he stepped away.

Damn. Amelia pushed the dress free of her shoulders and petticoats. "Can you untie my skirts?"

She didn't need him to, but she was obviously possessed by some sort of wicked spirit.

He stepped forward again, and when he was finished, she was left in her stockings, drawers, and shift.

Amelia crossed her arms over her chest and turned. "Will this serve?" Now that she could see him, he was flushed and having trouble meeting her eyes. He seemed to be focusing intently on a spot a few inches to the left of her head.

"Nick?"

"I need a moment."

Curiosity got the better of her. "For what?"

"I'm trying to convince myself you're Jasper."

Amelia laughed. "Why?"

"I'm not attracted to Jasper, and I think this will go a great deal smoother if I am in a proper frame of mind when I start touching you."

When I start touching you. Amelia shivered again.

"You're cold. I'm sorry, I didn't think. I'll…get ahold of myself." He moved close and started measuring her legs with quick, efficient movements.

Meanwhile, she was wishing he'd get ahold of her. Had he meant he was attracted to her? More than the usual, that is. She knew he considered her to be attractive in the general sense, but she hoped he'd meant in a specific, special sense. If he had…perhaps the feelings he inspired in her weren't such torture after all.

When it came time to measure around her chest, Amelia dropped her arms and met his eyes head on. He swallowed audibly. This time she was certain of it—he was as affected as she was.

The certainty made her bold. "Nick, are you attracted to me?"

"Wha...I—"

"I mean, really attracted. Not just passively appreciative."

Nicholas finished his measurement in a series of quick, jerking movements. "I should go. I have to get these to the tailor straight away or it won't be done in time."

All of the awkwardness she'd felt. All the effort she'd put into trying to quell her response so she didn't jeopardize their friendship. He felt it, too. "Nick."

"I'll let myself out!"

And before she knew it, he was gone and Amelia was left standing in her undergarments. It would not be the last he heard from her on the subject. If Nicholas was attracted to her, and she felt confident he was, she meant to explore it. She may have lost her faith in marriage, but if there was a chance she could investigate these tingles—she could think of no better person than Nick to investigate them with. He was her best friend and partner in all of her greatest adventures. It made perfect sense that he should also be her partner in this.

"How did you fare?" Jasper asked when Nick was shown into his library.

He'd been too flustered to go home to Philip's. They would immediately know something was amiss. "She asked if I ever am attracted to her—while she was in her underclothes."

"Well, that's progress." Jasper grinned. "Although the fact that she doesn't know is evidence of historical failure."

"It's too much progress. It's too soon." Nicholas threw himself into a chair, trying not to think about the perfect curve of her hips or the faint shadow of her nipples through the linen.

"By all accounts, it's been most of your life."

"But she's still engaged!"

"Barely."

"Not barely. Technically, she's still engaged to another man."

"A blackmailer," Jasper argued with a raised eyebrow.

"It doesn't matter. She's the love of my life, Jasper. I'm not going to have our first kiss—our first anything—tainted by unsavoriness." If he wanted Amelia to reconsider the possibility of marrying, everything must be perfect.

"That's utterly adorable."

"Don't patronize me."

"Don't make asinine statements."

Nick pushed his hands through his hair in frustration. "I love her, Jas. I want to spend the rest of my life with her. I can't start with a stolen kiss in her bedroom while she belongs to someone else."

"And that's where you and I differ," Jasper said, raising his glass. "Because I can imagine no better beginning."

They had chosen an early hour to minimize the number of firsthand observers to the scandal, but the stream of men and women riding through the grand entrance of Hyde Park suggested that word had gotten out. Being there to witness the Earl of Montrose's outspoken fiancée race Mr. Preston on Rotten Row was apparently well worth an early start to the day.

Nicholas waited outside the carriage, checking his timepiece. "Are you ready?"

"Almost," Amelia's muffled voice came from inside.

"Can I help? We're going to be late."

She popped open the door and stepped out. "What do you think?"

For a moment, he thought nothing at all. From the waist up, Amelia didn't look particularly out of the ordinary. The crimson jacket fit much like one of her usual riding costumes, with a fall of white lace and a fashionable topper perched on her head.

It was where the jacket stopped that Nicholas's thoughts became muddled. Bright crimson velveteen clung tightly to her full hips, making her gender unmistakable. Her calves were incased in black leather riding boots with a similarly expert fit.

"This is a bad idea," he said.

"Why?"

"I can see all of you."

Amelia looked down at her own thighs. She twisted around to check her backside. "I'm covered."

"But it…" Nicholas struggled for the proper way to word it. "It leaves nothing to the imagination."

She circled him, observing his own riding clothes. "Neither do yours."

"That's different."

"Why?"

"Women's minds aren't as vulgar as—"

Amelia cut him off with her laughter. "Is that what men think?"

"I'm certain of it."

"You've seen me in trousers before. You've never thrown me over your shoulder and had your way with me."

He might not be ready to declare himself, but he could start clearing up this misunderstanding of her not knowing he was interested. "Just because I haven't doesn't mean I haven't thought about it."

She blushed, looking away when he didn't. "Well, maybe you should have."

Nicholas took a steadying breath.

She grinned. "Come on. We'll be late for the race."

They retrieved their mounts from Nicholas's groom. Nicholas moved to give her a hand up but she waved him off, swinging into the saddle with ease. The provocative bouncing of crimson-encased flesh as she landed and found her seat caused Nicholas's own trousers to fit uncomfortably.

"We can call the whole thing off."

"And cause you to lose one hundred pounds?"

He didn't care. "It's only money. I can—"

"No need. I'm doing it." She clicked to her mare, setting the beast in motion.

Nicholas cursed, mounting his own horse in a hurry and chasing after her.

It felt deliciously wicked to be riding astride in public, especially knowing Nick was affected by her outfit. She wished he were the only one looking—there were plenty of people who could see her now that she'd turned the corner onto the long tree-lined row—but she wouldn't let it ruin the morning's triumph. Nicholas had flirted with her in earnest. There was a good chance he would be amenable to an affair.

It was enough to let her block out the crowd and concentrate on the race.

Amelia leaned down to whisper to her mount. "Steady, Dio. We mustn't be too tense or we'll lose speed."

The little mare's ears flicked in response. Dionysia did not need Amelia's advice on how to race. She was in fine form even with the trip to London. If anything, being cooped up had added an extra spring in her step.

Nicholas caught up with her as she reached Mr. Preston and his cronies.

"Wakefield," Mr. Preston said with a tip of his hat. "For a moment I thought you weren't going to show."

"I wouldn't miss this for the world," Nicholas said.

Preston turned his attention to Amelia and Dionysia. "Shouldn't you have brought a larger horse, or can't you control a true racing breed?"

Up until that moment, the wager had merely been a means to disgracing herself in Embry's eyes. Now, it was deeply personal. Amelia was bloody tired of people making side comments, disparaging her loved ones, telling her how to behave, sneering at her horse. Mr. Preston was going to rue the day he ever looked at Dio.

"I understand you have a wager with Nicholas regarding the outcome of this race," she said loudly enough to draw attention.

"I do," Preston agreed.

"Shall we make a wager as well?"

Preston scoffed. "I wouldn't want to rob you of your pin money."

"Oh, I'm quite confident you won't. Shall we say two hundred pounds?"

Mr. Preston blanched. "That's quite a wager."

"Nicholas, please assure Mr. Preston I am good for it."

Nicholas looked slightly concerned, but he nodded. "She is. You may consider me her guarantor."

"I, ah—"

"Unless you don't think you're going to win," Amelia added. "Three hundred pounds is a lot to lose in one race. If you'd rather play it safe, I understand."

Amelia let the murmurs running through the gathering crowd do her work for her. She could see Preston imagining his manhood being called into question with each whisper.

"Deal," he said.

"Excellent. Let's start the race."

"You don't want to run a lap or two to warm your mount up?" Preston asked.

"No, thank you." Amelia had already warmed Dionysia up before she changed clothes, but Preston didn't need to know that. Let him think she was an inexperienced horsewoman and underestimate her if he liked.

They lined up at the start of the row. Amelia tried not to think about the two hundred pounds she'd just put on the line. Good Lord, what if she lost? What on earth would Papa say? *Don't think about that. It's time to be Julia. Don't think about the risks.*

She leaned down again, rubbing the side of Dio's neck. "Shall we make our sisters proud today?"

The little horse pawed the dirt of the track.

They were in agreement. There would be no losing today— nor any other day. They were champions and they gave way to no man.

Chapter Nine

asper came to call on Amelia the day after the race and, because he was an imp sent by the devil, he brought *The Times*.

"Have you read it?" he asked.

"No." Amelia flopped against the arm of the parlor's sofa with distinctly un-ladylike grace.

"Why not?"

"I keep hoping if I don't look, it won't have happened."

Jasper's stare told her exactly what he thought of that foolishness. He struck a pose in the armchair and snapped the pages open. "Lady A, recently engaged to the Earl of M., scandalized the denizens of Hyde Park yesterday by engaging in a horse race along the riding track commonly referred to as Rotten Row."

Amelia cringed.

Jasper continued reading. "Lady A.'s vulgar inclusion into this predominately male pass-time was compounded by the nature of her dress, which included men's riding breeches, flashing her backside to all and sundry."

"Flashing my backside!" That was more than a bit of creative license. She sat up in indignation. "I was no less dressed than any man there."

Jasper choked a laugh. "'The sum of money rumored to have been wagered between the riders—yes, Ladies and Gentlemen, Lady A. added gambling to her incendiary behavior—is too ludicrous to be repeated by this reporter, lest they should inspire others to likewise irresponsibility.' How much did you wager?"

Amelia sighed. "Two hundred pounds."

"Well done."

"Nicholas bet a hundred, and then that awful man insulted Dio," she mumbled.

The paper snapped back to attention. "As to the race, we should like to say very little. Unfortunately, it's all anyone can talk about. While the racers appeared quite evenly matched, it was the moment of high drama, when two unattended children stumbled onto the track from the nearby walking path, directly in the way of the horses, that proved the winner of the day."

Just thinking about it made Amelia stand up and start pacing the parlor. It had scared the life out of her. Seeing those little boys come spilling out of the trees, practically under Dio's hooves—she would have nightmares for weeks.

"While her opponent's horse reared and its rider lost his seat—an unfortunate outcome for anyone who considers themselves a horseman of merit—Lady A. sent her mount into a leap, clearing the children and finishing the race." Jasper looked at where she was walking circles into the carpet in front of the hearth. "Truly?"

"Truly. It was awful."

"I say again—well done."

"It was awful. I never ever want to race again."

It had been traumatizing. What if they hadn't cleared the jump? What if Dio's hooves had clipped that poor child in the head, killing or maiming him for life? Amelia was not cut out for adventure, not in the slightest.

"There's a bit referencing the article about your getting into a women's rights argument at Lady's Chisholm's salon, but that's old news."

"They did *not* print that in the paper."

"They did," Jasper assured her. "The young misses of London going rogue is quite newsworthy."

Amelia was going to die of embarrassment. It was bad enough when she was committing the offenses, but to have them immortalized was mortifying. "If Embry was half as scandalized as the reporter of *The Times*, I'd be quit of this engagement already."

"Nicholas, may I speak with you a moment?" Philip called to him through the open library door.

"Of course." He was headed out to meet Amelia, but there wasn't really any rush. She'd promised to send word after she spoke with Embry and she hadn't sent it yet.

Nicholas joined his brother, where a pile of papers that looked suspiciously like the estate bills were strewn across one of the large tables. This time, though, it was Nicholas that had Philip's full attention.

"I've received a note from the tailor," his brother said, steepling his hands.

That was fast. "That should have come to me directly. I'll reimburse you for it."

"It wasn't a bill. Just a note."

A note. That didn't bode especially well. "Oh?"

"Is there a reason you can think of that they might wish to disassociate themselves from us?"

Oh bloody hell. "Perhaps."

Philip leaned back in his chair. "Thomas Hawkes dressed the last two King George's, The Duke of Wellington, and, as of yesterday, apparently, no longer dresses the Lords of Wakefield."

The only honorable thing to do was be honest. "I suspect he recognized the clothes."

"What clothes? And why should it matter if he recognized them? What the devil is going on, Nicholas?"

"They weren't for me." Their father was going to kill him—at least, he would if he received the news on a day when he didn't mistake Nicholas for one of the neighbors.

Philip waited for further explanation. When none was forthcoming he prompted Nick. "Who were they for?"

"Amelia needed my help."

"You outfitted Amelia Bishop with clothes from our tailor." Philip scrubbed a hand across his face. "Yes, I can see how that might offend the dignity of Hawkes and Company. Might I ask what the hell you were thinking?"

I was thinking I want to spend the rest of my life with her, and she looks absolutely sinful in trousers. That explanation wouldn't help the situation at all. "I'll fix it, I promise."

"Do you think you can?"

"I have to try." Philip finding out was one thing, but if his father caught wind of it on one of his lucid days God only knew what would happen. Perhaps they would conscript him to the church or the army after all.

Philip nodded.

Nicholas stood up and went to the library door. "Philip?"

"Yes?" His brother sounded extremely tired.

"I'm sorry. I didn't for mean it to affect you."

"We're family. Everything we do affects each other."

Indeed, it did. But when one family member wanted something so drastically at odds with what the rest of the family wanted, how could he keep from disappointing them? "Again, I'm sorry."

Philip waved his explanation off. "What's done is done. Fix it if you can. Once word gets out about father, we'll have more than enough gossip to attend to."

It was harder than ever for Amelia to sit quietly when Embry brought his mother for tea. She kept expecting someone to jump up and start making accusations about the race. Instead, everything was business as usual. She was agreeable, smiled adoringly, and generally played the role of devoted fiancée. Internally, she was on edge. When she did manage to pay attention, it didn't take long before she was seething. With every passing moment, it became ever more clear how little Embry actually saw her.

Amelia takes three sugars in her tea. No, no she didn't. She took one or none at all.

Amelia favors the classic Roman architecture. Actually, she preferred the giant cathedrals of the Gothic period.

Amelia would never dream of visiting America. She abhors sea travel. How could he possibly be certain of that when she wasn't certain herself? She'd never been on a ship.

"One does wonder how you've come to know me so well, so quickly," she said through clenched teeth.

Embry squeezed her hand. "Because you are the match to my soul, darling."

Ahh yes. That must be it.

How had she never noticed this about him? She must have been so desperate for someone to pay attention to her. Had she only taken his offer because he was offering? The last one sounded dangerously close to the truth.

Amelia had no one to blame but herself for the situation she found herself in. She'd accepted the proposal of a man she didn't actually want, purely because she'd wanted someone to propose to her.

She was at the end of her ability to pretend when Embry's mother pulled her aside.

"Amelia, dear, I want you to know how thrilled I am to have you join the family."

Of course she was thrilled. The paragon of amiable behavior Embry had painted couldn't help but be a blessing to any family.

Amelia did her best not to take it out on his mother. "Thank you, Lady Montrose."

"He told me what he said at your engagement party, and the way Olivia and Charlotte have been behaving. I know he is deeply sorry," Lady Montrose continued.

"They're hardly in the minority, thinking the way they do about my family."

"Be that as it may, I've spoken to the girls. My son has been through so much. For a time it looked like he might never find someone new. We must welcome anyone that can make him happy, no matter their shortcomings."

Amelia could think of a few shortcomings she'd happily develop to test that theory. For now, it couldn't hurt to highlight a few of the ones she already possessed. "You're so kind. I can only hope that our children aren't afflicted with the same difficulties my sister experiences. It was so hard on my parents, to say nothing of Julia."

Lady Montrose's face paled. Her expression settled into a mask of politeness, but Amelia could see her imagination running wild with images of a crippled grandson as heir to the Earldom. "My son assures me that is extremely unlikely."

"Oh, I do hope so. The doctors know so little about why these things happen, but I'm certain Embry knows best."

Amelia was not surprised when Lady Montrose soon excused herself from their tête-á-tête, and shortly after expressed that it was time for her and Embry to take their leave.

"Your mother seems pleased for us," Amelia said as she walked Embry to the door.

"Of course she's pleased. I found the finest woman in all of Britain to marry."

Unfortunately, she died, and now you're trying to cram me into her mold.

"Embry, there's something I need to tell you." Now was as good a time as any to tell him about the Rotten Row incident— he'd hear about it soon enough—but Amelia was interrupted by her mother letting out a distressed cry.

"Mother?"

The footman who had whispered in her ear left after handing her a note.

Lady Bishop pasted a stiff smile on her face. "A conflicting engagement I completely forgot about. I can't imagine what I was thinking, but we'd better make our farewells to Lord Montrose and his mother."

To the shock of all three of them, Lady Bishop shuffled the pair out with something very close to haste.

"What the devil?" Amelia asked once they were gone.

"It's your sister. She has an infection."

The world stopped.

Everything came to Amelia as if it was coming through

water. An infection. Julia hadn't had one in years, but they had been nearly fatal when Julia was young.

The last thing Amelia had told Julia was that she didn't forgive her. That she didn't need her.

What if they were their last words to each other? "When's the next train?"

"I don't think that's necessary. I just didn't want you to make a scene when you heard."

Enough was enough. "Never mind," Amelia said, rushing for the stairs. "I'll find out myself."

* * *

Due to Lady Bishop's newfound dislike of Nicholas, he was forced to arrange secret and accidental assignations with Amelia. Today, they had planned to frequent the same coffee shop once Amelia sent word that she was free. No messenger had come, but Nick was impatient, so he went to wait at the agreed upon place anyway. Construction on the new square near Charing Cross made the streets a nightmare, but Nicholas was in no hurry. He was feeling rather conflicted about his involvement in Amelia's scandals when he arrived at the coffeehouse, but they suddenly compounded tenfold—Lord Montrose was seated at a table directly next to the door.

Executing an about-face, he tried to make a stealthy escape.

"Wakefield."

Damn it. Nicholas turned back around. "Montrose."

He needed to get outside before Amelia showed up, so he could warn her.

"Sit with me," Montrose said. "I've been meaning to have a word with you."

"I really must—"

"Please, Wakefield."

There was something about the way he said it. Nicholas was a hundred kinds of fool and he was certain he would end up regretting it, but he turned and sat down at Montrose's table. "What is it?"

"It's Amelia."

Well, of course it was. She was the only topic they had in common. "And?"

The Earl pondered the edge of his napkin. "She's been behaving quite strangely lately."

Under different circumstances, Montrose's genuine distress would have garnered sympathy from Nicholas. Instead, it only fueled his irritation. "To be completely candid, how would you know?"

Montrose frowned, but was not dissuaded. "She's my fiancée."

In for a penny, in for a pound. "She's your prisoner."

Montrose's face became a sky before the storm.

"My point is, Amelia is as sweet as you imagine, but she's not livestock. You're trying to force her to do something against her objection. She will fight you every step of the way—that *is* her nature."

"I refuse to believe it."

"It does not require your belief to be the truth." Nick couldn't see it working, but he had to try. "Why don't you just let her go?"

"Excuse me?"

"She doesn't want to marry you. Let her go."

The Earl's rage bubbled over. "Why? So you can drag her down the road to ruin? So you can prey on her innocence?"

He shouldn't. Nick knew he shouldn't. "So I can marry her."

The kaleidoscope of emotions that crossed Lord Montrose's face—bafflement, surprise, and finally more rage—could have kept an artist busy for months. The sound of his cup connecting with the table rang out like a shot. The entire coffeehouse went silent, watching them. Montrose realized it at the same time Nicholas did.

"I think I've taken up quite enough of your time," Lord Montrose said through clenched teeth. "Excuse me."

Chapter Ten

The first thing Amelia did when she arrived was go straight to her sister's room. The maid, Nora, was sitting in a chair by the bed. Julia was lying still with her eyes closed, and she was so dreadfully pale. Amelia climbed into bed next to her. No more of people telling her she couldn't have her sister.

"Miss, I'm not sure you should—"

"She's allowed," Julia said, leaving her eyes closed.

"Miss Julia, your father said—"

"Mia has had a dreadful scare. She thought I was going to die without having forgiven her for being so horrible to me. You wouldn't want her to remain guilty and miserable would you, Nora?"

The maid's face settled into resignation. "No, miss."

"Has she been completely dreadful?" Amelia tucked herself in next to Julia.

Julia gasped. "I have been a saint."

Nora's expression told a different story. "None of us behave our best when we're feeling poorly, Miss Amelia."

"That's it." Julia coughed. "I want Mrs. Polk back."

"Well, you can't have her," Nora said without sympathy. "You scared her half to death, trying to die, and she's having a rest."

"You could have one as well," Amelia offered. "I'm not going anywhere for a while."

Nora looked between the two of them. "Miss Julia?"

Julia sighed. "Fine, but bring cake when you come back."

"Oh yes, Your Highness. Your wish is my command, Highness." The maid laughed her way out the door.

Amelia leaned in to whisper in her sister's ear. "You two seem to be getting on."

"She's growing on me," Julia whispered back. "Once she got over the pity and the mousiness, she's actually rather interesting."

A weight lifted off Amelia's chest. Julia hadn't been miserable and alone. She'd had Nora to keep her wickedness entertained. "You tried to die?"

"I didn't try, so much as it just sort of happened."

"Is it done happening?" Amelia asked.

"I think so."

The danger was past. Another weight gone. There was time to say what needed to be said and put things to rights between them.

"Are you going to go back to being cross at me?" Julia asked. "Because if you are, I might try to die on purpose to get you to see sense again."

Amelia laughed. "No, I'm not going to go back to being cross. Are you going to keep insisting I should marry Embry?"

"Yes. I think it's what's best for you. But you aren't required to agree with me."

"Well, that's a first."

"I know. I must truly be ill this time."

Amelia laughed. She laid a hand on Julia's brow. It was warmer than it ought to be, but not dangerously hot.

Julia closed her eyes again. "Mia, are you…can you stay awhile, or do you have to go back?"

"Would you like me to stay?" Amelia asked.

Julia nodded, sounding drowsy. "Only for a while. Embry can spare you for a little while."

Embry could spare her for a lifetime, if Amelia had any say in the matter. She snuggled in closer to her sister, running soft fingertips over her hair. "I'll stay as long as you like."

✦————◦❧❧◦————✦

When Nicholas arrived home from his catastrophic meeting with Lord Montrose, the estate agent was waiting for him.

"Mr. Fletcher? What brings you to London?"

"Lord Nicholas," the man said, bowing formally. "I'm afraid I must speak with you."

Dread seeped into his chest. "Of course. Is it about my father?"

Mr. Fletcher nodded.

"Perhaps we should include Philip, then. I believe he's at home."

They sent someone for the future Marquess. When Nick heard he'd been in the nursery playing games with the children, guilt settled in his stomach. Lady Wakefield was not right—Philip should know—but her wish to spare him was rooted in kindness. How many good days would be tainted by unfortunate news?

"Lord Wakefield's condition is getting worse," Mr. Fletcher explained when they were both assembled. "Yesterday, there was an episode with a tenant. He became violent."

"Violent?" Philip straightened, frowning. "Surely not."

"What was he doing dealing with a tenant?" Nicholas

leaned forward in his chair.

Mr. Fletcher answered them both patiently. "It was one of the new tenants—Mr. Allen—that recently moved in. He wanted to handle the problem directly, to show that the lord of the manor didn't take tenant issues lightly."

He could believe that. "What happened?"

"He was having a good day, and then suddenly he wasn't. He became confused. He didn't know the man, and the man kept insisting he did. Your father shook him, rather violently. I'd ask leniency for Mr. Allen. He had no notion of your father's condition."

"Of course," Nicholas said. "Was he hurt badly?"

"Nothing serious. I think the shock was the worst of it."

Undoubtedly, the poor man. This should never have happened. "I'll come back with you and set things to rights with him in person."

"I'm going also." Philip stood up.

"Philip."

"I can spare a few days, and I think it's time I see Father for myself."

Nick put a hand on his brother's shoulder. "Are you sure you want to?"

"Is there a chance he'll get better and this will all blow over?" Philip asked.

Nicholas shook his head. The running of the estate was their responsibility now, and they needed to accept it.

Philip's expression fell. "Better now, then, while there are still good days to be had."

That Philip had actually hoped it might be possible was a testament to his brother's optimistic nature. Nick wished he could spare him this, but they were all going to have to deal with it sooner or later.

"Pass me a roll, would you?"

Amelia took one from the covered bowl sitting in the middle of the bed and fired it with excessive force. It bounced off the headboard and over the side out of view.

Julia continued pulling pieces of cod apart with her fingers. "Brat."

They were in the palace, surrounded by Julia's recreated menagerie on a mountain of pillows. "I should tell Nora I heard you sniffle. Or worse, heard some sort of fluids building in your lungs."

"You wouldn't."

"Oh, I would."

"You're truly that cross?"

"How should you feel if I wanted you to spend the rest of your life with someone who only saw your limp? Who only saw something that's not you when they looked at you?"

Julia frowned at Amelia. "If they were good to me, I might—"

Amelia cut her off. "Don't lie to me, Julia. You don't even allow the servants to underestimate you, and you want me to believe you'd accept it from a husband?"

Amelia had always pitied the queen when they were children. She had been isolated as a child like the Bishops, though for wildly different reasons, but she didn't even have a sibling to keep her company. Amelia had often thought how miserable it would have been if she were Victoria, with no Julia to keep her company. Now, she had rather mixed feelings on the subject. On the one hand, Amelia was certain she couldn't survive it if something happened to Julia, but on the other—even from her sick bed, Julia could be so frustrating it made Amelia's eyes cross.

Julia broke into a fit of rough hacking. When she'd finished, her face was red and she sagged back against the pillows.

Amelia poured a glass of wine and handed it to her. "Are you all right?"

"Fish. I just swallowed it wrong."

Unfortunately, Amelia was as versed in her sister's lies as Julia was in Amelia's.

She cleared the food dishes away to the carpet and slid in beside Julia, pulling an extra blanket over them both. Amelia had known she was right, but it was confirmed when Julia wrapped her arms around Amelia and put her head on Amelia's chest.

How could she marry someone and build a new life away from Julia, when any moment something terrible could happen? No. She had to find a way to explore her new feelings for Nicholas without ending up right back where she was—engaged.

She would convince Nicholas to become her lover, and find her happiness here with her family. Where she belonged.

"That cough is God punishing you for meddling in my love life." Amelia stroked her sister's hair.

"God has better things to do than help you make terrible decisions," Julia retorted. It was followed by another fit of coughing, this one sounding worse than the last. Her skin was getting hotter by the minute.

Amelia was about to get up and call someone when their father came into the room.

"Abandoned the palace picnic already? I was just coming to join you."

"Papa." Amelia didn't need to say anything else.

Lord Bishop turned around and started shouting the

house down. Mrs. Polk was there in an instant, followed by an army of maids. A footman was sent for the doctor. Lord Bishop and Amelia were displaced from the room in the flurry.

"She was fine an hour ago," Amelia said as they stood staring at the closed door together.

"None of that, sweetheart. She'll be right as rain in no time, making you feel silly for worrying."

"Yes. Yes, she will." Amelia tried to force herself to believe it.

✦ ━━ ⟐ ━━ ✦

Nicholas was sitting down to tea alone—Philip had gone upstairs to see their father and Fletcher had pressing county fair business to see to—when Jasper arrived, full of righteous indignation.

"There you are!" Jas complained.

"Was I supposed to be somewhere else?"

"London, where I left you." Jas waved the question away. "Montrose raced out here this morning. Has it worked? Is he finally setting Amelia free? What the devil is going on? I hate being uninformed."

Nicholas ignored the dramatics, focusing on the oddity in Jasper's tirade. "How do you know about Montrose's movements?"

"I have a boy watching his house."

Nicholas stared at him.

"Don't look at me like that. Honestly, you should have thought of it, but at least one of us is taking your situation seriously." Jasper sat down. "So, is he?"

"I don't know." Nicholas hoped it had. Maybe what he'd

said to Montrose had an effect after all. "Did you ask Amelia before you left? She'd be the one to know for certain."

Jas shook his head. "She's here, too. Left before he did."

Dread struck Nicholas in the gut. "Oh no."

"What now?"

"He's chasing after her. What if he tells her? Oh, bloody hell."

"Tells her what?"

"I told him I wanted to marry her."

"Oh." Jasper considered for a moment. "Bloody finally."

"I haven't told *her* I want to marry her. She can't find out like this."

Comprehension dawned. "Ahh. Yes, I imagine his delivery might be somewhat lacking in romance."

He needed a solution. Fast. "Could I beat him there, do you think? Maybe he stopped to change."

"Afraid not. He arrived in the company of Lady Bishop an hour ago."

Nicholas didn't bother asking how Jasper knew that. "Don't spy on my intended."

"She's not your intended until you stop being a coward and declare yourself. And she accepts you. That's also a requirement, if I remember correctly."

"I'm not a coward."

"You have had every possible opportunity to tell her before this."

"The moment wasn't right."

"The moment will never be right. Coward."

Nicholas put his cup down. "If you keep calling me a coward, I will call you out."

"Admit that you've been a dolt for not telling her. You know I'm a better shot than you. You're only in a panic now because there's a chance you could lose her."

If she found out he was planning to marry her anyway, she'd think he was no better than Montrose. Amelia had made her stance on marriage very clear.

Nicholas stood up. He needed to see her. He needed to explain. If Montrose thought he was going to ruin this for Nick, he'd better be prepared for a fight.

Chapter Eleven

Embry sat across from her in the parlor. Amelia hadn't yet said two words, not that anyone would have noticed around the avalanche of adoration tumbling from her mother.

The doctors had come and gone, and Julia was on the mend once again, but it was one scare too many. That any of them, especially her mother, could think of idly socializing at a time like this was offensive. Julia was better, no longer sweating through her sheets, but still weak enough that moving around her room was about all she could manage.

"Your carriage was so comfortable, Lord Montrose. Is it new?"

Embry frowned. "No, not especially."

"Ah. Then it must have been the extraordinarily fine company. And fine looking as well, if I do say so."

"Thank you." He looked around the room uncomfortably, settling on Amelia.

"You're so splendid in grey," Lady Bishop continued. "Do you think you'll wear grey for the wedding?"

"Perhaps. Lady Bishop—"

"Please, call me Felicity. We're family now."

"Felicity," he said with a nod. "Perhaps Amelia and I could have a few moments alone?"

Lady Bishop sent him a knowing smile. "Of course, of course. I'm sure you two have quite a lot to talk about."

When Lady Bishop left the parlor, the silence stretched out between them. If he wasn't going to say anything, Amelia might as well. "Lord Montrose—"

"Amelia," he said at the same time.

They lapsed back into temporary silence.

"I wish you would go back to calling me Embry," he said.

"That was before."

"Before what?"

"Before I realized I couldn't marry you."

Embry stood up, pacing across the carpet. "Amelia, please. I didn't come here to fight with you."

He didn't belong here. If he wasn't going to throw her over, then he had no business in her house. "Why did you come?"

"To see you. To spend time with you." He sat down beside her, taking her hands. "To put this nonsense between us to rights."

Amelia pulled them back, scooting away to give herself more space on the settee. "My feelings are not nonsense."

His face clouded at her retreat. "This difficulty between us is my fault."

Not this again.

"I've given you too much time to think. The strain of all the preparations have caused you to doubt."

"Hardly."

He ignored her, scooting closer. "I thought by allowing you to hold off on selecting a date that I was allowing you time to adjust to your new social standing, but I've seen the error of my ways."

A feeling of dread crept in. "Lord Montrose—"

"I've spoken with your mother, and we have chosen a date next month. Once we're married, you can let all of this indecision go and devote yourself to the task of being my wife."

He was utterly delusional. So was her mother. "I won't marry you."

"You will. Need I remind you of the lengths I am prepared to go to make you see sense?"

No, he didn't need to remind her. Amelia was well aware of what was at stake.

His face darkened. "If you're thinking Nicholas Wakefield will find some foolish scheme to disrupt our union, please disabuse yourself of the notion."

"What does Nicholas have to do with anything?"

Embry took her hand again. His grip tightened when she tried to pull it back. "I know you harbor a great affection for each other, but I've written to the Marquess. Soon Wakefield will understand the impossibility of his position, and I don't want you to be heartbroken when that happens."

He'd written to Nicholas's father? Amelia pulled away from his grip, but he held tight. "What the devil are you talking about?"

"It's for your own good Amelia, and his."

This time, when she pulled away, he let her go. "I'm not entirely sure what you're talking about, but I am quite certain, whatever it was, that you have grievously overstepped!"

"You're my fiancée. It is my responsibility—"

"You have no rights where I am concerned."

He stood up and took her by the shoulders. "I have every right, and I will dare whatever I must to keep you."

His fingers bit into her shoulders and the hardness in his expression was extremely unsettling. Amelia's anger drained away, replaced by fear. She took deep breaths, willing herself to stand still and keep her expression smooth.

"Mia, do you know where I left my—" Julia came through the parlor door. "Oh, am I interrupting something?"

Julia? She wasn't nearly well enough to be walking around. Still, Amelia had never been gladder to see anyone in her life.

Embry's hands fell away and a polite smile fell into place. "Not at all."

"Excellent. You don't mind if I steal my sister away, do you?"

He obviously did mind, but his manners wouldn't allow him to say so.

Julia was already pulling Amelia through the door with a weak grip. "I'm afraid we'll be busy for a while, but I'm certain Mother won't mind keeping you company for the rest of your visit."

They left Embry behind, making it to the stairs before Julia's knees buckled and Amelia had to hold her up.

"You shouldn't be up," Amelia insisted. "What are you doing?"

"Nora was listening at the door for me." Julia's breathing was labored. "You should have told me he frightens you."

"It doesn't matter, Jules. You really shouldn't be—"

Julia stopped her until they made it to the top of the stairs. "I wanted to be selfless. I wanted you to have a husband and a family but...not like this."

The tension drained out of Amelia's shoulders. They were only words, so they shouldn't mean that much to her, but they did.

Julia smiled. "I've missed you all the time you were gone. I don't think I could bear it if you left me for good, and I hate myself for it because I should be a better sister. A better person."

"I'm not leaving you. Not ever." Embry could do his worst.

"You might, eventually. Embry isn't the only man in the world."

Amelia shook her head. "I was so wrong about Embry. I can't believe all the things I didn't see. I won't marry, ever. I won't run the risk of being wrong again."

"Mia."

Amelia regained her senses. They were standing in the hallway, having an utterly private conversation where anyone could hear them. She led the way back to Julia's room. "We can discuss it later. Right now, we need to get you back to bed and me out of this engagement."

Julia nodded. "You should get into a fistfight at a ball. Or visit a gaming hell!"

Leave it to Julia to suggest only extreme solutions. Amelia had hoped to stay relatively within her comfort zone while convincing Embry to jilt her. "Don't you think we could find something a little less—"

"Likely to succeed? Certainly. What color would you like me to wear to your wedding?"

Amelia sighed. "Fine. I can think of a few people I'd like to slap. Do we know of any gaming hells?"

Julia was asleep again, this time without any residual fever, when Amelia was summoned to the study by her father.

"Amelia. Sit down please."

She sat. The atmosphere was much like the times she'd been called to task for something she and Julia had done, only this time Amelia had done it all on her own.

"Lord Montrose spoke with me before he left." Lord

Bishop pressed two fingers to the bridge of his nose. "He's asked me to forbid you to see Nicholas Wakefield anymore."

"Was that all he said?" Convenient of him not to mention that he was blackmailing her.

"He feels quite passionately about it. Montrose believes Wakefield is a bad influence on you."

"Papa, that's ludicrous."

"I agree. Much as it pains me to admit it, I am well aware it is the other way around. I tried to explain that to him, but he refused to see reason."

"Yes, he does that."

"He's quite devoted to you."

Too devoted. "I won't stop being friends with Nicholas."

"No, I don't imagine you will. You two have been thick as thieves since you were children. Still, I'm concerned about you, Mia."

"Because of the race in Hyde Park?"

Her father's expression darkened. "Honestly, Mia. What on earth were you thinking?"

"Does it matter? What's done is done." She couldn't tell him, but she refused to lie to him.

"Mia, it might not hurt if you saw a little less of Nicholas." Her father fumbled with the pen on his desk. "Marriage lasts a very long time, and giving a little ground here and there can go a long way."

Amelia looked her father in the eye. "Nicholas is the only person who stood by us, Papa. Don't ask me to give him up."

Lord Bishop sighed. "I won't ask it of you. Just consider what I've said."

"Thank you." Amelia rose to leave.

"Was Montrose telling the truth? Did you truly win two hundred pounds in a wager?"

"I did."

"And something about using children as hazards?"

Amelia choked out a laugh. "Not intentionally. Some boys wandered onto the track. Dio jumped them. She was amazing."

"It sounds like you were amazing."

"I appreciate that you think so, Papa."

"I always will, darling."

It was a good moment, one she hated to ruin with less pleasant matters, but something had to be done and there might not be a better time. She settled back into her chair. "Papa, we need to talk about Mother."

"Is everything all right? She seemed fine when I saw her."

There was no easy way to approach this. "Did you know that mother has given Nicholas the cut? He came to see me in London and she refused him entry."

A frown creased his forehead. "That can't be right."

"It is," Amelia insisted. "She also told Julia not to go to my engagement party."

Lord Bishop frowned. "Your sister said she didn't feel up for it."

"Because Mother told her to say that. This engagement, the return to society, is turning Mother into someone else entirely."

"I know she's been exceptionally involved with your engagement and she can be trying sometimes, but—"

"Did you not wonder why I came on the train alone? Julia was *sick,* and Mother didn't want to leave London."

Suspicion tainted Lord Bishop's expression. "Your mother enjoyed society a great deal, before we were forced to remove ourselves."

"She enjoys it a great deal now. More, I lately suspect, than her affection for her children."

"I'm sure that's not true." Lord Bishop sighed.

Amelia crossed her arms. "I'm not sure of it at all."

Her father sighed. "I'll speak to your mother. I'm sure it's a misunderstanding, but I'll get to the bottom of it."

"Thank you, Papa."

It wasn't a misunderstanding and something had to be done about it. Amelia intended to rid herself of Embry and get her life back. That also meant returning her mother to someone Amelia recognized.

The walk to the Bishop house felt longer than ever, especially with his nerves causing Nick to perspire as if it were the height of summer. Amelia had to hear him out. She just had to.

Nick half expected to be turned away when he arrived, but was instead greeted by a very welcoming Mrs. Polk. "Lord, but it's good to have everyone home—including you, Lord Nicholas. The house doesn't feel right with Lady Amelia and Lady Bishop gone."

"Was there something in particular that brought them back?" he asked.

"Och! You don't know? Lady Julia took poorly."

Oh no. "I'm sorry. I can come back another time."

"No, no, no. She's turned the corner now. Feeling much better, and I imagine Lady Amelia could use some cheering. She takes it so hard, you know, and you always make her feel better," Mrs. Polk promised as she left to go find her.

Nick wasn't certain of that—he just hoped she wouldn't toss him out on his ear.

"Lord Nicholas. What are you doing here?" Lady Bishop stopped her path down the hall when she saw him through the open doorway of the parlor.

"I came to see Amelia."

"She's with Julia right now and I don't think—"

"Nicholas!" Lord Bishop boomed. "No one told me you were here."

"Just popping by to see Amelia."

"Of course, of course." Lord Bishop clapped him on the back. "I hear my wife has been playing a little trick on you in London, pretending to give you the cut."

"Ah, I..." Nicholas had no idea what to say to that.

Lady Bishop didn't, either. Her face was a picture of shock.

"You know, obviously, that it was only a jest. You are always welcome anywhere a Bishop hangs their hat." There was an element of steel in Lord Bishop's voice that Nicholas was starting to admire.

"Of course, Lord Bishop."

"Anyhow," the older man said. "Lady Bishop and I will leave you to it. Don't let Mia get you into any more trouble. I'm sure Lord and Lady Wakefield are up in arms about that race fiasco."

"I don't think they've heard yet, but I'll be sure to keep my wits about me."

"Good man." Lord Bishop led his wife out of the room with a firm hand on her arm.

Amelia came in as they left, not looking the least bit surprised at what passed between her parents.

"What was all that about?" he asked.

"My father has promised to rein my mother's ridiculousness back to a manageable level." Amelia collapsed in an unladylike puff of skirts onto the settee next to him. "Though how he'll manage it, I don't know. What are you doing back?"

"There was some trouble with my father. He's getting worse."

"I'm sorry, Nick." Her hand closed over his. The warmth of it spread out across his entire body. She wasn't screaming or giving him the cold shoulder. That was a good sign.

"And Julia? Mrs. Polk said you had a scare."

Amelia blew out a sigh. "A couple of them. She's all right now, but it's been awful. Somehow it's harder now that we're grown. I still feel as powerless as I did when we were little, but I'm too old to run away and live in the woods."

The first time Amelia had done that, Lord and Lady Bishop had been too busy with Julia to notice she was gone. Nick had noticed. He found her in a tree, crying and shivering. They stayed in the branches all night sharing his jacket and making up stories where the three of them featured as epic heroes overcoming insurmountable odds. The Wakefield search party found them in the morning when they came looking for Nicholas. They sent him to Eton shortly after.

Nicholas squeezed her hand. His decisions were his own now. No one would be sending him anywhere.

"We've made amends," Amelia said, perking up. "Julia no longer wants me to marry Embry, and I couldn't be happier to be in accord, even though the circumstances that brought it about were terrifying."

He couldn't help stiffening a little. "I heard Lord Montrose came to visit you. Did he have anything to say?"

"He only left an hour ago. How did you—don't tell me. The all-knowing Lady Wakefield." Amelia shook her head. "Yes. He had plenty to say, unfortunately."

"Was any of it about me?"

Amelia's eyes went wide. "How could your mother possibly know we talked about you?"

Damn, damn, damn. Montrose had told her. "This wasn't how I wanted to do this, but please hear me out."

"Nicholas."

He slid off the couch and onto one knee. Nick took a deep breath to calm his nerves. "Amelia Bishop, will you marry me?"

She blinked. Amelia looked down at him. Her brown eyes were full of surprise but still warm. Still—dare he hope— loving? "Nick, you know I can't."

It stung, but he'd been prepared for her objection. He pulled the little book of sonnets and the letters that had best expressed his love from the inside pocket of his jacket. "You have known me almost your entire life, and I have not changed. I am still the boy who wrote you letters every day I was away—I just lost the courage to send them, because they would reveal how much I care for you."

"Nick."

"And this book. I bought it for you in Paris. It speaks my heart better than I can."

She put the letters aside, holding the book gently, running her thumb down the spine and turning the pages. He watched her lips move faintly as she read the first sonnet.

"Please, Mia. Say you care for me, too."

She looked at him again. There was a sheen of tears making the perfect brown of her eyes sparkle. "Of course I care for you."

A giant weight lifted from Nicholas and he felt like he would float up through the ceiling. He pulled her to him and kissed her.

It was like touching lightning. All the tingles on earth, concentrated on one tiny point of contact. It hurt a little, feeling so much all at once. Amelia leaned into him, trying to spread it out across more of their bodies. Nicholas pressed against her, giving her the contact she craved. His tongue touched hers but it wasn't a conquest, it was a question. She answered it with enthusiasm.

She slid her hands inside his jacket, feeling the warmth of his skin and solid strength of his muscles through the linen. Her hands ran across the planes of his chest, up to his shoulders. She heard him groan in response and it called to something within her that demanded she answer. Abandoning her exploration of his chest, she wrapped her arms around his neck.

Nicholas seemed to know what she was asking. He pulled her forward across the cushions, his thigh shifting to a position between her own and his mouth moved over hers in a more calculated fashion. Amelia lost track of everything except the feel of his lips against hers and the delicious pressure of him all over. She was so far gone, she didn't understand when he lifted his head and pulled back.

Amelia looked up at him, finding adoration mixed with intensity and…Nick. Only Nick. The same Nick who'd tended orphan kittens with her in the barn and argued continental politics with her until they were both red in the face.

"Oh my," she said quietly.

He smiled. His eyes memorized her face and hers did the same to his as his fingers came to rest against the side of her neck. He stroked, ever so softly.

Amelia's lips parted of their own accord. There was still only a whisper's distance between them.

"We'd better not." His eyes traced the curve of her lips, undermining his words.

She couldn't quite get her thoughts to order. It felt like they were the only two people in the universe. "Why?"

"It's not proper."

"I should hope not," she said. "If there are proper things that feel like that and I've been missing them this entire time…"

Nick laughed. "We'll want to think about the proper way

to tell everyone, instead of letting ourselves be discovered."

Tell everyone? Had he gone completely mad? Oh. Oh no. "I told you, Nick. I can't marry you."

He froze. "But you kissed me back."

"I did." Amelia smiled. And this was the part that hurt. "I like kissing you. I like *you* and I would like to do a great deal more than kiss you. But I can't marry you."

"Then what—"

She could almost feel the pain radiating off him. Amelia took a deep breath. The scandals of the past few weeks couldn't hold a candle to what she was about to say. Even thinking it was exhilarating. "I think we should have an affair."

"You're not serious."

"Of course I am. It's the perfect solution. I can stay here with Julia, and you and I can—"

"Can what? Live in sin? Disgrace our families?" Nick set her away from him, standing up to pace the room. "This is ludicrous."

The anger in his voice hurt. Amelia had expected him to take some convincing, but she'd thought he would at least consider it. She tried to explain. "Nicholas, think how nice it could be. We care for each other. We're attracted to each other."

"Then marry me."

"No!" Amelia regretted raising her voice, but he wasn't *listening*. "I don't want to marry. I don't—"

"Do you think you don't know me?" Nicholas challenged. "Do you think I'm going to change suddenly?"

The answer to that was complicated. He was Nick—he was always Nick. But these feelings she had for him were so new, and for him to suddenly declare feelings for her after years of saying nothing... He was the same, but their relationship had changed. "Of course I know you, but—"

His face clouded over. His entire posture went stiff. "But you can't marry me. So it's not a matter of knowing me."

"Nick." Amelia ached to see him shut her out.

His movements were jerky, like he wasn't entirely aware of himself. "You accepted Montrose's proposal and he was a complete stranger to you. But he was a titled stranger." He picked up the packet of letters and tucked them back into his jacket. He refused to look at her while he prepared to leave. "He wasn't a second son, stupid enough to silently devote himself to you for twelve years, hoping you might someday see his value."

Twelve years. What did he mean? Amelia went to him, reaching for him. He had it all wrong. If he would only listen, she could explain. "That's not it at all. I just... I do see your value, Nick."

"As a contingency plan. As a pale replacement for a husband," he spat out. He pulled her hand from his chest, setting it back at her side as he stepped around her.

"Nick!" She moved to stop him but he shook her off. "Don't you dare leave. I know you're upset, but we're not done discussing this."

He kept his back turned to her. The rigid line of his shoulders was formidable. "No, thank you. I think I've played the fool long enough."

And then he was gone.

Amelia sat down hard on the settee. She squeezed her eyes shut against the tears, shaking her head. This was not happening. She had not reunited with Julia only to lose Nick moments later.

And how could he be so stupid? How could he think so little of her, that she of all people would give two damns about a bloody title? His pride might be hurt, but she expected better from him. He was supposed to be her friend. If he truly meant the things he'd said, then he didn't know her at all. They had no business in a marriage *or* an affair if that was what he thought of her.

She was well rid of him.

Amelia told herself she meant it. She ignored how much it hurt to watch him walk away from her. Ignored that she was still clasping the cushions in a death-grip to keep from chasing after him and telling him how sorry she was.

Good riddance, Nicholas Wakefield.

Chapter Twelve

"You're packing," Jasper said, standing in Nicholas's doorway.

"I am."

"Which fact should we address first, that you're robbing poor Bertram of his livelihood, or that you said you'd be staying a few more days at least?"

Nicholas continued to stuff items haphazardly into a bag. "There's nothing I need to do here that can't be done from London."

"Is Amelia going back?"

At the mention of her name, Nicholas gave up packing. Bertram could follow him later with his belongings. "Why don't you go ask her?"

"I'm asking you."

"Well, I wouldn't know." He picked up a book, only to slam it down on his dressing table. "Apparently, I don't know a lot of things."

"She refused you," Jasper said gently.

"She didn't just refuse me. She kissed me, like we were the only two people on earth and the world was unraveling around us, and *then* she refused me."

"Well done, Amelia."

"Well done?" Nicholas shouted. "Well done? This is the worst day of my life and you're taking her side?"

"Lord Nicholas," Smithson interrupted, frowning at his raised voice. "Your mother needs to speak with you at once."

"Fine. I'm on my way."

Anything to get away from Jasper or how miserable he felt. He'd finally declared himself and she turned him down. Not because she wasn't attracted to him. Not because she didn't care for him. Because she only saw him as being suitable for an affair, not for being her husband.

"I say 'well done' because it's an excellent opening volley," Jasper said, following him and speaking quietly over his shoulder.

"It's not a volley. It was a finality. She doesn't want to marry me."

"She kissed you."

"Yes." She'd kissed Montrose, too. How foolish Nicholas had been.

"Did she enjoy it?"

"That is not the problem." Nicholas didn't want to think about it anymore.

"So she likes you and she likes your kisses. She just doesn't want to marry you?"

Why did he have to keep repeating it? "Apparently."

"Does she want to marry anyone?"

Nicholas stopped mid-step. "She says not, which is ludicrous. Which means that I have been under the tragic misapprehension—"

Jasper started laughing, loudly and with an extreme lack of consideration for anyone around him. At one point he bent over, holding himself up with a hand on his knee. When he was finished, his eyes were watering and he was fanning his face to help with the redness.

"What on earth is so amusing?"

"You don't know a thing about women. Not your fault, really." Jasper clapped him on the back. "You've dedicated your entire life to knowing this one woman and she's gone and confounded you. This is where some diversity of experience would come in handy."

"I know plenty about women. I do not need your help."

"You do, desperately. Go and see your mother." Jasper took a seat on a chair outside the study. "And when you're done, we'll go to London and I'll take you to see the expert on women who do not wish to marry. She'll know what to do to convince Amelia to change her mind."

Nicholas wanted to ignore him. He wanted to stay angry, but if there was a chance, he had to take it. "Who's this expert?"

Jasper's grin was triumphant. "Lady Ruby De Vere."

"Your sister?" It served him right for believing a single word that came out of Jasper's mouth. Nicholas continued his path to the study.

"The legendary breaker of hearts who has turned down no less than three dukes and a crown prince. Who, yes, also happens to be my sister."

He was an idiot. He was a fool. He turned around. "You think she can really help?"

"Obviously. She's a De Vere."

Nicholas wanted to marry her.

She hadn't asked him for help with the next stage of her and Julia's plan. How could she, with the way he'd stormed out? It was a good thing she didn't want to marry, because her history with proposals was proving dismally unexceptional.

"Did you ask him? Will he do it?" Julia was waiting impatiently.

"No," Amelia said, still in a haze. She sat down in the chair next to the bed, rubbing her fingers over the cover of the book of sonnets he'd left behind.

Julia followed her. "No, you didn't ask him? Or no, he won't do it?"

"I didn't ask."

"Why ever not?"

"Because he asked me to marry him."

Julia was stricken silent for perhaps the first time in her life. Amelia stared at the wall, not actually seeing it.

"Nicholas asked you to marry him just now?"

Amelia shook herself, sighing. "Yes. I said no, and then he kissed me, and then I said no again. He stormed out."

"Oh, Mia." Julia climbed out of bed and wrapped her arms around Amelia's shoulders. "Why did you refuse him?"

"I told you; I don't want to marry. I want to stay here with you. I thought, of all people, Nick would understand but he thinks it's because he doesn't have a title. I've never seen him so hurt."

Julia hummed her sympathy. "Men and their pride. Unfortunately, that puts a damper on our plans for your next big scandal."

It put a damper on more than that. Nicholas was her best friend, next to Julia, and in some ways more than Julia. He was the person she turned to when she couldn't see her way clear of something. She'd never seen him so upset.

Well, so be it. He'd misjudged her as badly as he thought she'd misjudged him. If he expected to hold the monopoly on hurt feelings, he was in for a surprise. "I think I know someone else I can ask. Lord Bellamy. I think he'll help."

"The man who punched Lord Montrose?"

"Yes."

"You hardly know him."

"We've become good friends. If there's mischief involved, he'll help if he can." Unless he'd decided to take Nicholas's side. But there would be no knowing until she spoke to him.

"He sounds intriguing."

It was Amelia's turn to wrap her sister in an exuberant hug. "I can't wait for you to meet him. I'm certain you two will get on."

Julia's whole body stiffened. "Mia, no."

"Julia, he's not like that."

"He's the heir to a dukedom! I'm not meeting him."

Amelia scowled at her sister. "Why am I the only one who has to take risks and expand my horizons?"

"Because you're not a black mark on the family name, inveterately shunned by society."

Amelia wasn't done with that line of discussion, but she was prepared to leave it for now. "Well, give it a moment. If I do half the things we've planned, I'll have earned my place right next to you."

"Goodness. Poor Mother and Papa."

"I know. They'll start to wonder if our bloodline really is morally corrupt."

"I think we can safely say it is," Julia said with a grin.

Amelia jumped up, putting Nicholas out of her mind. "All right, then. We must make haste. I wish to be rid of Embry as soon as possible and get this whole mess behind us. How do we convince Papa to let you come to London?"

Based on the coldness of his mother's greeting and the rigidness of her posture, Nicholas was about to be treated to an encounter with yet another woman who didn't think he amounted to much.

"What did you need to speak with me about?" he asked, willing the encounter to end quickly.

"Smithson tells me you've called for the carriage. You're leaving again?"

"Yes."

Lady Wakefield's eyes narrowed. "What happened at the Bishops'?"

"Nothing."

"Do not lie to me, Nicholas. You were going to stay all week, and then you went over to that…that…" She was incapable of vulgarity even in her anger. "And now you're leaving. Your father received a very distressing letter from Lord Montrose, so don't pretend not to know what I mean."

"It's none of your business, Mother."

"It is every bit of my business! Do you think it's easy, being here alone with your father? Watching him fade? Watching him become violent?" Her hand flew up, hovering near her mouth. "You were supposed to be here with me, helping. Instead, nothing has changed. Wherever Amelia Bishop is, that's where you can be found."

It was the wrong day for her to challenge him on this. Any other day, he wouldn't have argued with her. "Has it ever mattered to you in the slightest that I am in love with her?"

Her face shuttered into stubborn denial. "Don't say that."

"We both know it's the truth. That's why you sent me away. She's the one person who makes me truly happy, but you care more about reputation than whether I'm happy." He'd gone too far to stop now. He'd broached the unbroachable subject. And he should have done this a long time ago. "That's why you're alone. You could be surrounded by friends and family to help you through this, but you can't dare to let anyone think the Wakefield bloodline might be as fallible as the Bishops'. Not after all the venom you've spewed."

His mother went pale. She was shaking from the strain of not shouting at him. Nicholas wished she would. He wished she'd give up appearances once and for all and be his mother.

Instead she said, "You're clearly overwrought. We'll discuss this another time."

"We won't, actually. The issue of Amelia Bishop is closed." God, it hurt to say it. "I offered her our name, but she didn't want it."

Lady Wakefield gasped. "You what?"

"I'm not good enough for her." And honestly, could he blame her? Why on earth would she want to join a family that despised her when she could stay with her own? "So now you can rest easy. Amelia Bishop has refused the opportunity to become a Wakefield. Twice."

"Thank God for that," she breathed.

"No, Mother, not thank God. I shall spend the rest of my days miserable without her. I doubt God wants much to do with any of that."

And if He did, Nicholas wanted nothing to do with Him. He left the room and headed for the train station with Jasper in tow. Hopefully Lady Ruby had some miraculous answer for them. Otherwise Nicholas would be spending the rest of his days alone.

✦ ⁃⁃⁃ ⳩⳩⳩ ⁃⁃⁃ ✦

With Julia's help, Amelia convinced Lord Bishop that London was the best place for Julia, given the proximity of the world's leading physicians. She had also convinced him that it would be best for them to return immediately, while Julia was relatively well, instead of waiting for a relapse to come along and ruin Julia's chances for receiving the best medical care available.

It was a testament to Julia's love for her. Agreeing to go along meant Julia would spend her time in London being tested and poked by every doctor Papa could get his hands on. Meanwhile, Amelia would be undergoing her own version of torture, attempting to brazen through the scandals Julia came up with. If only they could trade places. Amelia would much prefer private prodding to making herself a public spectacle.

They were barely settled at the new London house—Julia hated it, just like Amelia thought she would—when Lord Bellamy answered her summons. Amelia tried her best to convince Julia to meet him. "I swear to you, he might behave badly, but it won't be because of your leg."

"Absolutely not."

"Julia!"

"Enough. Get out there. You've left a duke's heir languishing in our parlor."

Amelia sighed. She left the downstairs linen closet, the closest room available that Julia had ducked into when the butler asked if they were available to receive Viscount Bellamy, and made the short walk to the parlor. It served Julia right if she ended up trapped with the tablecloths for the duration of Jasper's visit.

Lord Bellamy's smile lit up the room when she entered. "Amelia, it is lovely to see you again."

"I'm so glad you accepted my invitation. I wasn't certain you would." She left the parlor door open for propriety's sake. Lord and Lady Bishop were out for the afternoon.

"Nicholas is being ridiculous. Don't worry. He'll come around."

That wasn't why she'd asked to see Jasper. "I need to ask a rather alarming favor of you."

Jasper let the subject of Nick drop with a smirk, taking his ease in the wing-backed chair, looking as if he'd always belonged there. "Yes, your letter was intriguing, if a bit mysterious, but I like a good mystery."

Amelia sighed in relief. "Well, in that case, I need your help creating my next scandal."

Jasper's smile was a slow spread across his face. "Finally off the reserve list, am I? Nicholas should abandon his senses more often."

"I must up my game to be rid of Embry, and I think you are uniquely suited to what I have in mind."

Jasper's face lost its mirth. "So Montrose's visit to your father didn't cancel the engagement?"

Amelia scowled. "No. He is proving to be quite resilient. First, he claimed I was being hysterical. Then, that I was acting out from neglect. And now I'm to be married next month to save me from the altering strain of wedding jitters."

Jasper frowned with her. "How many others can he blame before he must admit he's engaged to a dragoness? So, what did you have in mind?"

Amelia couldn't stop the blush that spread across her cheeks. "I wondered if you might take me to a gaming hell tonight."

Lord Bellamy whistled. "Up your game indeed. Any one in particular?"

She straightened her shoulders. "I thought perhaps Crockford's. Do you know it?"

Jasper laughed. "I do, though how you should, I'd like to know. Yes, my dear. I will take you to Crockford's."

They made plans to visit the hell the following evening when it was certain to be packed, and then it was time for

Jasper to rush off to some other appointment.

"Thank you, Jasper."

"On the contrary," he responded. "I rarely have such a willing participant to my distractions."

Amelia laughed as she walked him out.

"You didn't tell me he was so handsome," Julia accused as soon as the front door closed behind Jasper.

"You didn't ask. Besides, what does it matter?" Amelia relished the opportunity to taunt her sister a little.

"It matters because what if I had agreed to meet him? Good God."

"He would love you." No one with any sense could meet Julia and fail to absolutely adore her. Someday she would see that. She just needed to meet more people who didn't treat her like a pariah.

"You don't know that. Anyhow, will he help?"

"He will." Amelia burst into a huge grin.

Julia squealed with delight. "I can't believe it. You're going to a real live gaming hell! There will be rowdy men and loose women and foul language!"

Amelia's stomach immediately dropped into her knees. "Oh God. I'm going to a real live gaming hell."

"Don't. Amelia Marie Bishop, do not do this to me."

"I can't do it. What was I thinking? The kinds of people that will be there—"

"Will still be well-bred, just badly behaved. Like us."

Amelia rolled her eyes. "Like you, maybe. All I ever wanted was to be left alone in the country."

"Well, that ship has sailed. We're on a new ship bound for debauchery." Julia flung herself against the wainscoting in a pose of extreme drama. "You must remember absolutely everything so you can tell me about it."

"Why don't you come?"

"Don't be ridiculous."

"What's ridiculous? I'm sure Jasper won't mind, and it's not like you're worried about your reputation."

Julia's joviality disappeared. "No."

"Julia." Amelia wondered if her fearless older sister might not be quite so fearless after all.

"It's all right. You'll just have to tell me about it, that's all." Julia's smile reappeared. "Goodness. We have to find you something suitably unsuitable to wear."

"Why can't I wear my normal clothes?"

Julia scoffed. "If you show up looking like yourself, they'll never let you in."

She had a point. This plan was getting worse by the second.

"You're late," Nicholas told Jasper when the carriage door opened. "You said we were going at four and it's half past."

"Heart-broken Nicholas is a bit of a killjoy." Jasper moved over to make room. "She's my sister. It doesn't really matter when I show up."

"It matters to me."

"I had pressing business come up."

"What sort?"

"The Amelia sort."

Pain spiked through his chest. He stayed silent. Jasper was baiting him.

"She's asked me to help her with the scandals," Jasper offered, watching him closely.

It didn't matter. It wasn't his business anymore. Nick focused his attention on the passing buildings as the carriage turned off the mall, heading north toward Mayfair.

"I'm taking her to a gaming hell tonight."

Nick spun around to face him. "Are you out of your bloody mind?" It was too much. It was beyond irresponsible. It was fine for Jasper, but to drag Amelia into a place like that was completely unthinkable. His objection wasn't due to his feelings, it was common sense.

Jasper shrugged. "It wasn't my idea. I merely agreed to accompany her."

Affairs? Gaming hells? It was too far. She had lost her damned mind. "You can't take her. Tell her you won't go."

Jasper raised his eyebrow. "No."

"Yes!"

"She wants to go and I am inclined to be her escort." Jasper studied Nick. "Of course, you are welcome to apologize to her and offer calm reasoning on why she should reconsider."

Absolutely not. Not after she'd relegated him to the position of concubine. She'd even replaced him with Jasper as her ally in getting out of her engagement. No. She clearly didn't value his opinion or listen to it.

"You could come with us. Make sure nothing untoward occurs."

"No."

"Suit yourself."

The rest of the ride passed in silence as Nicholas made a list of all the reasons he should cease being friends with Jasper De Vere. He was only halfway finished when they pulled up in front of the early Georgian palace Jasper's grandparents called home when they stayed in London.

His mouth dropped open. "You didn't tell me we were going to the ducal residence."

"My sister is unwed and my parents are dead. Where else would she live?"

Nicholas tried his best, but he couldn't find a way to

attribute the misunderstanding to Jasper. He must have been too distracted to have thought it out clearly. "Did you tell them you were bringing me?"

"Why would I? It's my home, too."

· Nicholas should not have come. Imposing on a duke. His parents would have simultaneous heart attacks.

They ascended the wide front steps and entered a foyer done entirely in marble. Jasper didn't wait to be announced. "Ruby, where are you?"

His voice echoed down the halls.

"Good God," Nicholas muttered.

"Lady Ruby is in the flower garden," the butler offered, unfazed. "Would you like me to tell her you are here?"

"That's all right. We'll surprise her."

Tandem apoplexies due to shame—both his parents gone in one fell swoop. Could he be sent to the tower for a social affront?

In the garden, a woman who was Jasper-but-not sat painting in the dying light of the early winter evening. She shared Jasper's dark hair and sharply aristocratic features, but her elegance was purely feminine. Seeing his friend in female form was an odd sensation that left Nicholas quite disconcerted.

"You're lucky they're at a musicale. Grandmother promised to skin you the next time you went bellowing down her hallway."

"Our hallway."

"Really? Is your name on the deed?"

"Lord Nicholas Wakefield, may I introduce you to the most irritating woman alive—my twin sister, Lady Ruby De Vere."

She finished the flower she was painting and set down her brushes to stand and present Nicholas with her hand. "A pleasure."

Nicholas bowed over it. "I'm delighted to make your

acquaintance, Lady Ruby."

"Manners, how novel. What foul elements conspired to see you mixed up with my brother?"

Nick almost smiled. "I ask myself that every day."

"Enough of that," Jasper said, sprawling in his sister's chair. "Nicholas has a problem to which you are uniquely suited to give advice."

"Not a social call then." Lady Ruby shoved his boots off the opposite chair and reseated herself. "Well, I don't have any plans this evening, so I suppose I'm game."

Jasper raised his eyebrow. "Fresh out of admiring suitors?"

"I'm spending the week at home. Giving Duke Atherton time to cool off before we see each other again."

"Atherton proposed?"

"Unfortunately. But you're not here to talk about my romantic troubles." She turned to Nicholas. "What can I help you with?"

Jasper gestured vaguely. "The woman Nicholas loves has refused his offer of marriage and made a counter-offer of an affair."

Lady Ruby sighed. "Is the turning down of proposals all anyone imagines I'm an expert at? I'm quite accomplished, you know. Well-read, well-traveled, generally considered to excel in many areas that have nothing to do with failed attempts at matrimony."

"We're all famous for something, dear sister."

She ignored him, turning back to Nicholas. "Did she say why she doesn't want to marry you?"

"Does it matter?" Nicholas immediately regretted saying that. Lady Ruby was every inch the granddaughter of a duchess and knew exactly how to make a man feel utterly inconsequential with a look.

"It matters a great deal."

Under the force of that unmanning stare, Nicholas had no choice but to tell her everything—twice. Once in his own way, and once again when she demanded to hear his and Amelia's story from the beginning.

When he'd finished, Lady Ruby was nodding slowly. "So to make sure I have it right, this woman has been abruptly ripped from a lifetime of isolation, nearly lost her sister, and her sole experience with being betrothed thus far has been blackmail. Do I have all that correct?"

Nicholas didn't trust himself not to say the wrong thing, so he nodded.

"And you think her objection is because she has been playing you false for over a decade, secretly despising your social status while pretending to be your closest friend and confidant?"

When it was put like that, he could see more than a gap in the logic. *Oh God.* He was an idiot. The things he'd said to Amelia—how could he have botched it so completely? She was terrified of everyone around her turning into strangers with secret motivations, and he'd shocked her with a sudden declaration of feelings and then had gone completely mad.

"How do I fix it?" Nick begged Ruby. "What can we do?"

"Well, for starters, Jasper can ring for tea."

Chapter Thirteen

"Are you certain about this?" Amelia looked at herself in the mirror.

Julia put down the shears after taking yet another strip of cloth away from the front of Amelia's gown. "I don't know. It might need to be a little lower still."

Lower still? Was she trying to expose Amelia's navel? "Absolutely not."

"We could rouge your nipples."

Of all the scandalous notions. Amelia gasped. "Julia! Where do you even come up with something like that?"

"You're not the only one who reads." Julia sighed. "I suppose that will have to do. We'll shorten the skirt up a bit to show your petticoat though."

Amelia made a small sound of distress.

"Do you have a good one? One that's not plain?"

"Why would I?"

Julia shrugged. "I had one made of fuchsia silk for fun. Mother was aghast but she didn't stop me. I'll loan it to you."

Amelia narrowed her eyes. "When did you do that and

why didn't I ever hear about it?"

"Last year. It was my secret for myself. Everyone needs one."

Amelia looked at herself again. They'd chosen a white satin gown to alter, the one meant for her wedding breakfast. Another small stand in the name of defiance. Since she didn't intend to marry Embry, she doubted it would be missed. If she pretended she were someone else, if she didn't think about all the strangers' eyes on her, she could see how it might be quite provocative.

A scrap of silk fell to the floor from the skirt. Julia looked in the mirror and caught her admiring herself. "You can borrow the matching corset as well," she said with a knowing smile.

"There is something truly wrong with us." Amelia took a deep breath and watched her breasts lift obscenely.

"Nonsense," Julia said. "We're just more honest than most people. Well, I am. You'll learn eventually."

Amelia twisted to see around the back. "Should we pin up the sides? Show a bit more flash?" The prickle of nervousness running through her was turning into a thrill of excitement.

Julia clapped her hands. "Now you're getting it. Take it off, and we'll sew it up."

They sat together on the bed, using their years of embroidery for a purpose that would give their governess an apoplexy if she were there to see it.

"You know I'm going to try to back out again when I actually have to wear it," Amelia said.

"But you won't. You won't like it, but you'll go through with it."

Of course, she was right. After they'd finished sewing and under much duress, Amelia found herself dressed and ready for scandal.

"What will you tell Mother and Papa?" Amelia asked as she pulled the cloak around her shoulders. Like the petticoat and corset, it was Julia's, and cut longer for her sister's taller frame. It wouldn't do to have Lord or Lady Bishop accidentally catch a flash of fuchsia on her way down the stairs.

"I'll think of something brilliant, don't worry."

"I know you will." She took another look at herself—a vision of impropriety, with her hair piled high to expose as much creamy flesh as possible. "Oh God. I can't do this."

"Since we know you're going to, why don't you skip all the worrying and enjoy yourself instead?"

Could she? Could she just decide to enjoy herself?

No, she couldn't. "Oh, God."

Julia laughed. "It was worth a try. Here, drink this."

Amelia took what she was handed and downed it in a gulp. It lit her insides on fire the whole way down. She came up coughing. "What was that?"

"Papa's best whiskey. Here, have another." Julia lifted the bottle.

Amelia was still coughing from the last one. "You're a demon sent to torment me."

"You'll care a lot less if you're intoxicated. Everyone else will be. No one will think it unusual."

She did notice a slight lessening of her tension now that the burn had settled into a warmth in her chest and stomach. Amelia held out her glass. "All right."

Julia giggled. "This is almost as good as going myself."

"You—"

"Don't even try," Julia interrupted. "I'm sorry I brought it up."

Amelia sighed. Before she closed the cloak, she turned to her sister. "How do I look, honestly?"

"Like a woman who is up to absolutely no good."

Amelia nodded. "Well, then I suppose I'm ready."

She snuck down the back stairs—the same ones Nicholas used when he snuck in to measure her—and out the garden. *Don't think about Nick. He made his choice.*

In the alley, Jasper was waiting by a carriage. "My lady," he said with an overly flourished bow. "Your carriage awaits."

"My lord." Amelia giggled as she executed a curtsy.

He handed her up and they were off. Amelia couldn't quite sit still. She kept fidgeting with her dress.

Jasper raised an eyebrow at her. "Are you all right?"

"I'm nervous."

"About what, my dear?"

Amelia laughed. "About going to a gaming hell."

"And what do you imagine you'll find there that unnerves you so?"

Good question. "I don't know. I'd imagine it's the things I don't know about that frighten me."

"Well," Jasper said with a smile. "I know everything there is to know about gaming hells, and I assure you, you have nothing to worry about. Especially at Crockford's."

"Is it not disreputable?"

"For a lady to visit, certainly it is. But by gaming hell standards, it is fairly reputable. There is no cheating or violence there. Only the sort of debaucheries you'll find pleasurable."

"Oh." Amelia wasn't sure what any of that meant, but it didn't sound too terrible.

They pulled up in front of an unassuming door on Saint James Street. Jasper stepped down and held out his hand. "After you, my lady."

She took his arm. They went up the steps and straight into Sodom and Gomorrah.

The women were fascinating. They were leaning over tables, sitting on laps. They were like beautiful flowers, just past their bloom. The man at the door took Amelia's cloak and Jasper gave a low whistle. "Lady Amelia."

"I thought I ought to look the part."

Jasper stepped back, looking her head to toe. "Oh my dear, you are something quite above and beyond the part."

She blushed.

"None of that now," he whispered. "You must pretend to be worldly."

She whispered back, "I don't think I know how."

Jasper laughed. "Follow my lead and pretend everyone is very boring and saying something you've heard a hundred times before."

And then he led her to the hazard table. Amelia didn't know the rules—she didn't need to. Jasper laid the bets and she threw the dice. The first time she threw them, everyone yelled. It startled her, until she realized she'd done something good. She threw them again and they yelled again—this time with a strange man kissing her on the cheek—so Amelia assumed she was doing well.

It went on that way for what felt like an eternity. The cheering and the praise made her forget to be nervous. Now and then someone brought her a drink. She lost count of how many she'd had.

"Ahh, darling," one of her new admirers declared. "Come away from this place and let me lavish you with queenly riches."

Intoxicated Amelia remembered what Jasper had told her. She raised her chin at the man. "Why would I want the riches of a queen, when I can have the worship of a goddess?"

Jasper arched an eyebrow at her and smiled. She leaned into him. "Was that the right thing to say?"

"Quite. Come, let's move to the card tables."

Amelia nodded and turned too quickly, stumbling into

the back of a gentleman. "I'm sorry, I—"

He turned. It was Mr. Preston. His eyes widened, and then dropped to her extremely exposed cleavage. "Lady Amelia. How surprising to see you here, and in a dress no less."

She narrowed her eyes, in part because it made it easier to keep him in her field of vision. "I am not in the least surprised to see you. I know how much you enjoy losing money, Mr. Preston."

"Perhaps on a riding track under extenuating circumstances, but cards are my game, Lady Amelia."

Amelia looked to Jasper. He shrugged and handed her his winnings from the hazard table.

"Mr. Preston, may I interest you in a game?"

Nicholas was in the library when the footman came to find him. Lady Ruby had given him a great deal to think about and left him feeling very much like an ass. He was sitting with a book, hoping no one would realize that he was just lost in thought.

"My lord, there is a messenger here from Viscount Bellamy. He says you must come at once."

"Jasper?" Nicholas put his book down. "What's the matter?"

"I'm afraid I don't know, my lord. He said you must come at once, nothing more."

"Right." Nicholas struggled to collect his thoughts. "Could someone—"

"Your coat and hat are in the foyer and the carriage is being brought around, my lord."

"Thank you." At this hour, even Jasper wouldn't send a

messenger unless it was truly urgent.

Once he arrived at Jasper's house, the staff let him straight in and led him to the small library. Jasper was standing next to the fireplace, but Nicholas barely saw him. Laid out on one of Jasper's leather couches was Amelia. Her eyes were closed.

Nicholas raced to her side. "Amelia. Amelia, love, are you all right?"

"I didn't realize…" Jasper's words faded as Nick blocked him out.

Amelia's eyes opened, hazy and unfocused. His heart lurched in his chest.

"You're a handsome man," she slurred. "Do you worship me, too?"

It took a moment to register. When it did, Nicholas was flabbergasted. "She's drunk?"

"Utterly soused." Jasper acted as if he didn't know how it had happened. "I tried to take her home, but she refused to get out of the carriage. Didn't want to go. She kept demanding to see you."

Nicholas stood up, ready to strangle Jasper. "How could you let this happen?"

"We were having a good time. She seemed fine."

She seemed *fine?* "Jasper, I swear to you—"

"Nicholas, why are you so angry? Look how fancy I am." Amelia stretched on the couch.

To his credit, he hadn't noticed her clothes before then. There was entirely more of Amelia on display than he was used to, and all of it was lifted or accentuated to its best advantage. He swung back around to Jasper.

Jasper held his hands up. "I had nothing to do with that. All her idea."

Amelia pushed herself up on the couch. She had her eyes closed and she was frowning. "You're a bad friend. You were supposed to understand."

"I know, love. I'm sorry."

She nodded, accepting the apology for what it was. "I don't like these clothes anymore. I want to take them off."

She meant immediately. Amelia started pulling at her bodice, managing to get a sleeve completely free of her shoulder. Nicholas had to dive to stop her. Fortunately, her dress hadn't been designed for someone without the services of a maid.

"I can't. I can't wear it anymore. I want to breathe."

"You are breathing, Mia. You're breathing just fine."

She shook her head. "No."

And who could argue with that sort of logic.

Nicholas turned to Jasper. "I have to take her home."

"Are you certain that's a good idea? It might be easier if she sobers up a bit."

Amelia was reaching around her back again, trying to undo the buttons of her dress.

"I'll have to risk it. Sneaking her in naked will be much more dangerous than clothed."

Jasper considered. "Probably easier, though."

"Much easier," Amelia hummed. She'd gathered her skirts in a puff on her lap, showing off a great deal of leg from the knee down.

Dragging her skirt back down, Nicholas fended off her hands as she retaliated by trying to undo the buttons on his waistcoat. "Amelia, you can take off as many of your clothes as you like if you let me take you home."

She looked at him, weaving slightly on the couch. "I don't want to, though."

"But don't you want to get undressed?" Jasper asked helpfully.

She squinted at them. "This is a trick."

"It's not. If you let me take you home, you can be nice and comfortable in your own bed."

Her hands went wandering again. "Can I be comfortable in your bed?"

Nicholas groaned. Jasper, meanwhile, was having an excellent laugh.

"No, Mia. You can't come to my bed."

She frowned. "You keep saying that. You're mean."

Jasper gave him a look and sat down next to her on the couch. "Amelia, darling."

"Jasper, darling," she echoed, lips splitting into a wide smile.

The viscount leaned close. He pitched his voice in a loud whisper. "I bet, if you're very tricky, you can convince him to join you in your bed."

What the devil? Nick had to put a stop to this. "Jasper, what are you trying to do?"

He held up his finger. "You can be tricky, can't you Amelia?"

Her nod was exaggerated. "All right. Take me home, Nick."

Nicholas watched her stand up and stumble her way to the door and out into the hallway. "What are you doing?" he demanded.

"Oh please. If you can't outsmart her in her current state, you're not the man I thought you were."

Someday, Nicholas was going to tally up all of his and Jasper's encounters. He suspected their friendship had caused him far more trouble than good. But right now, he had to tend to the love of his life, whom he could hear having an involved conversation with her own reflection in the hallway mirror.

Amelia felt wonderful. Every once in a while, the world tried to spin on her and then she did not feel wonderful, but for the most part she felt better than she ever had. She was also discovering things she'd never noticed before, like the way her face made the strangest shapes when she crinkled it this way and that.

"You're my face," she told her reflection. "I should be quite familiar with my own face."

Nicholas appeared from nowhere. "Come on, Mia. Let me take you home."

She leaned into the arm he put around her waist. Nicholas was nice. So nice. Except when he was being an ass, but he'd said he was sorry for that. She'd like to take his clothes off. Hers, too, but also his. She hoped he'd let her. It seemed silly that she'd never seen him without his clothes on and she desperately wanted to.

Nicholas held her fingers. She realized she'd been unbuttoning his waistcoat again. And why shouldn't she? "You want to marry me," she told him with a wide smile.

"I do," he agreed. "Some days more than others."

Amelia wanted to do married things with Nick. They could hide away in the woods and be naked all the time. And she told him so.

"I think the groundskeepers might object. And what about our families and your fiancé?"

Amelia told him what she thought about families and fiancés using one of the vulgar expressions she learned from her new friends at the hazard table. She was still telling him when she tried to navigate the step up into the carriage, but the driver kept moving it. She stopped her story to give the driver a piece of her mind.

"She doesn't mean it, I'm sorry," Nicholas called up.

"I certainly do!" Amelia heard a sigh, right before a

forceful shove to her backside sent her tumbling into the coach. "Why did you push me?"

"I told you I was going to give you some help up." Nicholas climbed in behind her and shut the door.

"You did not."

"I did. Not three seconds ago, I said 'We'll never get there if you keep clinging to the handle for dear life. Let me help you.'"

"I don't remember any of that."

"Later, when you're safely tucked in bed, Jasper and I are going to have a great deal to say to each other."

Amelia didn't care about that. They were friends, so of course they would have a lot to talk about. Just now, her major concern was why she was so cold. "It's freezing."

"Amelia? Amelia, you're shaking."

"Because it's cold."

Nicholas crossed over to her bench and gathered her to him. He took off his coat put it over her, trapping his deliciously warm body heat inside the cocoon he'd made for her.

She snuggled deep, trying to crawl into his warmth. "Mmm. Coffee."

"You want coffee?" he asked.

She laughed. "You smell like coffee."

"Oh."

"And oranges."

"I—" His voice cut off in the oddest sound as she pressed her lips against the exposed column of his throat and tasted him.

"You don't taste like coffee or oranges." She tried a different spot. "Not there, either."

"Amelia." He sounded choked. "While I am elated that you are not cross with me, I think we should save this line of exploration for another time."

"Why?" She slipped her fingers between two of the buttons she'd managed to get undone, running her hand against his chest. So warm. Like fire.

"You're not yourself right now."

She trailed her fingers lower, exploring the crisp little hairs on his stomach. "Of course I'm myself. How could I be anyone else?"

"I just don't think it's a good—" There was that odd sound again as she reached the waistband on his breeches.

"Do you have hair everywhere? How far does it go?" She reached for the buttons on the fall, but his hands trapped hers, bringing them to his lips.

"Yes, I do."

"May I see?"

"Not tonight. Perhaps someday, but not tonight."

Amelia frowned. "But I want to now."

"You're making a very compelling argument, but—"

Suddenly she was too hot. Amelia shoved off the coat and pushed herself out of Nick's lap. His hands caught her as she narrowly missed being dumped on the floor of the carriage.

"Amelia?"

"Hot, too hot." She needed to get this damned corset off. And the dress. All of it needed to go. She reached for buttons and Nicholas stopped her again. Amelia glared at him. "Why do you hate me?"

"What?"

She didn't have time to explain it. The driver lurched to a reckless stop.

Nick looked out the window. "We're here. Shall we get you inside so you can take off your dress?"

Finally, someone was making sense. She opened the door for herself and stepped out. The driver moved the carriage again, or the ground, and suddenly she found herself face down in the dirt. "Nick. Something has gone awry."

"So it would appear. Are you all right?"

"Of course. I don't know about your carriage driver, though."

"I think he's in better shape than you are."

"I think he might be drunk."

Nicholas helped her up off the ground. "I'll be sure to look into it. Let's get you inside first."

There were things in Nicholas's life that he was not exceptionally proud of, and the tactics he'd employed to get Amelia quietly up the back stairs were among them. Letting her walk on her own would have been a catastrophe. She'd managed to fall flat on her face twice, traversing the garden. In the end, the only sensible thing had been to pick her up and carry her. If only that had been the end of it, Nicholas could have counted it as chivalry and maintained his sense of honor.

Amelia, while intoxicated, was quite talkative. She wanted to chatter on and question everything. The only time she wasn't attempting to get them both in serious trouble was when she used her lips and tongue against his skin—God above—in ways Nicholas had only imagined in his most memorable of dreams.

And so he encouraged her.

He let her slide her hands under his clothes and wreak havoc with his senses for every agonizing step up the stairs, down the hall, and into her bedroom. By the time he deposited her on the plush carpet in front of her dressing table, he was rock hard and thoroughly ashamed of himself. It had seemed the only way, but his enjoyment of it with the state she was in was reprehensible.

When he set her down, she was not inclined to stop.

"Amelia," Nicholas groaned as her fingers rubbed him through his trousers. "You must stop."

"I don't want to."

"Don't you want to go to sleep?"

She shook her head, tracing her tongue across his nipple. Thanks to her efforts on the stairs, his shirt was hanging from a single shoulder. "Nope."

Nicholas was in very real trouble.

Fortunately, her assault stopped briefly when she started tugging at her own clothes again. She turned her back to him, gesturing for him to undo her buttons. He certainly couldn't leave her like this. Helping her undress was a necessity, not taking advantage. He kept repeating that to himself.

Unfastening her clothing with businesslike efficiency, Nicholas stepped away. He began refastening his own clothing while she was distracted with freeing herself from the dress. If he could just get his own clothes back in place, he'd make it out of here in one piece.

"Nick."

He looked up. She'd managed more than the dress. Amelia was completely naked. She was a nymph, all soft curves and hair curling down to her waist. She was a predator, the way she was eyeing him with dark intention.

There are certain occasions in every gentleman's life where he is compelled to behave in an ungentlemanly fashion. This was one of those times for Nicholas. Confronted with Amelia's perfect, naked form and his own overwhelming arousal, he gave in to a primal instinct as old as life itself.

He turned for the door and fled.

Chapter Fourteen

Morning was not kind to Amelia. Immediate analysis suggested she had been simultaneously poisoned and hit in the head with some sort of blunt object. It was very likely that it would be easier to just give up and die, rather than try and make it to the bell pull to ask someone to bring her a glass of water. She lay there, poised between life and death, hoping for once that Julia would interrupt her and come through the door.

Julia did not come.

Eventually there was no hope for it. Dying would take a long time, and it was clearly going to be agony for every horrid second. Amelia leveraged her legs off the side of the bed and—slowly—stood up. The change in elevation increased the throbbing in her head tenfold. Her stomach threatened to overturn right then and there. She almost laid back down, but then she'd just have to get up again. Hobbling to the pull, she yanked on it and sank down against the wall to wait.

No one came.

What the devil? Maybe she'd died already. Was this the

hell she'd been condemned to for her wickedness? Amelia used the wall to help her stand back up and open her door. She made slow progress down the hall, and even more laborious progress down the stairs. Each step jostled her body to new heights of misery.

She opened the first door she came to—the drawing room. In it, Julia was sitting with her embroidery kit. Of course there would be a version of her sister in hell. Who else could torment her so thoroughly?

"Amelia," Julia said entirely too loudly. "You look awful."

"I rang the pull. No one came."

"Oh. Mother and Papa are out and it seemed like you would sleep forever, so I gave everyone the afternoon off. There's a fair or a play or something. I don't quite recall."

Amelia blinked. She looked past her sister to the leftover tea tray sitting on the table. Rushing forward—a definite mistake, but it was too late to correct—she poured herself a cup of cold tea and gulped it down. She made it through half the liquid before her stomach revolted. Setting the cup down, she sank onto the couch and curled up in the corner, whining.

Julia watched the whole thing, fascinated. "What the devil is the matter with you?"

"I drank too much."

"And?"

"And I drank too much."

"That's all? This entire state is from drink?"

Amelia nodded into the cushion. She was on the verge of tears.

"Fascinating." Of course Julia would think so.

"I think I'm going to die."

Julia scoffed. "Don't be ridiculous."

"Please, Julia. Be nice me to today." Amelia turned the cushion over, sighing in ecstasy at the coolness of the fabric.

"It's really that bad?"

She nodded gently. The couch shifted next to her and she felt Julia's hand stroke the hair at her brow. It was like being touched by an angel.

"Should we call a doctor?"

"And say what? What does Mother do for Papa when he drinks too much?"

"Tells him he's a fool and slams doors around the house all day."

Amelia laughed. She immediately regretted it.

Julia made a sympathetic sound. "Come on, Mia. Let's get you up to bed."

"I won't make it."

"Sure you will."

They struggled their way back across all the hard-fought ground Amelia had covered. When she was back in bed, she pulled a cool pillow over her face to block out the light. Was it natural that she should be sweating? Surely that must be an indicator of some other malady.

Julia laid down next to her, radiating entirely too much heat. "So, what happened? How was it?"

"I honestly don't remember much."

"What do you remember?"

Amelia sifted through her hazy memories. Lights, laughter, so many little refreshment glasses. "I played hazard. I think I won Jasper a lot of money. He used it to stake me in—"

"What is it? Used it to stake you in what?"

One memory in particular surfaced with glaring clarity. "Mr. Preston was there."

"The one you raced in Hyde Park?"

The very same. "I said incredibly rude things to him, and then challenged him to a card game. It became quite the spectacle. Everyone was watching."

"Did you win?"

Leave it to Julia to be completely unfazed. If Amelia had even half her disregard for convention, she'd have been jilted weeks ago. Or never proposed to in the first place. How odd, and supremely unfair, that she should suffer for being the better-behaved sister. "I think so."

"Poor Mr. Preston," Julia said, obviously not meaning it in the slightest. "Trounced by a woman twice."

"I don't know what I was thinking."

"Well, then you shouldn't think more often. You've likely made an enemy for life, embarrassing him. He'll make sure everyone hears about what you've been up to."

That, at least, was good news. Amelia would hate to have pickled herself near to death and have everyone politely keep it to themselves. God, what if she had to do this again?

It took three days for Embry to call on Amelia. It was probably just as well, because she wouldn't have been in any state to receive him until late on the second day. The delay allowed her to appear in the parlor looking for all the world as if nothing out of the ordinary had happened.

Embry did not look ordinary. He was tapping his foot and scowling while he waited for her.

"Amelia."

"Lord Montrose."

He frowned at the formal title. It was only the two of them in the parlor, and for a long time there was silence. Amelia let it stretch. He could take as long as he liked to get to the point, as long as she ended up thrown over when he was finished.

"What were you doing at Crockford's, Amelia?" He stared

at her the way her father tried to when she was called to answer for her mischief in the study.

Amelia stared back. "Having a great deal of fun."

"This behavior is not like you."

"Isn't it?" Amelia kept her face impassive and her tone flat. "The fact of the matter is, Lord Montrose, that you don't know me."

"Don't be ridiculous. You're my fiancée. Of course I know you."

"I don't take sugar in my tea," she interrupted.

"What does that have to do with anything?"

"You told your mother I take three sugars. I don't. I don't take any."

He blinked at her like she'd lost her mind. "Of course you do, I've…"

Amelia watched the doubt creep in. "Might I hazard the guess that Lily took three sugars?"

His face shuttered. "It's one detail. You can't honestly be angry with me over how many sugars you take in your tea."

"I don't care for Roman architecture and I've never been to sea, but if I had, I suspect I would take to it marvelously." She kept her shoulders straight and her voice even.

"Amelia, you're being ridiculous."

"Am I? You do not know me, Lord Montrose, and you've been trying to paint me with the colors of some other woman. A wonderful woman, to be sure, but she is not me."

Montrose stood up from the settee, pacing the carpet in front of the fireplace. Amelia shifted to keep her distance.

"You're talking nonsense." Embry shook his head. "This is Wakefield's doing. He's been poisoning you against me ever since he returned because he has dishonorable intentions toward you."

"Nicholas had nothing to do with my going to Crockford's.

In fact, we've had a falling out and I don't expect we'll be seeing much of each other in the future."

There was a hint of satisfaction in his face then. Amelia didn't care. Let him think her father had forbid it if it removed Nicholas as an excuse. "I am not the girl you think I am. Your family doesn't like me. Society does not like me. Can you not see that we're unsuited to each other?"

"No, I cannot." He crossed the room to stand in front of her. "I want you for my wife, Amelia."

"Why?" she demanded. There was nowhere for her to go. An end table blocked her retreat.

"Because I love you." He took her hands.

Amelia shook her head. "I'm sorry, but no, you don't. You loved Lily, and I remind you of her. That's not love."

He seemed lost in thought for a moment. She held her breath. If he would only hear what she was telling him, they could end this amicably. It didn't have to be this difficult.

"You're upset by my feelings for Lily. I'm sorry, Amelia. I hadn't realized—but yes, I suppose it must be upsetting, to feel you're in competition with a woman who's out of reach."

Amelia screamed her frustration.

Montrose dropped her hands, stepping back in surprise. Amelia was a little startled she'd actually done it as well, but the entire situation was so bloody infuriating. It was like she was shouting into the void.

"Do you never hear anything I say?" Amelia demanded. "Is it that impossible for you to actually listen to what I am telling you?"

"Amelia, you're overwrought. Perhaps you ought to—" He came toward her.

Amelia picked up the closest thing to hand, a large porcelain vase. "Embry, I swear to God—"

"What's all this, then?" Lord Bishop came into the parlor.

Montrose turned, bending at the waist respectfully and blocking Amelia's view of the door. "Your daughter is not feeling well."

"You do not speak for me, Lord Montrose." Amelia stepped out from behind him, not bothering to lower her voice, the vase still in her grip. "I am frustrated because my fiancé refuses to listen to me or believe that I am a sentient being capable of making my own decisions."

Lord Bishop put a hand on Embry's shoulder. "Why don't we give Amelia a bit of space?"

"I don't think that's—"

"I'm afraid you'll have to trust me on this one, Montrose." He led Embry out of the parlor.

Julia appeared in the doorway in their absence, sending surreptitious looks down the hall after them. Amelia put the vase down and took deep, calming breaths.

"I suppose bludgeoning him to death with crockery is one way of getting out of it. You'll be hanged, but Papa will get to keep his money."

"Don't joke. At this point I'm considering it." Amelia flopped back down on the couch. "Jules, what if I can't get him to throw me over?"

"You can, don't worry."

"I *am* worried."

"Everyone has a breaking point." Julia patted her shoulder. "We just have to find his before he drives you mad."

"It may be too late."

When Montrose and Amelia were announced at the Chesterfield ball, the entire room went silent and then immediately erupted in a thunder of murmuring. Nick watched her from across the room. It had been a week since he'd snuck her back into her room after she'd visited the gaming hell. He hadn't seen her since.

Amelia must be hating every second of the attention, but she did a marvelous job of not letting it show. She lifted her chin and stared the room down in a look she most certainly had borrowed from her sister.

"...surprised she had the gall to attend."

"We can't imagine what Montrose is thinking."

"...better get his fiancée in hand."

"You hear she took Pembroke for a pretty penny at Crockford's?"

"I wouldn't mind another look at her in those trousers."

The last comment had Nicholas's fingers tightening around his glass. He turned to see who it was, but the crowd shifted and the man was gone. Not that Nicholas could really blame him—Amelia's backside in a pair of breeches was a sight to behold—but Nicholas wanted it to be a sight for him and him alone.

The crowd shifted again, and he caught a flash of Lord Bishop on the edge of the crowd. Amelia was bound to head in her father's direction eventually, so Nicholas made his way over. On the way, he passed the Chisholm sisters scowling into their punch.

"Honestly. Must she make a spectacle everywhere she goes?"

"And who even cares about horse racing?"

Nicholas grinned. He kept moving past them, only to be stopped by someone grabbing his arm. He looked up. "Montrose."

"If you're looking for Amelia, I'll save you the time. She is no longer going to be entertaining your company."

She wouldn't have confided in him. Anyone else, perhaps, but not Montrose. Nicholas pretended not to know what the man was talking about. "Oh? And why is that?"

"Because I've told her father to forbid it."

Nicholas laughed. "Lord Montrose, Amelia said you were a serious sort of man, but I see now that you just have an unusual sense of humor."

Montrose's face turned florid. "She is my fiancée."

"She is your hostage," Nicholas growled. "If you have to hold a woman's family ransom to get her to accept your affections, perhaps you're going about it the wrong way."

Nicholas shook off the earl's grip and kept moving through the crowd before their discussion erupted into violence. Arriving at Lord Bishop's elbow, he bowed as best he could in the packed crowd. "Lord Bishop."

"Nicholas! Thank God. These things are dreadful. I can't imagine why I agreed to come."

Nicholas experienced a flash of guilt. He should wait and give Amelia the time she deserved to be angry with him. That's what Lady Ruby had suggested. Still, he couldn't help but be worried about her. "I haven't spoken to Amelia in a few days. Is she all right?"

"Well enough. You know how women get when they're planning a wedding."

He didn't know, actually, and with Amelia swearing off the institution, he likely never would.

Amelia and her partner executed the last turn of the dance, coming to a stop a few feet away from her mother. He bid her good evening and she couldn't even remember his name. There had been so many of them. She must have been introduced to a hundred people tonight and danced with half as many.

Would she ever get used to being surrounded by strangers? Lord Montrose never missed an opportunity to escort her. Amelia found him in the crowd and glared. He was proving impossible to get rid of and she was at her wits' end.

"Hullo there, lovely." Jasper's voice came from over her shoulder.

She turned. "Jasper! Thank goodness."

"Miss me, sweetheart?"

"Desperately."

He swiped two glasses from a passing footman and handed her one. Amelia forced herself to take a drink. Never much of a drinker to begin with, ever since their escapades at the gaming hell, Amelia had paused at even the tamest of liquors. She tried another timid sip. The second one wasn't so bad.

"Bellamy!" A tall man wove through the crowd toward them.

Amelia saw Jasper's eyes narrow before he put on a brilliant smile and turned. "Renton. What a surprise to see you here. I thought respectable balls were beneath you."

"Quite right, but this one is for some daughter of a friend of my mother's. I've been blackmailed. I wouldn't have expected to see you here, either."

"Don't you know? I'm full of surprises." Jasper tasted his champagne and looked out over the crowd.

"I hope you'll save a few for *la balle du pécheur*. I heard you've made the list." Renton looked downright envious.

Jasper stared down his nose at the other man. "I'm sure I don't know what you mean, but if I did I would advise you to watch your tongue."

"I doubt anyone heard."

Jasper sighed. "Go away, Renton."

The other man looked shocked for a moment, but did as Jasper said.

"Is everyone afraid of you?" Amelia asked, curious.

"For the most part."

"How odd." She didn't find him intimidating in the slightest. "What's the *Sinner's Ball*?"

His eyebrow lifted. "Nothing you want to know about."

She blinked prettily at him, tilting her head to the side and fluttering her fan.

Jasper laughed. "Fine. Take a walk with me on the terrace."

She took his arm and let him lead her outside. They didn't stop at the terrace. Jasper kept going, down the gravel path and out onto the torch-lit lawn until they were out of earshot of everyone else.

"*La balle du pécheur* is an extremely exclusive masquerade ball attended by the wickedest, most debauched members of society."

"And you're one of them?"

Jasper gave her a sideways glance. "Of course I am."

"Will you take me?" Surely Embry would be forced to throw her over if she went to something like that.

"No, darling. Gaming hells and drinking to excess are one thing, but that is not the place for you."

"Please?"

"Even if I were willing to babysit your innocence all night, it won't serve your purpose. It's discreet. No one would know."

"But if I let my masque slip, they would."

"Amelia, you must trust my judgment on this. We'll find you another way, I promise." Jasper turned them back toward the party. As they approached the house, Amelia saw Embry standing on the terrace.

"Lord Bellamy."

"Montrose."

"May I borrow my fiancée?"

Jasper didn't answer right away. The delay clearly infuriated Embry. "I suppose, but do give her back. These functions are hellish without decent company."

Embry dragged her to the deserted end of the terrace. "What were you and Lord Bellamy talking about?"

"I can't imagine it's any of your business."

"You're my fiancée. All of your business is my business."

Amelia lifted her chin. He and his staggering presumption could go hang.

Embry grabbed her arm. "Perhaps I had it wrong. Perhaps Wakefield isn't the corrupting influence. Lord Bellamy was extremely upset at our engagement party."

"Let go of me this instant."

"I will not be made a fool of, Amelia."

"Really?" she demanded. "Because you're making a fool of yourself right now, grasping at straws, blaming anyone and everyone to avoid seeing the truth."

"No. These men are toying with you. They're making you act this way and say these things."

His eyes had gone a little wild and Amelia felt a sour, stabbing sensation in the pit of her stomach. She scanned the terrace, looking for an escape. Her savior came in the most unexpected of forms.

Nicholas stood outlined by the gaslights of the ballroom. "Amelia, your father is asking for you. It sounds urgent."

Embry dropped her arm and turned to Nicholas. "She doesn't need you to deliver her messages."

"And yet, her father has entrusted me with one." Nick looked only at Amelia, holding out his arm. "Shall I take you?"

"Yes, please. I shouldn't keep him waiting." She accepted

his arm and the feeling of safety that washed over her when she touched him.

"Are you all right?" he asked. "You looked frightened."

"I'm fine." And she was, now.

She expected him to mention her atrocious behavior from the other night. It was cruel, throwing herself at him and knowing that he thought she didn't value him.

Instead all he said was, "Your father didn't actually ask for you. It just seemed like you could use a rescue."

"Oh. Thank you." Nick, always so thoughtful. Her chest spasmed with pain.

He stopped her, just shy of the circle surrounding her parents. "Amelia, I know haven't been the best friend to you lately, but please believe I will always be here for you, even if I sometimes behave like an idiot."

"Stop." She reached into her hair, untying the tiny tube of rolled paper hidden beneath her curls. She pressed it into his palm. "I know. And Nicholas. Look."

He frowned down at the paper, unrolling it. His thumb rubbed over the wax seal, cracked from years of being rolled and rerolled.

"Never think I don't value you. You mean more to me than you will ever know." She stepped past him, joining the group around her parents before he could say anything that might encourage the moisture gathering in her eyes to fall.

"Amelia!" her father boomed. "Did you have a nice walk around the gardens?"

She brushed the corner of her eye, obscuring a tear that had managed to escape. "Very much. It was lovely."

There was no denying it. Amelia needed Nicholas. She felt too alone when they were apart and warmth bloomed in her chest when he was near. Somehow, she needed to find a way to fix what was broken between them.

Chapter Fifteen

Nicholas knocked on the door of Philip's study. "Do you have a moment?"

"A few," Philip answered. "What do you need?"

"I'd like to apply to one of the Inns of Court. Mr. Fletcher seems capable and…"

"And I've taken on all the rest of the estate work even though I promised I wouldn't," Philip said, setting his pen down. It looked suspiciously like he was balancing one of the manor ledgers. Lady Wakefield would be livid, but Nicholas could hardly demand Philip relinquish his birthright.

"I'm not needed," Nick said honestly. "I'd like to get started being useful somewhere." He was finally changing his life. Making it his own. And it had given him strength in ways he hadn't expected.

Philip sighed, nodding. "You're far from useless. I don't mention it enough, but if more men in the House of Lords had your intelligence and patience, we wouldn't be having so many problems. But I'm happy to help. What do you need?"

Nicholas took a moment to recover himself. "I'd like your

advice on where to apply, firstly, and then your endorsement once I actually do it."

"The second is yours. As to the first,"—Philip tapped his chin—"Lincoln is the best, in my opinion. All of them produce fine legal minds, but I think Lincoln does the best job of instilling fundamentals. Plus, I have a few more connections there."

"Lincoln's Inn it is." Saying it out loud was thrilling. He was really going to do this.

"Do you plan to live at the Inn? You'll get more out of it that way."

"Somehow I don't think Lord Wakefield is going to volunteer to pay my lodging." He still remembered their conversation, even if his father didn't.

"I'll pay for it."

It was Nicholas's turn to be surprised. "Are you certain?"

Philip leaned forward. "I've seen what it's like for you. We have two sons. One will be the Marquess eventually, but the other—when he comes of age I hope you'll smooth the path for him to do the same, to be productive and a contribution to the family."

Nicholas felt himself warm. "Of course."

"Good," Philip said, the matter seemingly settled. "I imagine it will be quite difficult. Learn all the things to do and not to do, so you can help your nephew do it better when the time comes."

"I'd like to get started as soon as possible." It would take at least three years before he could practice the law. It had seemed like such a long time when he thought of Amelia waiting for him.

"I'll draft a letter of recommendation right now."

Letter in hand, Nicholas's next stop was Lincoln's Inn. There was no sense wasting any time, since it would take long enough as it was. With any luck, they would have him. If not, he would try the others until someone accepted him. He hailed a hack and ordered the driver to take him to Chancery Lane.

It deposited him in front of the brick wall surrounding the Inn. Nicholas wasn't entirely sure where to start, so he figured he might as well try the hall. He was lucky enough to find an older, robed gentleman passing through the other direction.

The words came so easily, like he'd long been ready for them. "Excuse me, sir. Do you know who I might speak to about attending?"

The man looked him over and nodded. "Hilary term has already started. You can see about Trinity term, though. What is your name?"

"Nicholas Wakefield."

The man squinted. "The Marquess of Wakefield's son?"

"Yes, sir." Nicholas wasn't sure if this man knowing his father was favorable or not.

"You're Viscount Melton's brother, then. Good man. Takes his seat in Lords seriously."

Nicholas breathed a sigh of relief. "He does, indeed. I have a letter of endorsement from him."

The man took it, looking Nicholas up and down again. "You mean to apply yourself with the same dedication?"

"I do, sir." He stepped closer. "I'd like to live at the Inn and learn as much I can."

The man's eyebrows raised. He made a thoughtful humming sound. "I'll see what I can do. What's your direction?"

"I'm staying with my brother, near Charing Cross."

The man nodded. "You'll have an answer by week's end."

Nicholas left the Inn feeling better than he had in days, weeks maybe. It gave him the courage to write to Amelia. He was finally following his dream and no matter what was between them, she was the only person he wanted to share it with.

Waiting for Nicholas was one of the most nerve wracking things Amelia had ever had to do, which was saying quite a bit considering her recent activities. He'd written asking if he could see her and she had responded, telling him he could. Since then, the minutes had ticked by with excruciating slowness. Every creak of the house sent her head whipping around, checking her bedroom door.

The house creaked and Amelia's gaze snapped to the door again. This time it really was Nicholas. The evening damp had curled the ends of his hair and darkened his eyelashes. His collar was up against the cold. Amelia's heart thudded in her chest so loud she was certain he could hear it.

He shut the door behind him.

"Hullo," she said quietly.

"Hullo," he said back. "I'm glad you agreed to meet me."

"You might not be after we talk."

"Even then, I'll still be glad."

Amelia stood up. She'd intended to pace the floor to help her say what she needed to say, but instead she drifted toward Nick like he had some sort of gravitational pull. "I haven't changed my mind about marriage."

"I know."

He did? "I want you to know, I've never cared that you don't have a title."

Nicholas held his fingers up to her lips. The shock of the contact surprised them both. "I let my insecurities run away with me. I know you better than that."

Amelia found her voice. "And now you're here."

He nodded.

"Does that mean what I think it means?"

The movement of his throat as he swallowed was mesmerizing. "I still want to marry you. I always will. But what I want isn't the only thing to consider. If you're still interested in pursuing an affair…"

His words died off as she leaned in close, lips a hair's breadth from his. The deep rise and fall of his chest as he breathed in drew her hand up in fascination. She played her fingers along the edges of his cravat. "I'm still interested. Are you certain?"

His hand brushed her rib cage. His thumb whispered against the underside of her breast. "It is not in my power to deny you."

She couldn't think anymore, couldn't talk anymore, with him touching her like that. Every inch of her was charged with lightning and she needed to let out. "How do we— Where do we start?"

Nicholas used his hand to guide her around until her back was against the door. "You want to begin right now?"

Amelia nodded.

"So be it." He kissed her. He buried his fingers in her hair and kissed her senseless. The solid muscle of his thigh was between her legs and she clung to him for support. Nicholas picked up right where they'd left off in the parlor as if no time had passed, leaving her dazed and overwhelmed with the pleasure arcing through her body.

When he let them both up for air, her bones felt like liquid. How could she feel so safe and so completely undone at the same time? He held her close, but she felt like she'd lost her hold on the earth. This time, when she leaned in to kiss him again, he didn't stop her.

Where do we start? Amelia would be the death of him. Her boldness and her innocence would bring him to his knees with their perfect contradictions. She might not want his name, but she wanted him. He would give her everything in his power to give.

Nick had thought to slow things down, coming up for air, but she wasn't having it. One look from her through those impossibly thick eyelashes and he was helpless. She slid her palms inside his jacket and he lost all semblance of control.

Nicholas captured her hands, trapping them above her head. This new Amelia, queen of scandal, was not so easily tamed. She leaned back against the door and shifted herself against his thigh. Once. Twice. A third time. A flush crept up her chest and her expression turned languid.

Good God. "Amelia."

"There's something about this, isn't there?" she asked, rocking against him. "You keep putting your leg there and it feels impossibly wicked."

Nicholas leaned in, burying his face against the side of her neck while he tried to catch his breath. The honeysuckle smell of her filled his nose. Amelia kissed the edge of his jaw, the sensitive skin beneath his ear.

"I'll show you, if you want," he promised.

He felt her smile against his neck. Nicholas took one last deep breath and commended himself to the devil. Kissing her wrists, he let them go and sank down to his knees on the carpet. He slipped his hands under her dress, rubbing them lightly against the skin of her ankles.

Amelia's eyes went wide, but she didn't say a word.

Nicholas stroked up the sides of her calves. Goosebumps sprang up under his fingertips. His hands reached her knees — even her kneecaps were perfect — and nudged them apart.

A tiny squeak escaped her. Her knuckles were white

against the inlay of the door.

"Are you all right? Do you want me to stop?"

She shook her head.

"Amelia?"

"I'm all right. It's just new. Don't stop." The words came out breathy.

He cleared his throat. "Tell me if anything frightens you or doesn't feel good."

"I will, but Nicholas?"

"Yes?"

"It all feels wonderful."

Nicholas groaned. He pushed her knees a bit farther apart, setting her off-balance against the door. The soft skin of her inner thighs was under his palms. He took his time—stroking lightly, kneading the tension from her muscles.

She moaned when his thumbs brushed against the curls at her apex.

Nicholas stood up, the weight of her skirts trapped up against his forearm. He took her hand, massaging the tension from her palm while his other hand stayed poised at her entrance.

"We can stop. We don't have to do this now."

"Nicholas, if you stop I will kill you."

Her certainty undid him. Leaning down to kiss her, he slid his fingers forward. Silky wetness met them and it was his turn to moan. His Amelia; so incredibly, wonderfully perfect. He stroked in a slow back and forth motion, helping her explore the sensation. She shifted her hips against his hand and increased the pace, a steady stream of cries being swallowed by their joined lips. Nicholas could feel the tension building in her. More than anything, he needed her to come apart in his arms.

Adjusting his position, he started light circles against the collection of nerves that he knew would take her there. His first finger made a shallow inquest, and he felt her clench around the sudden intrusion. Amelia's head dropped back against the door. She gasped.

"Shh," he cautioned, working her body to a frenzy with his fingers.

She clapped her own hands against her mouth and bucked against the doorway as she rode the rising pleasure. Everything about watching her was magnificent. She was completely lost, abandoned to the sensations. As she crested the peak, poised to come crashing down, her eyes met his. Her pupils dilated, fear and wonder meeting before her eyelids slammed shut and she shuddered against him.

Nicholas held her close as she made her way back to rational thought.

"That was incredible," she whispered.

Downstairs, the front door closed. Lord and Lady Bishop's voices reverberated through the house.

"I have to go," Nicholas whispered. "Was it what you wanted?"

"More than I knew," she said, still looking half lost as she stared into his eyes.

He placed a gentle kiss on her lips, careful not to start them off anew. "Then I'm happy to have been of service."

If an excruciating feeling of loneliness took root in his chest as he slipped back down the stairs and left her behind, that was just the price he would pay to be the man she needed.

Jasper was going to kill her, but she didn't care. Nick's visit and the events that followed had locked Amelia's resolve into place in a way it hadn't been before. She needed to be with him. She needed to be free of Embry and to have the time to explore what was happening between them.

Whatever she must do to make that happen, including stealing Jasper's invitation to *la balle du pécheur*, she would do. It was time to put an end to this nonsense.

Amelia pulled the hood of her cloak farther over her face before she stepped out of the hired carriage. It was broad daylight. If anyone recognized her she would be in the worst sort of trouble. Walking up the steps of the townhouse, she steeled herself. It was just a knocker. She could sound it. Men did it all the time.

Knock. Knock. Knock. Goodness. Her heart was pounding like she'd sounded the opening volley in a battle.

The door opened and Lord Bellamy's butler appeared in front of her. "Yes?"

"Is Lord Bellamy at home?" Amelia knew that he wasn't. He'd told her he had luncheon with his grandmother.

"He is not."

Amelia checked to be sure no one was on the street to see her and lowered her hood. "Do you remember me?"

Disapproval emanated from the man. "I do, Lady Amelia."

"I am deeply sorry for my previous behavior. I have never been intoxicated before." This was the tricky part. Amelia had never been a very good liar. "The trouble is, I left something extremely valuable here and I need to retrieve it."

"Perhaps you should come back when Lord Bellamy is at home." The butler glared down at her and added, "With a proper escort."

Looking embarrassed wasn't difficult, because she was. "I'd like to, I really would. Only, the thing I left was a gift from my fiancé and he expects to see it when I see him in an hour."

The butler blinked at her.

"If I don't have it, I'll be forced to tell him where it is."

For a moment it looked as though he might refuse her.

He ought to have. What in the bloody hell was she thinking, coming here? In the end, though, he seemed to have more care for his employer's reputation than Jasper did himself.

The butler ushered her inside and shut the door. "What are you looking for and where did you leave it?"

"A necklace, with a big pink sapphire. As to where." Amelia did her best to look apologetic. It wasn't difficult. "I'm afraid most of my memory of the evening is a bit muddled. I think I was in the study?"

The depth of his frown lines made them appear etched in his face. "This way."

Amelia searched the room under his eagle eye. She took her time, waiting for the second half of her haphazard plan to take effect. Eventually an unholy pounding started up on the door. The butler swiveled, looking for all the world like he wanted to glare the noise into silence.

He looked back at Amelia as she was crawling her way around the room searching under furniture. He sighed. "I will return shortly."

Once he was gone, she hopped up and went to Jasper's desk. There was a stack of invitations to one side. It didn't take long to find the one she wanted. All the rest looked like the usual sort of invitations, but one of them at the bottom of the pile was black with no sender and no explanation. Only an address and a date written in white.

La balle du pécheur. Surely if it was as wicked as Jasper said, Embry would have no choice but to throw her over. Embry's stubborn refusal to listen to her was frustrating, but the frightening intensity of their last interaction had inspired Amelia to desperation. If attending the sinner's ball would free Amelia from her engagement, she would do it.

She heard footsteps in the hall and dropped back down to the carpet.

"Lady Amelia?"

She popped back up, pulling the necklace from the pocket sewn inside her cloak and slipping the invitation inside. "I found it!"

"Your hired carriage is outside. The driver is insisting you must leave now if you're to make your next appointment."

"Of course. I mustn't be late or there will be questions." She hurried from the room, nerve endings on high alert, certain the butler would somehow know. "Thank you so much for helping me."

"Think nothing of it, miss." The set of his mouth gave Amelia the impression he'd like to forget it had happened entirely.

"Everything is sorted," she called up to the coachman. "Let's be off."

More than sorted. The driver had done his part marvelously. She'd promised him double the fare, but she ought to throw a bit more on top. Everything had gone according to plan.

Every dress Amelia owned was laid out on the various surfaces of her bedroom. She was standing in the middle of them, frowning.

"None of these look particularly sinful," she told Julia.

"Whose fault is that?" Julia answered from her place on the bed. "Remember this moment the next time we're dress shopping and you're refusing to order anything interesting."

"I don't usually need anything interesting."

"Until you do. It's always good to have something unexpected to hand."

Amelia couldn't argue. She'd already been saved once

by Julia's predilection for inappropriate clothing. "What if it doesn't work? What if I do this and it still doesn't put Embry off?"

"Then we will try something else."

And something else, and something else, and something further still. *Whatever she must.*

"I stole from Jasper." To give her and Nick a chance. To be free. But it was all so selfish. What if she was wrong? What if having an affair with Nick was a mistake, and she destroyed their friendship? "I don't know who I'm becoming, Julia."

"Pretending to become, more's the pity. If this were an actual change of temperament, I would rejoice." Julia leaned off the edge of the bed, flashing teal stockings as she sifted through a pile of cotton day dresses with a scowl.

"How do you know it's not?"

Julia lifted her head. "If you could be anywhere right now, where would you be?"

"Home," Amelia answered instantly.

"Do you know where I would be?"

Amelia shook her head.

"Beijing."

"You would not."

"I would."

"Doing what?"

Julia shrugged. "Who knows? Seeing sights. Meeting people. Lounging in a cloud of opium smoke. I could be doing anything."

"You wouldn't actually go." The whole notion sounded terrifying.

"Yes, I would," Julia pinned Amelia with a serious stare and a raised finger. "And that's the point. You like to think about art and faraway places, but your heart is at home. No matter how many wicked things you do, you'll always secretly be sitting with a teacup and a book."

God, what she wouldn't give to be sitting in the window seat in her bedroom at home right now reading. "Am I the docile homebody Embry thinks I am?"

"Homebody, absolutely. Docile? Never. You're still my sister, after all."

"High praise."

"The highest. Montrose thinks he can wrap you up and box you in to being just one way. You are a member of the scandalous Bishop family. We accept no limitations, regardless of our natural predilections."

Amelia laughed as she always did when Julia started waxing lyrical on the virtues of their status as outcasts. "All right, I believe you, but I still don't have anything to wear."

"I think I know what's missing," Julia declared.

Thank goodness. "Oh?"

"We've only dragged out the dresses."

What else would they drag out? The only other things she had were trousers. She realized belatedly that was what Julia meant. "I can't wear the riding costume to a ball."

"Not exactly as you did before. That would be boring. But if we use the trousers for something, you would be immediately recognized without having to take off your mask."

So much for the window seat and the book. Nicholas's poor tailor was going to have an apoplexy when he heard she'd gone back out in his creation. At least it wouldn't be quite so public this time.

Julia's face lit up with inspiration. "I've got it. I know exactly what your costume will be."

Chapter Sixteen

Nicholas was firmly ensconced with Mr. Fletcher and Philip, the wicks of the oil lamps burning low as they finalized the details of Philip's takeover, when Jasper's unmistakable tones rang through the house.

"For God's sake, let me pass and I'll do it myself."

"My lord, if you'll only wait."

Nicholas excused himself and leaned out into the hall. "Jas?"

"Thank God," Jasper said, sidestepping Philip's butler. "You must come at once. It's an emergency."

Emergency was a widely defined term in Jasper's world. It covered everything from inebriated love-interests to invading hostile troops.

"I'm in the middle of something important," Nick explained.

Jasper went rigid with affront. "More important than Amelia's safety? Or her virtue?"

What the devil had happened now? "I'm sorry, Mr. Fletcher. Philip."

"We have it from here," Fletcher promised.

Heart racing, Nicholas left them to it.

"You need a dress coat."

Nicholas stopped. "Jasper, this had better not be another one of your schemes."

"They won't let you in without a dress coat. They may try to not let you in anyway, but we've got to get in to get her out."

"Who is they? Where are we going? Where is Amelia?"

"The Sinner's Ball."

Mother of God. Nicholas had never been to *La balle du pécheur,* but he had heard enough stories in Paris to know Amelia did not belong there. They were rumored to combine the showmanship of the old Italian masques with the secrecy and sexual depravity of a Greek orgy.

"We have to hurry," Jasper told him.

Hands already turning clammy with nerves, Nicholas led the way to his rooms to grab his coat. "How do you know she's there?"

"Goddamn Renton mentioned it in front of her at that Chesterfield soiree and she got it in her head that I should take her."

"Which you wouldn't."

Jasper glared at him as they took the stairs two at a time. "Of course I wouldn't. I'm eccentric, not an idiot."

"So how could she be there? It's bloody impossible to get in without an invitation."

"She has one."

"What? How?"

"She stole mine."

"Stole it?" Nicholas had a hard time imagining Amelia as a thief. "Are you certain?"

"Completely. Are you going to keep questioning me like I'm simple-minded, or can we get on with it? We're already late."

Nicholas changed into evening dress faster than he ever had in his life. Still, every minute it took for them to get back down the stairs and into Jasper's waiting coach felt like an eternity.

"How do you know she took it?"

"Because it's missing, and apparently Amelia paid a secret visit to my house today."

"That doesn't mean she took it."

"She lied to my butler, claiming she left a necklace that she was decidedly not wearing the night we went to Crockford's."

"Are you certain?"

Jasper sighed. "Have you ever known me to misremember anything to do with a woman's bosom?"

Fair point.

"She took it, Nicholas. Points for cleverness and all that, but she doesn't know what she's getting herself into."

Even Nicholas wasn't entirely certain, but what he did know made him stick his head out and shout for the driver to pick up the pace. Looking out, he realized they were on a road headed out of London. "Where are we going?"

"Not far."

Nicholas clenched his teeth, silently willing himself not to lose his temper. "Jasper."

"There are rules, Nicholas."

"And you care about them?"

"I ought to. I made them."

So Jasper was one of the founders of *La balle du pécheur*. It wasn't terribly surprising. They had a tendency to crop up in cities Jasper haunted, and decadence and debauchery were two of his favorite pastimes. "If anything happens to Amelia, I am going to blame you."

"As you wish. I won't notice, because I'll be busy blaming you."

"Me?" Nicholas exclaimed.

"You." Jasper leveled a glare at him. "You should have shot Montrose and put an end to this ages ago."

The sight when Amelia entered the ballroom froze her in place. Bodies—naked, exposed bodies—were everywhere. Not three feet in front of her, a woman was bent over the lap of a man who was gasping in pleasure, while another man lurched rhythmically against her backside. She met Amelia's stare with a wink as she increased the bobbing motion of her head.

Was that…were they…

It was, and they were. Amelia was suddenly thankful her masque was covering most of her face. As it was, the skin across her throat and chest felt impossibly warm.

To the left, a woman was stretched out across a table while another woman dripped honey across her skin. A couple sat on a couch a few feet away, touching each other intimately as they watched the second woman bend down and lick the honey from the first. To the right was a scene much like the woman with her two male companions, but all three were men.

Amelia's eyes widened as far as they would go. She should have listened to Jasper. This was not what she'd thought.

Whatever she must do to get rid of Embry.

An arm slipped around her, coming to rest not at her waist but between her legs—stroking the trouser-clad juncture of her thighs. Amelia's shock came out as a squeak.

"Aren't you delightful," a man's voice growled in her ear. His teeth scraped her earlobe and a rigid protrusion pressed against the small of her back. He dragged her hand back, cupping it against his arousal. "What's your pleasure? Do you like to command or submit?"

Her eyes flicked back to the couple on the couch. The man had joined the women with the honey and his partner was stretched out on the couch alone, pleasuring herself. "I... like to watch."

"Don't we all." He chuckled, still moving his fingers between her legs. "But you know the rules. Everyone participates."

Everyone participates? Oh, hell. She had to get away from here, but first she had to get away from her extremely amorous new acquaintance. "I've only just arrived. I haven't yet decided where I'll start."

He turned her around, cupping her backside in his hands. "Start with me."

"I don't think—"

"Don't think. Just wrap those sweet, pink lips around my cock." He let her go to undo the buttons on his trousers.

Amelia backed up and spun straight into a wall of masculine chest. The smell of coffee and oranges filled her senses. Her head snapped up, finding a familiar shadowed jawline and rigid set of lips beneath the edge of a black domino. That feeling of being completely safe dropped over her again. How could he feel so right, just standing there?

"Ni—"

He put his fingers to her lips. "Names aren't allowed. Are you all right?"

Amelia nodded.

Nicholas glared over her shoulder at the man she'd stepped away from. "Are you certain?"

"I am now."

Jasper joined them, distinct even with his bright harlequin mask, and inspected her from head to toe. The usual twinkle of mischief was missing from his eyes. "Ah, yes. She'll do nicely.

Bring her, we'll find a room."

"She's mine," the man with his trousers open protested.

"Is she?" Jasper sounded doubtful. He looked the other man up and down with a smirk before turning back to Amelia. "Lady's choice. Will you stay with him or come with us?"

Safely standing between Nicholas and Jasper, Amelia felt much bolder than she had a moment ago. She pretended to consider the question. Looking Jasper over the way he'd done to her, she pursed her lips. She circled Nicholas, running her hands along the lines of his back and legs. There was an edge of warning in the look he gave her when she came back around to his front.

"I'll come with you."

Jasper smiled. He sketched a bow to her acquaintance and led Amelia and Nicholas through the ballroom. The sounds and smells of passion surrounded them as they stepped carefully past prostrate forms and outstretched limbs. All three of them received their fair share of groping before they made it to the other side. Only Jasper appeared to be enjoying himself, returning the fondling in kind.

"Shouldn't we be going back toward the carriage?" Nicholas asked.

Jasper didn't answer. He motioned for them to wait while he went to speak with an attendant. After a moment, the attendant handed him a key and Jasper returned, gesturing that they should follow him. They went up a flight of stairs and down a short hallway, stopping in front of a door.

Jasper handed Nicholas the key. "Lock it behind you. I'll come back for you in a few hours."

Nicholas did not look happy. "We need to take Amelia home."

"Amelia should never have been here in the first place," Jasper said with a flat stare in her direction. "But since she is, we might as well follow through with her plan."

"You can't be serious."

"Why not?" Jasper asked. "In a few hours, the worst of the depravity will be over. Most people will be too exhausted. You and Amelia can put on a bit of a show without any real danger."

Amelia blushed. The idea of doing any of the things they'd passed on their way through the ballroom, especially where anyone could see her, was scandalizing indeed.

"And now I must go make amends for bringing not one but two novices to the ball," Jasper announced.

Amelia wondered what form the amends would take.

"Must?" Nicholas mused.

Jasper shrugged. "Must, desire. It's all the same at the Sinner's Ball. I've done my part. You can lock yourselves in, or not. Who knows, maybe you'll find something that interests you."

They watched him walk away down the hall.

"Is he terribly cross?" Amelia asked.

"He was. Mostly he's just glad we found you and that you're safe."

"And you?" she asked Nicholas.

He didn't answer, but the set of his jaw was not encouraging.

The click of the lock sounded overly loud to Nicholas's ears. Now that they were alone, the fear he'd been carrying on the ride turned into nervous energy and threatened to burst through his skin. "You're sure you're all right?" he asked. Her face hadn't been visible beneath her mask, but he'd felt her tension when she'd run into his chest.

Amelia nodded. The ostrich feather in her cavalier's hat bounced with the motion.

"I wanted to strangle that man for touching you."

Amelia put her hand on his forearm. "He didn't hurt me."

It was Nicholas's turn to nod. He wrapped his arms around her, satisfying a primal part of himself that needed tactile confirmation that she truly was unharmed.

"It's my fault really," Amelia said. "From what I gather, his behavior was perfectly acceptable for where we are."

Yes, it was, which begged the question. "What are you doing here, Amelia?"

"I thought it could finally put an end to the engagement. Surely Embry wouldn't want me if he thought I'd…"

"Been servicing strange men in a public ballroom?" Nicholas offered.

"Precisely."

"Did it not occur to you that you might be expected to actually give truth to some of the rumors you were hoping to spread about yourself?"

Amelia leaned back to look at him. "I thought there would be a wandering hand or two, but that it would be like Crockford's. I'd planned to be seen, and flirt, and then come home."

Sweet, naïve Amelia. "And how did you plan for Montrose to hear of it?"

"Surely someone would mention it."

"The point of the Sinner's Ball is that it isn't talked about."

"Except it absolutely is," Amelia argued. "I heard about it and so did you."

"Through our association with Jasper. I doubt Montrose consorts with any of tonight's attendees."

"So it was for nothing."

Nicholas wanted to yell and chastise her, but he didn't have the right. She was her own woman. He didn't get to be angry about what she chose to get herself into. Instead, he feigned a lightness he didn't feel. "Not for nothing. I've gotten to see you in trousers again, which is always a torturous delight."

"Do you like my costume?" She backed away and did a turn. "It was Julia's idea."

The crimson trousers fit her like a second skin. There was a sword belted to her hips and the billowy white shirt was open in front, exposing the smooth skin between her breasts as if she were a lothario lounging in dishabille. "It's very compelling. You're a cavalier?"

"I am La Maupin, the famous seductress who made conquests of men and women alike, and fought duels over honor." She bowed with an extra flourish.

Nicholas was given an uninhibited view of her breasts all the way down to her navel. "Have you bowed to anyone else?"

"No." Amelia righted herself. "Why?"

"No reason."

She reached up and ran her fingertips along the edge of his half-mask. They dipped down, tracing his lips. They fluttered there while she said, "Hullo, Nicholas."

A different man would have let her continue. A different man would have taken what she was offering and been thankful. But Nicholas could only be himself. He'd thought he could manage an affair, but he couldn't. Seeing her with that other man's hands on her downstairs had nearly killed him. He'd been in love with her from the day they met and he wanted more from her than curiosity. "Amelia, don't."

She frowned. "What's wrong?"

"The other night was amazing, the best moment of my life, but I can't. It's not good for me."

"Why?" At the rejection, bold Amelia turned back into the shy girl she'd been growing up.

Nicholas hated to be the cause, but he had to stand up for himself. "I can't turn my feelings off. I will be your friend, always, but I can't do this to myself."

"I'm hurting you," she said. There were tears at the edges of her words.

"It's all right. I just can't go through with it."

She ducked her head, worrying the sleeves of her shirt. "Would it hurt less if you knew I loved you?"

The air grew thick around him and the room suddenly felt ten degrees warmer. "Do you?" *Please let it be true. Please let it.* He could live a thousand scandals, survive whatever was in front of them, if it were true.

"I need you—as much I need Julia. And in a different way. When you're around, I feel safe. Like everything's been made right. And when you're gone I don't entirely feel like myself. And I want you. Desperately. So yes. I think that's what that means."

"Say it." He needed to hear it from her gorgeous, perfect mouth again.

Her lips curved up and her forehead creased. She sounded it out slowly, like a foreign language she wasn't sure of. "I love you."

Nicholas pulled her into his arms, sliding his hands down to the small of her back. "It hurts much less. It might not even hurt at all."

"Say it back to me," she said, wrapping her arms around his neck. "Unless you don't. If you don't, you don't have to."

Nicholas laughed. "How can you doubt it? I've said it a hundred times."

Amelia looked at him with uncertainty in her eyes. "Never to me."

Was it true? Had he told everyone on earth *except* Amelia? He had so much to make up for. "I love you, Amelia Bishop.

I have loved you every day since the day we met. And I will love you long after I am gone from this earth."

She blushed under her mask and it was breathtaking. "That's quite poetic."

"I've had a great deal of time to work on it."

"Will you kiss me now?"

He lifted her hat from her head, tossing it on the bed. When he untied the strings of her mask she tilted her face up to his. "Yes."

"Will you do other things with me now?" Amelia's hands slid down his chest, popping the first of his buttons free.

"That depends." Nicholas pushed her shirt free of one shoulder. It fell to her elbow, exposing one exquisite, pale breast. "It might start to hurt again. I shall need you to keep telling me."

"I love you," she interrupted.

Nicholas covered her breast with his palm. Her lips parted. The peak of her nipple tightened and raised against his hand.

"I love you."

Nick brushed his thumb across it. Amelia's surprised inhale filled him with a deep satisfaction. He dropped his hand back down to her waist and lowered his head. He took her nipple between his teeth, teasing it with his tongue.

"I love you," she gasped.

He pushed the other shoulder clear, baring her to the waist. Amelia moved against him. He pulled her closer, easing his thigh between her legs. He covered the newly bared breast with his palm while he continued to pay homage to its twin with his mouth.

"Nick," she said again, a demand this time.

He smiled against her skin. "We have plenty of time, Mia."

"But I want—"

"You'll have it. I promise."

She gave in, leaning back to give him unhindered access. Nicholas took full advantage. He worked them both into a fervor as he worshipped each tiny detail of her breasts. When he finally lifted his head, she pulled him back down and claimed his mouth for her own.

It was a desperate, breathless kiss. Amelia was trying to communicate a need she didn't have a name for. There was a hollow, aching void inside her. More than tingles, more than pleasant friction. She needed Nicholas in places he couldn't possibly be. She wanted him inside her, around her, surrounding her. All she had was their joined lips and mingled tongues. She used it, trying to fill herself with him as best she could. It wasn't enough.

He knew. Amelia felt his muscles flex and she was being lifted. Her legs wrapped around his waist. His hands molded themselves to her backside and then the mattress was at her back. Soft, downy pillows framed her head and Nicholas rested above her. She was surrounded.

"I love you." She said it as a demand, kissing him again.

Nicholas ground his hips against her, pressing her further into the bed.

Ecstasy.

He pushed against her, matching the rhythm of their tongues to the rhythm of his hips. Amelia buried her hands in his hair. She pulled, urging him on. Urging him closer. She bit his lip. Nicholas bit back.

"I love you," she begged.

He sat up, pulling off her boots. Amelia tore at his shirt. He shrugged it off along with his jacket. She took a moment to admire the beauty of him. Hard planes and angles that rippled under her touch, like he was the one on the brink of coming apart instead of her. The buttons of her trousers gave way under his hands.

It was the strangest feeling as he pulled the fabric clear of her legs. She was completely naked. The feeling of being so exposed made her want to cover herself, but the expression of admiration in Nicholas's eyes made her want to fling her limbs wide and let him look his fill. She settled for doing neither. "You still have your clothes on, and I am completely naked."

"I like you completely naked," Nicholas teased. "And I don't want to frighten you."

What a ludicrous concept. "Why would I be frightened?"

"It might be a bit surprising."

"I should think so, but it's still you, isn't it?"

He grinned. "Yes, it is still me."

"Then I couldn't be frightened by it." The one thing on this earth she would never be frightened of was Nicholas.

He took a deep breath. The buttons of his trousers came free one by one and he pushed the fabric past his hips.

Oh my. Amelia couldn't stop her eyes from going wide. She'd seen sketches of Michelangelo's David, but Nicholas's manhood was so much more…upstanding. It was very like the men she'd seen in the ballroom. For some reason, she'd thought they might be anomalies based on the perversity of their activities.

"Are you all right?"

"I am." Amelia sat up on her knees to get a closer look. "Are you? Does it always stick out like that?"

"Not always."

"What makes it…" Amelia made a raising gesture with her hands.

Nicholas's smile was lopsided. "Beautiful women. Friction. Inconvenient timing."

It was too interesting not to investigate. Her hand hovered above it. "May I?"

He took a deep breath and nodded.

Amelia ran her fingertips across the length of him. It was fascinating, hard and soft at the same time. She closed her hand around him, squeezing as she marveled at the combination of velvety soft skin and rigid core.

Nicholas groaned. His hips flexed, pushing forward into her closed fist. The look on his face was something she'd never seen before. Amelia repeated the motion, dragging her closed fist to the head and back down to the base. He gasped out loud.

Truly fascinating. She did it again.

Nicholas's hand flew out, grasping her shoulder. "Amelia."

"You like that." It wasn't a question. She repeated the gesture.

"God, yes." His eyes were closed and he was taking deep breaths.

"Does it make you tingle?"

He smiled, but his expression was tense, almost tortured. "And then some."

The effect she was having on him made her bold. It was a powerful feeling. "Where?"

He took her free hand, cupping her palm gently around the soft orbs between his legs. "There."

Amelia tested them with her hand. They were nothing like anything she'd ever felt before. There was no rigidity there, like liquid forced to choose a form. Nicholas reacted to every movement. His fingers tightened on her shoulder.

Testing a theory, Amelia rolled them in her palm while she stroked up and back with her hand. Nicholas groaned again and suddenly she was being pushed back into the mattress with her hands pinned above her head.

"I wasn't done."

His mouth interrupted her. Amelia could feel the rigid hardness of him against the inside of her thigh. She moved against it. When it slid against the moisture that had escaped her center, slipping up to rub against the knot of sensation between her legs, the pleasure intensified—coiling and magnifying at her core. She shifted, rubbing him up and back against it. Nicholas groaned against her lips, matching her movement.

Little jolts of electricity pulsed through her with each movement. She wanted more. She moved faster. The sound of their bodies slipping against each other grew louder. Amelia cried out with each completed journey. Nicholas reached between them, sliding his finger inside her. Heaven. That was what she wanted. He pushed in time with their movements, adding another, and then a third. Her body stretched to accommodate the new sensation. She felt full, so very close to what she needed, but not quite.

"Nicholas. I need—"

"I know. I need it, too." He kissed her lips, resting his forehead against hers. Nicholas withdrew his fingers and positioned himself in their place. "I love you, Amelia."

"I love you." Something important was about to happen. She could feel it in the air, in the tension of his body. In the way her nerve endings and his seemed to reach out for each other, especially in the place between her legs where he was waiting.

He moved. It *was* different. There was a heat to him, and a perfectness of fit, that his fingers could never replace. Amelia felt him in places that had never been touched. He pushed deeper and deeper still. When he came the last of the way, fully encased by her body, he pressed against something that sent a wave of heat and pleasure through her. She cried out.

"Did I hurt you?" Nicholas tried to withdraw himself.

Amelia trapped his hips with her legs. "Again. Do it again."

Nicholas surged forward. Amelia couldn't help it—she moaned.

"You'll be the death of me with those sounds, Mia."

She didn't care. She couldn't have been quiet if her life depended on it.

They rocked together in a rhythm that set the headboard thudding against the wall. Little beads of sweat broke out on Nicholas's brow. Amelia chased the feeling higher and higher. She urged him on with her body and her words. The frissons of pleasure arced through her. She lost track of time, of the room, of everything except Nicholas and the way he felt inside her.

When she crashed, it was in a crescendo of sounds. Nicholas's arms tightened around her as he found his own release. He murmured broken curses and words of adoration as he shook against her. When he settled, he rolled to the side, bringing her with him.

He kissed the top of her head and stroked her back. With her head on his chest, Amelia could feel his heart hammering against his ribs.

"Why did we wait so long to do that?"

The chuckle rumbled against her cheek. "I don't know."

Amelia looked up at him. "Promise me we won't wait so long before the next time."

"We're never going to leave this room."

That suited Amelia perfectly.

Chapter Seventeen

melia made it home barely in time to be discovered in her bed when the family woke for breakfast. She didn't tell Julia about the masquerade before they went down, and the suspense was clearly causing her sister a great deal of distress. Amelia couldn't help but be glad of the reprieve. She wanted to keep what she and Nicholas had shared to herself for a little while longer.

"You're in an exceptionally good mood this morning," her mother commented.

Amelia choked on her juice. "Am I?"

"You've been smiling to yourself since you came down."

Amelia's father looked up. "You do seem happier. Have you and Montrose stopped fighting?"

"No, not exactly." Amelia set her glass down. "About Montrose. I need to tell you something."

Julia's fork clattered to her plate. "Mia, can I speak to you a moment in the hall?"

Amelia knew what Julia was going to say, but she was tired of living the lie. She just wanted her engagement over so she could figure out the rest of her life. Nicholas loved her. She wasn't certain how she would manage it, but she would find a way for them to be happy. "We're in the middle of breakfast."

Julia kicked her under the table.

"Whatever it is, it will wait until after breakfast," Lord Bishop declared.

Lady Bishop frowned at Julia. "What were you saying about Lord Montrose, darling?"

Amelia met Julia's stare. If she told Papa about Embry's threats, he would be livid. He would insist on getting involved, and it would likely go wrong. She sighed. She couldn't tell them. Even though she felt unstoppable after her night with Nicholas, she couldn't do that to her family. "Nothing. I've quite forgotten it."

Lord Bishop looked between his daughters. "I won't pretend to know what you two are up to. Just promise me it's harmless?"

Having spent last night making love to Nicholas at an orgy for England's debauched nobility, Amelia wasn't certain she could promise that. She'd never been a good liar.

Fortunately, Julia had no such limitations. "We promise."

Lady Bishop pretended like the entire exchange hadn't happened. "I'm sorry to hear you and Embry are still at odds. Do try to work it out when he comes to call today. It wouldn't do to be out of sorts when you say your vows."

"Embry is coming today?" Nicholas had convinced her he wouldn't hear about the Sinner's Ball, so he couldn't be visiting for any reason Amelia was likely to enjoy. Since his accusations on the terrace, Amelia had been avoiding him, letting other appointments run long or forgetting he'd intended to call.

"Did I not tell you?" Lady Bishop's tone was a little too innocent.

"You did not."

"Well, if you've made other plans you'll have to cancel them."

"I'll be here." Today was as good a day for an Embry confrontation as any. Today she was unstoppable.

"Good." Lady Bishop sipped her coffee in satisfaction.

"I'll be here as well, in case anyone still cares about what I get up to," Julia announced.

Lady Bishop frowned at her oldest daughter. "Don't be dramatic, dear."

"Don't be so obvious, *Mother*."

"Actually, Julia. I wanted to discuss a physician I heard about in Manchester with you." Lord Bishop speared his eggs enthusiastically. "He has some interesting ideas."

Julia set her fork down with a clatter. "I am not going to Manchester."

"No, no. I'm going to go, today in fact, but I didn't want you to be surprised if I bring him back with me."

"Hooray!" Julia said sarcastically. "More doctors. I am the luckiest girl in all the land."

The rest of breakfast passed quickly. After, Lord Bishop left for the train station and Lady Bishop went up to prepare for her day. Amelia and Julia stayed in the dining room, sipping chocolate and lingering over their eggs.

"I sometimes wonder, if Mother wasn't wildly in love with Papa, if she wouldn't rather it were her who was engaged to Embry instead of me."

Julia didn't laugh. "What was that nonsense earlier?"

"Hmm?"

"You were going to tell them."

Amelia sighed. "But I didn't."

"But you were going to," Julia insisted. "I'm not suffering through all this poking and prodding for you to lose your nerve."

"I'm not. Nicholas and I…" She couldn't say it. Not in the dining room where anyone might overhear her. "I just want to be free of this mess so we can all get on with our lives."

"Abandoning the plan isn't the answer."

"I know."

Julia stared at her over the breakfast dishes for a moment longer, then she relaxed. "What do you think Embry wants?"

The air in the library was unduly warm. Memories of Amelia kept replaying in Nicholas's mind. The curve of the small of her back, the tiny gasps she made, her hair trailing across his skin as she explored his body with her mouth. He was held hostage by his mind as each scene played over and over on an endless loop.

Amelia loved him. They hadn't spoken about the future. Hadn't spoken much at all, really, but she loved him. It was enough for now. Everything else could be worried about later.

"Lord Nicholas, a message arrived for you." One of Philip's footmen handed him a letter and disappeared when Nicholas indicated he needed nothing further.

It had the Lincoln's Inn seal. He took a deep breath. If it was good news, he stood a decent chance of providing for himself if Amelia changed her mind about marrying him. If it was good news, he had three years of hard work and study ahead of him. Was he ready for that? Could he spend that much time away from Amelia?

Still, he wanted to become the sort of man she *could* marry, if she changed her mind. He wanted to be ready to build a future with her if she decided she wanted to. And, if he was being honest, he wanted it for himself. It was time for him to build a life of his own—with or without Amelia as his wife.

He opened the letter.

Dear Mr. Wakefield,

We are pleased to accept your application to study at Lincoln's Inn beginning with the Trinity term. Please contact the treasurer no later than a fortnight from the first day of term to settle your tuition and arrange for your accommodations at the Inn.

Congratulations, and welcome to the fraternity of legal minds.

Sincerely,
Dean of the Chapel
W.H. Tinney

He let out an un-Wakefield-like *whoop*. Caroline rushed in, concerned. "Is everything all right?"

"It truly is." Nicholas jumped up, kissing Caro on both cheeks. "Is Philip back?"

"Just now. Shall I get him?"

"Please."

His sister-in-law came back with Philip in tow, and Nicholas handed him the letter.

Philip read it over and nodded with pride. "Well done, little brother."

"You're sure the timing is all right?"

"Couldn't be better. I'm relinquishing the last of my committee seats at the end of Hilary term."

Caroline squeezed his arm. "I'm so happy for you, Nicholas. You're going to make a wonderful barrister."

"And an even better representative in Commons!" Philip insisted.

"One step at a time, I think." There was so much that could

go wrong between now and then. Right this instant, Nicholas just wanted to celebrate.

"You've been avoiding me," Embry said, once they'd been left alone.

She was unstoppable, Amelia reminded herself. Unstoppable women didn't waste time being polite. "The last time I saw you, you accused me of having an affair with Lord Bellamy."

"I'm sorry, I—"

"Was wrong. You're wrong about a lot of things, like wanting to marry me."

"Amelia, please." Embry cast his eyes toward the ceiling. "I only came to find out why you haven't accepted Charlotte's invitation to her coming out ball tonight."

"Because we hate each other and I don't want to go?"

Embry pulled at his cravat, loosening it due to some imaginary warmth. The shadows under his eyes stood out in the bright light coming through the window. At least she was making him as exhausted as he was making her.

"She's my family, Amelia. You two are going to have to learn to rub along together amiably. For what it's worth, she's promised to behave."

"Has she?" Amelia laughed. "Well, I make no such promises. In fact, I've become rather good at misbehaving lately."

"I've noticed."

"You don't know the half of it." Perhaps, just perhaps, she could end this here and now. He couldn't possibly want her if she told him.

She hoped Nick would forgive her. "I made love to Nicholas Wakefield last night. Many times."

Embry recoiled from her. The lines of his face constricted into a mask of revulsion—of pain. "You're lying."

"I don't love you," she said, enunciating each word so he couldn't mistake her. "I love him."

Embry put a hand up, trying to physically stop the words from reaching his ears. He shook his head. "You're young and inexperienced. You only think you love him because you don't know any better."

Disbelief pushed a choked laugh from her throat. Recklessness spurred her further. All or nothing. "I've had his cock in my mouth, Embry, and I liked it."

Emotions flashed across his face too quickly to identify. The last one had Amelia backing toward the door.

"Is that what it takes to get your attention?" he asked, stalking toward her. "To earn your loyalty? Have I been mistaken in behaving like a gentleman?"

"Embry, stop."

It seemed for a moment like he might do something drastic, but he regained his composure. When he spoke again, his voice was cold and controlled. "I will consider your confession and decide what to do with it. In the meantime, be ready when I come back this evening."

Amelia listened to him storm out; his heavy footfalls in the hall, Lady Bishop begging him to stay a little longer. She went upstairs to Julia's room to avoid the lecture she knew would be coming.

"What was all that about?" Julia asked when the door slammed downstairs.

"I told Embry I made love to Nicholas."

Julia eyes flew wide. "Did you say it, or did you actually do it?"

"I did it." Amelia nodded, rushing past that confession. The adrenaline was starting to wear off and shock was setting in. "I was quite graphic when I told him. I said *cock*."

"Well," Julia said. "If that doesn't do it."

I will consider your confession. "Jules, if I have to marry him, I think I might die."

"Don't be ridiculous. It will not come to that."

"It might. He should have thrown me over right then and there, but he didn't. You know I can't let…"

Julia finished what Amelia wouldn't say. "Let me suffer through life without a fortune to insulate me from people's disgust?"

The matter of fact way her sister spoke about being reviled broke Amelia's heart. "You're not disgusting."

"Obviously not," Julia said imperiously. "But it doesn't stop people from thinking it."

"It's not only you. Mother and Papa would suffer as well."

"But me most." Julia refused to let it go. "Admit it. If it were just Mother and Papa, you would have called the engagement off weeks ago."

Amelia couldn't deny it.

"Promise me, Mia. Promise you won't marry him, no matter what happens."

"I can't."

"You can. It's time for you to be selfish."

As if it were that easy, to suddenly decide to become selfish. "Maybe it won't come to that."

"Perhaps," Julia agreed. "We do have other options. For instance, we could drug Montrose and have him shipped off somewhere awful."

The corners of Amelia's mouth turned up.

"Or we could have him killed," Julia suggested.

"Julia." Her sister's tone was a little too earnest for

Amelia's comfort.

Her sister's enthusiasm rose. "Better yet, marry him and *then* we'll have him killed. Then you'll be a widowed countess and you can do whatever you like."

Amelia shook her head. "All of your solutions sound like something a villain in a play would do."

"Then let's be villains," Julia said seriously. "Honestly. Montrose is using the fact that no one likes us to blackmail you, so to hell with it. Let's be unlikeable."

It probably wouldn't take much more before Amelia agreed to something of this sort. She was tired and she was frightened. "If it comes to that, I'll think about it."

"If it comes to that, you won't have to. I'll see to it."

"Julia!"

"Don't." Julia took Amelia's hands in hers. "I won't be used to hold you hostage much longer, Mia. I am not some helpless pawn."

She certainly wasn't. Amelia envied that. She'd spent more time feeling helpless in the last few weeks than she'd ever thought possible.

Flopping back onto the bed, Amelia asked, "How did we go from racing horses through the meadow to pondering the murder of my fiancé?"

Julia fell back beside her. "You tried to get married before me."

"How foolish of me."

Getting dressed to go out took longer than it should have. Her every movement weighed with dread. Her life was closing in around her, a noose ready to strangle her.

"Honestly, Amelia." Lady Bishop sailed into the room without knocking. "Why aren't you dressed? Embry will be here any minute."

Embry might be the one holding the rope, but her mother was certainly cheering him on.

"Mother." Amelia watched her mother in the mirror's reflection. "I need to ask something of you."

"Of course, dear. Anything."

"Stop conspiring with Embry."

Lady Bishop's features masked themselves in neutrality. "I haven't been doing anything of the sort."

"You have. You are. Please stop."

Her mother's nose tilted slightly into the air. "I'm only trying to keep you from making a grievous mistake."

Amelia turned to her mother. "So you know I don't want to marry him?"

"You've just got a case of nerves, darling."

"Does Papa know?" Amelia asked. "That I don't intend to marry Embry?"

"Of course not." Lady Bishop's affront was evident. "And he doesn't need to, because you're going to give up this foolishness."

"I will not. I don't love him."

Her mother's expression turned mulish. "Well, you should have thought of that before you accepted his proposal. But I'm sure you'll change your mind once you…"

She would not be changing her mind, but her mother's sudden trailing off drove another spike of apprehension through Amelia. "Once I what?"

"Nothing. Marry. Once you marry, you'll grow used to him."

She didn't care that Amelia would be trapped in a loveless marriage. "Please leave my room, Mother."

"Embry is almost here."

"Leave. Now!" This new habit she was developing of shouting at people was strangely satisfying.

At the door, Lady Bishop turned back to her daughter. "Being an outcast was never difficult for you, but going back will be agony now that you know what you're missing."

"You mean it will be agony for you. You're the only one of us who ever cared." *And you're willing to sacrifice me to get it back.* Betrayal sluiced under Amelia's skin like hot water. It rushed past her eardrums and left splotchy patches of crimson on her skin. It reached her eyes, leaking out in tears of accusation.

Her own mother.

"Mia?" Julia came in.

Amelia tried to wipe them away before Julia could notice. It was hopeless.

"What's she done now?" Julia tipped Amelia's chin up, forcing their eyes to meet.

"She doesn't care that I'm unhappy. She wants me to marry him anyway, so she can keep going to parties."

Julia's eyes narrowed. Her head tilted the way it did when she was plotting one of her elaborate revenges, but she smiled reassuringly. "She can want all she likes. We make our own decisions. Haven't we always?"

Amelia nodded. Since the very first, from their earliest moments. She dried her eyes, standing up. "I'm all right now."

"Are you certain?"

"I am. I should get ready. Embry is probably here by now."

Frown lines creased Julia's brow. "You don't have to go, Mia. We can say you're ill."

Amelia shook her head. "No, It's all right. I'll be all right."

"Do you want me to go with you? I will."

The feeling of betrayal disappeared, replaced by a new ache. Julia, who hadn't set foot outside of the townhouse since she'd arrived, who hid upstairs when anyone visited, was offering to go to a ball. Just to make Amelia feel better. Any other day, Amelia would have jumped on the opportunity, but she knew now that it wasn't because Julia wanted to. It was because she loved Amelia that much.

"I'm really all right. If you want to come anyway, of course, you may."

"No, thank you," Julia said, relief evident.

Someday. Someday Julia would be ready, for her own reasons. For now, Amelia would be strong enough to face her problems on her own.

"So what do you think?" Amelia asked, turning to the ballgowns laid out on the bed. "Which one of these is more suited to evading one's fiancé? Amethyst with seed pearls, or peach chiffon?"

Jasper's summons came with a request that Nicholas dress for dinner. As usual, no explanation was included. Honestly, the man ought to write penny dreadfuls for all his love of mystery and cloak-and-dagger communications.

When he arrived, Jasper was already seated in the dining room with a course in front of him.

"It is customary, when one invites someone over for a meal, that one wait until that person has arrived to begin eating it."

"Customary is for the boring. Sit down."

A place setting appeared, and a chair was pulled out for Nicholas. The footman and Jasper stared at him expectantly.

Nicholas sighed and sat down. "Your message said you had news."

"It's bad manners to discuss business during dinner."

Jasper tasted what looked to be pea soup.

"Sod off."

Jasper grinned. "The boy I have following Montrose sent some interesting information today."

"Amelia loves me. Montrose and his movements can go hang."

"What a lovely picture, but I think you want to hear what he had to say."

"Fine." Nicholas waited in vain. "Are you going to tell me?"

"Not yet. If I tell you, you'll rush off and I would like to enjoy a meal with you."

"Jasper, if it's important, just tell me."

"I will tell you, if you give me your word that you won't do anything rash until after we finish our meal."

Nicholas looked at the table. "What course are we on?"

"The third."

"Of?"

"Eight. I assure you, there will be plenty of time. The information pertains to something happening tomorrow."

Not even Jasper's mysterious ridiculousness could ruin his mood today. "You'd better get me some wine, then."

Jasper grinned in triumph. The footman jumped to attention, filling his glass with a rich gold chardonnay. Nicholas tested his soup. Cucumber and mint, served chilled. "This is delicious."

"I'm glad you like it." Jasper beamed. "I think Montrose is planning something."

"Beyond blackmailing Amelia?"

Jasper swirled his wine in its glass. "He has booked passage for Upper Canada, leaving tomorrow."

Nicholas set down his glass, daring to hope. "That sounds like he's finally given up."

"He booked passage for two. Himself and his wife."

The hope evaporated. "Amelia wouldn't have changed her mind."

"No, I don't think so," Jasper agreed. "I entertained the idea that you were a terrible lover and you'd horrified her back into his arms, but I taught you everything you know, so that can't be it."

He ignored Jasper's Jasper-isms and sifted through to the heart of the words. "You think Montrose means to kidnap her." His stomach was already churning.

"I think he might."

He had to get to her. If Montrose managed to get her on that ship, Nick might never see her again. He stood up.

Jasper waved him back into his chair. "The ship doesn't leave until tomorrow, and you promised you'd stay until the end."

How was he supposed to eat when the love of his life could be in the midst of a kidnap attempt? "Amelia is in danger."

Jasper gestured his fork. "My messengers assure me she is at home, right where she ought to be."

"I thought I told you to stop spying on her."

"Aren't you glad I never listen to you?"

"Not particularly." Nick looked down at his bowl. The soup had suddenly lost all flavor. "If you expect me to stay, you'd better serve the fish early."

Montrose would not win.

Chapter Eighteen

"Are you listening, Amelia?"

"Hmm?" Amelia abandoned her introspection. She had a great deal to think about and the last place she wanted to be was in the middle of a crowded ballroom with Embry watching her like a hawk.

"Charlotte complimented you on your dress."

"I adore seed pearls," Embry's younger cousin repeated with a sneer at Amelia's dress.

Amelia blinked at her. Montrose might think he'd tamed his cousins, but Amelia did not share his faith. They would continue to be wretched, horrible creatures whenever the opportunity presented itself.

"Amelia," Montrose said through clenched teeth. "You're being rude."

"Am I? I can't imagine why."

Embry looked like he wanted to drag her off and strangle her. Charlotte put her hand on his arm. "It's quite all right, Embry. Besides, I'm sure the Canadians won't mind her manners as much."

Canadians? What the devil? "Excuse me?"

"Charlotte." Embry changed the focus of his ire.

"The Canadians," she said, ignoring him with vicious delight. "Embry swears it's quite civilized, but it's basically a frontier. I doubt they have enough society to care about your lack of social graces, or your atrocious family."

Amelia still didn't understand. "I'm not going to Canada."

"Aren't you?" Charlotte's smirk was unbearable.

"Charlotte." Embry glared at his cousin.

Amelia turned to Embry. "What is she talking about?"

"It's nothing." Montrose scanned the crowd over her head.

"I doubt that. Tell me."

"Not now, Amelia."

The youngest Miss Chisholm giggled maliciously, curls bobbing in her mirth.

"Yes, now Embry." Amelia shot his cousin a glare. "You will tell me, or I will cause a scene that London will talk about for the next ten seasons."

Embry ignored them both.

Right, then. There was only one scandal left on Julia's list, and Amelia had to admit it was the only one that she thought she might actually enjoy.

She turned to Charlotte Chisholm. "Charlotte, I have a gift for you."

The girl's eyes lit with avarice. "Have you? How wonderful."

Amelia nodded. Her hand whipped out, landing a slap that echoed throughout the ballroom. The entire party went silent.

Miss Charlotte stared in shock with her mouth gaping wide and a pink handprint on her cheek.

"Amelia!" Embry shouted. His knuckles were white on his champagne glass and a fascinating shade of crimson was climbing up his neck.

"I warned you," she said.

Before anyone else had time to react, he was hauling her by her arm out of the house and calling for his carriage.

"Of all the unmannered, ungrateful behaviors." He stomped around the driveway. "It's her coming out ball!"

Amelia didn't have any sympathy to spare either of them. "And now it will be remembered for years. Tell me what she was talking about."

The carriage arrived, interrupting his answer. He told the driver to take them back to the Bishop townhouse and sat glaring at her across the cab.

"Embry."

In the straightforward fashion she used to admire, Embry delivered his news. "I've taken a position representing the crown in Upper Canada."

"When?"

"Effective immediately."

Hope leaped in Amelia's heart. Embry was leaving. He would be thousands of miles away. "Congratulations."

Embry looked surprised. "I'm pleased to hear you're not opposed to it."

"Why would I be?" She wouldn't have to be afraid anymore and there would be plenty of time to find a way out of her engagement.

"It's somewhat sudden. I expected you to object."

"If you must go to Canada, then you must."

"Not just me, Amelia."

Who else would be going? No. Oh no.

"We'll be married at sea once we leave port." Embry was staring at her with an unnerving intensity. "I won't dishonor you by coming to your bed before I become your husband, but it's obvious that a lover is required to quiet your wilder nature. I am prepared to do what must be done."

"I won't go."

"You will, even if I have to carry you up the gangplank over my shoulder. I will not lose another fiancée. I will not start over again."

It was too much. It was too far. "This engagement is over, Embry. Sue my father for breach of promise if you like, but I will not marry you."

"It's too late for that, Amelia. Your mother and I have made all the arrangements. For your own good, you'll be locked in your room until it's time to leave for the harbor. Once you're away from here and properly bedded, you'll see sense."

Nicholas was making a spectacle of himself on the doorstep of Amelia's house, but propriety could go straight to hell. Someone was going to give him some answers or he was going to stay there all night.

"I know she's here. You have to let me speak to her."

"My lord, you must leave. We will be forced to call the constable."

"Call him! A woman is being held against her will in this house. You cannot kidnap someone in this day and age!"

There was a commotion behind the butler and he stepped aside.

Lady Bishop presented herself with folded arms. "Mr. Wakefield, go home."

"I demand to speak with Lord Bishop."

"He's gone to Manchester. He won't be back anytime soon."

So that was how they'd managed it. Amelia's father would

never have allowed something like this to happen. "You can't do this to her."

"I can and I will. It's for her own good."

"No. No, call the constable," he told the butler. "We'll let him get to the bottom of this."

"The bottom of what, exactly?" Lady Bishop asked. "My daughter is not of age. I am her parent and it is my legal right and duty to decide what is best for her."

"You cannot force her to marry him."

"And I won't," Lady Bishop said with alarming cheerfulness. "But I can force her to get on that ship. After that, convincing her is up to Lord Montrose, but I am certain he is up to the task."

Nicholas was stricken speechless. Lady Bishop took his silence as defeat and closed the door in his face. The bolt clicked audibly on the other side.

There would be no satisfaction through the front door, but Nicholas was all too aware that was not the only way into the house. He took the alley entrance around the back, only to find a footman posted at the back door. She truly was a hostage in her own home. There was no way to slip past him to her window, and no trees or moldings to climb if he could.

He tried to think of a way to get her out, but short of setting the building on fire, he was at a loss. It was time for Nicholas to admit he needed help. Not the Jasper sort of help, either. They really would end up setting the building on fire if he left it up to Jasper. No, he needed the rational help of someone who commanded respect and authority.

He just hoped Philip would agree.

Amelia could hear Nicholas yelling. Then she heard her mother, the slamming door, and nothing. Had he given up? The situation was too ludicrous to be imagined, except that she was living it.

There were footmen posted at both doors and one by her bedroom. Her room had been stripped of everything, including the sheets. Under different circumstances, she'd appreciate the lengths her mother had gone to. It showed a healthy respect for Amelia's ingenuity. Unfortunately, since that respect was being shown as utter disregard for Amelia's wishes, the compliment was negated.

The door creaked open. Amelia jumped up, ready to fight her way free.

Julia slipped in, looking behind her. "Well, she's officially lost her mind."

"You don't say." Amelia tried the door, but it was locked again from the outside.

"I begged visitation. I told her I thought I could talk you around so you'd fight it less."

"You what?" If Julia had changed her mind about Embry again, Amelia would lose hers.

Julia rolled her eyes. "It was a lie, silly goose. I needed to talk to you."

"Oh." Amelia slumped back down on the bare mattress. "Please tell me you have a plan."

"Not yet, but that's why I'm here. We think better together."

Amelia was having a hard time thinking at all. She was in dire peril and the situation was quite daunting. "I am open to any and all suggestions."

Julia sat down next to her, tapping her finger against her chin. "What we need is to remove the possibility of you marrying Embry. Then there'd be nothing in it for Mother. He'd lose his most powerful ally."

"It's a shame convents have fallen out of style." Hopelessness was making her delirious.

"You could marry someone else," Julia said. "And by someone else, I mean Nicholas."

She loved Julia for suggesting it, but it was exactly what she'd been trying to avoid. Any marriage at all would take her away from her sister. "Surely there's another way."

"Circumstances have become somewhat more dire than we originally anticipated."

"I promised I wouldn't leave you alone."

"And I appreciate that." Julia turned, forcing her to meet her eyes. "But I think it's time, Amelia. I can't hold you back forever."

"You don't hold me back," Amelia insisted.

"I do. Look at you—two marriage proposals from eligible men, even though we're disgraced and disreputable. Think what you could pull off with a decent start."

"Julia."

"I know. You don't care about all that because you're a lunatic—I suspect you get it from Mother—but you do care about Nicholas. I dare you to tell me you don't."

She couldn't. They both knew it would be a lie.

"It's Nicholas!" Julia threw her hands up. "He's my friend, too. He's the perfect husband for us."

Us. God. She could just imagine it. Julia mediating their arguments. Julia deciding where they should send their children to school. Julia sticking her nose into every aspect of their relationship.

"I don't know, Jules."

"I do. He's the best man we know—of two, one of whom is blackmailing you, but I like to think he'd hold up favorably in a larger contest—and he's in love with you. What choice do you have?"

Amelia had made a promise. Julia needed her, and they needed each other. That hadn't changed. "I don't want to live away from you. What if something happens? What if you get sick?"

"You mean what if I die." Julia squeezed her hand. "Nothing is going to make that easy, Mia, but having Nicholas to get you through it will help. Marry him. He won't keep us apart, and you need him as just much as you need me."

Amelia couldn't wrap her mind around a world without Julia in it, but she knew Nick. He would hold her. He would help her through it. He would be the only person who could truly understand what she would have lost. She'd been thinking marriage would keep her away from Julia, but marriage with Nick would be different. She could see that now.

She should think of another way. Her heart shouldn't be leaping at the thought of keeping Nicholas forever, but it was thudding like it wanted to burst from her chest and run to him. She could actually have this. "You're going to miss me dreadfully if I marry."

"Of course, but think of all the lovemaking you and Nick will be doing. You can visit once a week to tell me all about it."

Amelia let out a hysterical laugh. "Oh, God. All right. But it's all a moot point because I'm stuck in this house."

"All we have to do is get you out of this room. My room still has sheets and basic necessities. I know what I can do. I'll be right back." Julia knocked on the door, asking permission to leave.

"Wait!"

But it was too late. She was gone and Amelia was alone in her barren prison once again. Not a long time passed before the door swung open again, though. Julia came back through carrying an armload of books and Amelia's keepsake box. Once the door was closed, she dropped them all on the floor.

"Why are all of your favorite books so heavy?"

"I like long stories. Thank you for bringing them. It will make the time go much faster."

"Don't be a ninny. It was a diversion." Julia pulled her skirts up to her waist and started pulling sheets and table cloths from where they were tucked in to the waistband of her drawers.

"You replaced your petticoats with linens?"

"It was Nora's idea. She's rather genius in a pinch." Julia held out a steak knife to Amelia. "Pretend you're reading aloud. We need to cover the sound while we cut these into strips."

"To what end?"

"We're going to throw you out the window," Julia announced.

Amelia fished out a book for inspiration. "What's the box for?"

"You'll need things," Julia said, getting to work ripping strips off her sheets. "For your wedding. There's a pair of my slippers for you to borrow. I want them back. The blue hair ribbon you put away after Nick took you to the county fair. The rest of your mementos."

Sweet as the gesture was, it wasn't the most practical list of items for Amelia to be hauling around while she was fleeing the city. "I think I can probably manage without those."

Julia stopped cutting and stared at her. "You're getting married and I won't be there. You're going to need the things that mean the most to you."

Amelia was getting married, alone and on the run.

"Cut! We don't have all night."

"I told you not to involve me in Amelia Bishop's engagement, Nicholas."

Nicholas paced the study. He'd explained the situation, but his brother was being remarkably stubborn. "Does it not matter to you that she's being wrongfully imprisoned?"

"You're being dramatic."

"How about the fact that I love her?"

"That's not new information."

He slammed his hand down on the desk. "Philip, I need you on this."

The butler knocked on the study door. "My lord. Lady Melton requests both of your presences in the parlor."

"We're a bit busy. Please tell her it will have to wait." Nicholas radiated tension.

The butler was clearly struggling with decorum, clearing his throat and shifting on his feet. "I think it might be pertinent to your current discussion."

Philip's eyebrows rose. "We'd better go and see."

The trip to the parlor was silent. Nicholas was livid. This meant more to him than anything else. More than any endorsement or confidence or—his brain stopped short.

Amelia was sitting on the settee with Philip's wife with a box on her lap.

She was safe. She was here. *Why* was she here? It didn't matter. She was within arm's reach, and the weight that lifted from his shoulders at the sight of her was a glorious gift.

Caroline's expression was bemused. "Amelia has been telling me the most scintillating story."

"I'm sorry," she said, mostly to Philip. "I wouldn't have come if it weren't important."

Philip's head tilted to the side. "My brother was under the impression you were a hostage."

"He was correct, Lord Melton."

"And yet, here you are."

"My sister made me an escape rope out of sheets. I climbed out the window."

Nicholas couldn't have stopped the smile spreading across his face if he'd tried.

"How intrepid," Caroline murmured.

Amelia grinned. She sent a sideways glance at Nick, blushing. "Would it be all right if I spoke with Nicholas alone?"

"I doubt we could stop you." Philip held out his hand to his wife, who was staring at Amelia like a newly discovered exotic bird.

As soon as they were gone, Nick rushed to her side. "You're all right?"

"I've had an unusual evening."

"So I gather. I tried to break you out."

"I know, I heard. I love that you tried."

"I love *you*." He wanted to spend hours soaking up the sight of her glowing cheeks and windblown hair. He pulled a leaf from the silky strands resting on her shoulder.

"About that." Amelia looked down at her hands. "You wouldn't still want to marry me, would you?"

Nick's heart actually skipped a beat. She couldn't be serious. After everything they'd been through the last few weeks. How could she ask that, like she didn't know the answer? Of course he did. More than anything. More than ever. The thought of her sailing away out of his life had driven him mad with the need to find a way to make her want to be his wife.

Still, she'd been so adamant about not marrying. What could possibly have changed?

"I could probably drum up some enthusiasm for it," he joked. "Are you certain you want to?"

"I think it's the best way to be rid of Embry once and for all."

Ouch. Not exactly the romantic declaration he'd been hoping for. Still, she needed him. What did it matter why, as long as they were…no. No. He wouldn't do that to himself. "I can't marry you, Mia."

Amelia stilled. "What?"

"I'm sorry. I'll help you—we'll run away. Somewhere far where Embry won't be able to find you. But I won't marry you as a contingency plan. I'm more than that." He was more than that, no matter what his parents or the rest of the world thought, and his life was his own.

She frowned. "Nick. We love each other."

Nicholas took her hands. "I know you don't think I'm not worthy of it. But I also know you don't want this. It's all right. We'll find another way."

She yanked her hands away from his, taking the lid off the box and riffling through it like a mad woman.

He saw the little book of sonnets he'd given her and one of his old handkerchiefs. "Amelia, what—"

"Shh!" She pulled out another small book and flipped rapidly through the pages. "September seventeenth, year of our Lord eighteen hundred and thirty-two. Dear Diary, Nicholas has been gone for a fortnight and I'm not sure I can take it. Every time I walk past our tree I burst into tears. I miss him so much."

He would have been away at Eton when she wrote that. "I'm not questioning your feelings for me."

She flipped forward, interrupting him. "February second, year of our Lord eighteen hundred and thirty-six. Dear Diary, Why am I so selfish? I shouldn't want Nicholas for myself. If he could marry one of us—which he can't—it should be Julia, but I can't stop imagining it. I think of him always."

Nicholas couldn't breathe. She'd written that about him when she was fourteen? She had felt that way about him then?

More furious page flipping. "June twentieth, year of our Lord eighteen hundred and thirty-six. Dear Diary, I hate the Wakefield's new dairy maid. She seems quite boring, and Nicholas pays her far more attention than she deserves. I also hate Nicholas. He is stupid."

He couldn't help it—he laughed. All this trouble over a ridiculous comment about a dairy maid's eyes.

"I have loved you for a very long time," Amelia told him. "But first I didn't think you wanted me, and then—I can't lose Julia, Nick. I can't have a marriage that takes me away from her. You know how important we are to each other. But I do *want* to marry you. Since long before I ever heard Lord Montrose's name."

For a moment, Nick didn't say anything. He just wanted to sit in the feeling for a moment. She loved him—possibly as long as he'd loved her. She wanted to marry him.

They were going to be married. Imminently, if they could manage it. The corners of his mouth crept up on their own, impossible to repress.

"I would never dream of trying to separate you from Julia." He reached for her hand, running his thumb across the lines of her palm. "So since I don't have a special license to marry you here, I guess we should go to Scotland."

Amelia grinned, nodding. "The first train leaves at nine in the morning."

He couldn't help himself. He kissed her. Soon, he'd be able to do it as often as he liked. Amelia was going to be his wife.

"The thing is," she said, kissing him back between words. "We can't stay here. Embry knows about us and once they realize I'm gone it's the first place they'll look."

Right. They had to keep her out of Montrose's clutches until they could get on the train.

"Jasper's isn't safe, either. That will be the second place

he'll look. And I don't know who else I could call on."

Nicholas had a sudden bolt of inspiration. If he was right, it was guaranteed to keep Amelia safe. If he was wrong, they'd throw him in the tower for sure. "I have an idea."

"Are you going to share it?"

"I think you'd rather I didn't."

✦ ⬥❈⬥ ✦

Amelia looked up at the towering facade. "Who lives here?"

"Jasper's grandparents."

She reached up into her hairline, but the familiar bump of his seal wasn't there. She'd given it back to Nicholas. This was exactly how Amelia imagined a duke's house would look. The Bishops had never been invited to visit a duke, so she had only her imagination to go on.

Now she was knocking on one's door in the middle of the night. She tried not to faint on the spot.

When the door opened, Nicholas did the talking. "I apologize for the late hour. Is Lady Ruby at home?"

The butler looked them over. "Please wait in the foyer."

He disappeared, leaving Amelia and Nicholas to stand silently in the enormous marble entryway. Everything about it was imposing.

"It's a miracle he didn't slam the door straight in our faces," Amelia whispered. The sound carried through the hall like she'd shouted.

"I've visited before. I think it weighed in my favor."

"Only time will tell," a young woman's crisp voice answered. The dressing-gown clad body followed it, coming into view as she descended the sweeping staircase. "Since we previously established that you have manners, I assume there is an emergency of some kind."

"There is," Nicholas answered.

There was a long pause. When she spoke again, there was an undertone of fear in her voice. "Is my brother all right?"

"Yes," Nicholas rushed to assure her. "Jasper is fine. I sent a message to his club. He's on his way here right now."

Her entire demeanor relaxed. Amelia sympathized. Fear for one's sibling was a crippling thing. "Well, then. Come and sit down. I'm sure we'll hear him when he gets here."

Jasper's sister ushered them into a parlor where a warm fire was lit. She offered them both port, which they accepted. "Am I correct in presuming you are Amelia Bishop?"

Amelia jumped. How would the granddaughter of a duke know her name? "I am."

"I am Lady Ruby De Vere. Am I also correct in presuming you have forgiven Nicholas for his egregious male presumption?"

It surprised a laugh out of Amelia. "I'm afraid you'll have to be more specific."

Lady Ruby smirked. "When I first met Nicholas, he couldn't fathom why a woman would ever wish to remain unmarried."

"Could he not?" Amelia cast a speculative look at Nicholas.

Nick held his hands up. "I have since been suitably educated."

There was a commotion in the foyer, followed by the swift arrival of Jasper. He immediately made himself at home, crowding his sister on the settee. "I was right, wasn't I? Montrose tried to kidnap Amelia. Bloody hell."

"How did you know?"

"Jasper has been spying on you." Nicholas smirked. "Feel free to tell him how you feel about that at length."

"I would rather find out what we're doing here," Amelia answered.

"Begging refuge," Jasper explained. "Your fiancé might have the gall to come looking for you with Nicholas's family or my townhouse, but even if he thinks to look here he wouldn't dare."

"I couldn't possibly stay the night."

"Of course you can," Jasper scoffed. "It's not like we don't have the room."

"Has it occurred to you that our grandparents may not want to get mixed up in whatever nonsense you're part of this time?" Lady Ruby asked.

"Amelia's fiancé held her hostage in her own home and planned to put her on a ship to Canada where he would force her to marry him at sea," Jasper announced with relish.

Lady Ruby's nose twitched. She reached for the cord, giving orders when a servant arrived. "Have a room made up for Lady Amelia, please. She will be staying with us this evening."

Jasper kissed his sister on the cheek. "You have a kind heart, dear sister."

She rolled her eyes. "What about you two? Are you staying as well?"

"If it's not too much trouble," Nicholas answered.

"We can't," Jasper said at the same time. "Nicholas and I have to throw off the scent, as it were."

"What?" Nicholas asked.

"Unless you want Lord Montrose chasing us all the way to Scotland, you and I have to stay out all night being highly visible and appearing suitably desolate."

Amelia hadn't thought of that. He might not be able to find her, but it wouldn't take much for Montrose to realize where she was headed. Fear shivered down her spine. She clutched Nick's hand. "He's right."

"I don't want to leave you."

"I'll be fine," Amelia promised him. "Like you said, even if he thought I was here, he'd never dare to demand they give me back."

"Though he is welcome to try," Lady Rose said with menace.

"Indeed. Julia was right. If he's willing to assault the residence of a duke, it's high time somebody shot him." She would take extremely un-Christian-like relish in putting a bullet somewhere non-vital on Embry's person.

Nicholas lifted her hands to his lips and kissed them. "You're sure?"

"I'm sure. We'll rest easier on the trip north knowing he's not following us."

"All right."

Jasper was grinning ear to ear. "We're going to have so much fun. It will be like Paris all over again. And you're getting married. It'll be your stag party!"

"I thought I was supposed to be desolate."

"Just be yourself. No one will be able to tell the difference."

Amelia fought the urge to chase after them when they disappeared into the hall. It was just one night. Tomorrow they would all board the train together and then she and Nicholas would be married. Everything would be perfectly fine.

Chapter Nineteen

The train whistle blew, marking their departure in three minutes. Amelia was wearing a dress she'd borrowed from Lady Ruby after sleeping in the grandest house she'd ever encountered. Lady Ruby sat next to her, having volunteered to serve as their second witness. Nicholas and Jasper were nowhere to be seen.

"Perhaps we should disembark. We can always take a later train when they get here."

"They'll be here," Amelia promised. There was no sweat on her palms. No lurching of her heart. He was going to make it.

Lady Ruby patted her hand. "I admire your faith, but reliability isn't one of my brother's more prevalent charms."

"He's never let me down and neither has Nicholas."

Their first-class compartment descended into uncomfortable silence. The whistle sounded again. One minute.

Where was he?

"Honestly, Amelia, I'm all for getting out of town, especially with my Atherton troubles, but perhaps we should wait on the platform, just in case."

"They'll make it. They promised they would."

The train wheels chugged into motion.

"Too late now," Ruby muttered, pulling a book from her reticle.

Amelia's heart fell. Something must have happened. Oh God. What if they'd been hurt? What if they had a run-in with Embry and—

The door to their compartment lurched open. The view of the hall was blocked by a pair of unfairly wide shoulders, and the compartment filled with the smell of coffee and citrus. Amelia's vision blurred with relieved tears. He'd made it. Nothing awful had happened to him. He was all right and they were on their way to be married and she would spend the rest of her life blissfully married to her best friend.

"Sorry we're late," Nicholas said, breathing heavily. "Montrose was watching us like a hawk. We had to make a dash for it at the last minute so he wouldn't suspect."

"Move in or move over, Wakefield. It's undignified for me to be loitering out here in the hallway."

Nicholas rolled his eyes, taking the seat next to Amelia. "Are you crying?"

She shook her head. It was all right now—he was here. Embry hadn't stopped him. The universe hadn't played any cruel jokes during the night. Amelia wiped at her eyes. "Just something in my eye."

He squeezed her hand as Jasper slid in, taking the seat next to Lady Ruby. She put her book down and stared at him in disgust. "You smell abhorrent."

"I smell like I had an excellent time," Jasper countered. "Not to mention a great deal of adventure."

"You were right," Nicholas told Amelia. "Montrose showed up at Jasper's and Philip's, with a constable and everything."

"No!" Amelia gasped.

Nick nodded. "Turned both houses upside down. Philip is livid. I think it's safe to say he's firmly on your side now."

"Well that's something." Embry had finally done her a favor—accidentally.

"They turned your house over?" Lady Ruby asked her brother.

"Indeed, they did."

"I'm sure Grandmother will have a field day with that. Storming the heir's house like he's a common criminal."

"For once, I welcome her righteous indignation."

They all watched out the windows as the train left London behind. No men in uniforms chased after it. There was no unexpected stop on the edge of the city, just a smooth beginning to a long journey north. They all breathed a sigh of relief.

Except Jasper. "God, I'm starving. Ruby, did you bring anything to eat?"

"I am not dining anywhere near this odor you are currently producing."

"Then let's walk the train and eat. We can trail it behind us." Jasper's unsubtle glance at Nick and Amelia silenced her objection.

"Fine," Lady Ruby said. "But you're carrying the hamper."

Nicholas watched the door slide closed, blocking out his view of the De Vere siblings. As soon as they were gone, he leaned over and pressed his forehead to Amelia's. The entire night while he'd been pretending to carouse with Jasper, he'd been panicking inside. Logically, he knew Montrose wouldn't assault the house of a duke, but illogically Nick kept imagining Montrose dragging Amelia out by her hair, never to be heard from again. It made it extremely easy to appear desolate.

"You made it," she whispered.

"I would have had to be dead to miss this train."

Amelia shivered. "I thought maybe you were, when the engine started moving without you."

He hated that he'd made her worry. He covered her hands with his. "Even then, I'd have tried to get here."

She nodded, grinning. "I know."

Nicholas kissed the tip of her nose. Nothing could have kept him from her—nothing. "I have something for you." He pulled out the packet of letters he'd written her while he was away on the continent.

Amelia's smile lit up the compartment. "Where did you get those?"

"I went back for them. It's not all of them. I'll get the rest later, but they belong to you and I wanted you to have at least some of them."

"You didn't need to do that."

"I did. They've been delayed far too long." He handed them over. "Besides, it's a long way to Gretna Green. I thought you might need something to entertain you."

She unsealed the top one of the stack. "Entertaining, are they?"

"Some of them."

He watched her while she read. The flush in her cheeks. The widening of her smile. At one point, she lifted her hand to her mouth and her eyes teared up. It was so much better than sending them. He got to see the effect his words had on her.

When she opened one a third of the way down the stack, Nicholas recognized it and snatched it back. "Not that one."

"Why not?" She leaned over him, trying to grab it back.

"I was…erm…missing you quite a lot, that day."

Her frown was adorable. "Surely you missed me in all

of them."

"Yes, but in that one I was a bit more—" Nicholas coughed. "Graphic. About the *way* I missed you."

Amelia's eyes went wide as saucers. In a quicker move than he'd ever seen her make, she snatched the letter from his hand and scrambled to the far side of the bench.

"Don't—" It was no use. Her mouth was already forming into an *o* of shock. Then it softened, her lower lip getting trapped between her teeth.

He cleared his throat. "I told you."

"Nicholas Wakefield," Amelia whispered. She returned to his side, sliding next to him until there was no space between them. Her fingertips brushed across the rough weave of his trousers. "Read it to me."

Someone could walk in on them. The porter could come. Ruby and Jasper could come back at any moment.

Mia's lips found the sensitive space beneath his ear. She grabbed his hand, sliding it under her skirts. "Read it to me."

Bloody hell. He took the page from her, clearing his throat. "Today I saw a tree that looked like ours. I imagined pressing you against it and hauling your skirts up until you were bare in front of me and begging me to touch you."

She spread her legs, pushing fabric out of the way without hesitation. He brushed her center, finding her already damp. Amelia's hand closed over his arousal, squeezing.

"Amelia," he groaned.

"Touch me. Now."

She was everything he ever wanted. The reality of her was so much better than the fantasy. Nick poised his fingers at her entrance, testing her. Her approval came in the form of a moan.

"Ahem," Jasper's voice came from the other side of the door.

They both froze.

"While I have no difficulty sharing the compartment with you while you carry on like that," Jasper announced, "it is unlikely my sister will be similarly open-minded."

The mirror Ruby had managed to procure reflected Amelia's image back at her. She didn't look like herself. She looked so much more elegant. She looked like a woman with confidence and backbone. A woman who had taken control of her life.

"You're a miracle worker," she told the maid Lady Ruby had brought along for both of them.

"Hardly, miss. All I did was pin your hair."

They'd arrived in Gretna well after dark, having been delayed when the train let them off in Manchester to try to locate her father. If he had still been in Manchester, they'd been unable to find him. Amelia hoped he'd gone home. She'd also hoped to find some time alone with Nicholas to finish what they'd started on the train, but they had all been so tired when they finally stopped traveling. She'd gone straight to bed and not woken up until breakfast was brought in on a tray and it was time to get ready.

Now here she was, in a dress borrowed from Ruby and the slippers Julia had sent her with, looking like a princess in ivory silk and pearls. The maid had somehow managed to arrange her hair in a way that made her neck look longer and her cheekbones higher. A tear slipped down Amelia's cheek.

Lady Ruby's concerned face appeared over her shoulder. "What's wrong, Amelia?"

"I wish my sister was here. And my parents." Even her mother, though Amelia wouldn't be ready to forgive Lady Bishop for a long while. Still, it was strange to be doing something so important without her family.

Ruby reached down, squeezing her gloved fingers. "It's hard. Sometimes I think that's half of why I haven't accepted anyone. My parents will never be able to give me away."

Amelia squeezed back. She couldn't imagine losing both of her parents. "This is going to sound odd, but will you remember everything and write it down? My sister will want to know all the details and I never explain well enough for her."

"Your sister sounds a bit like my brother," Ruby teased. "And yes, I will."

Amelia nodded. "I think I'm ready, then." She gave herself one more look in the mirror and took a deep breath. Nicholas was waiting for her.

February was dismal, especially this far north, but the forge fire in the blacksmith's shop made the air comfortably warm. Nicholas stood beside the anvil with Jasper, waiting for Amelia to appear. He should have been nervous, but instead he was strangely calm. He'd been waiting for Amelia his whole life. Waiting for her notice him. To love him back. Now he knew that she'd loved him the entire time, and it made him feel like he could fly. This was the last time they would ever be apart. This wait was easy.

On him, at least. Jasper was handling it with significantly less grace.

"What is taking so damned long?" Jasper demanded, pacing. "Did they go all the way back to London to get ready?"

"Be patient."

"I can't. It's not in my nature. How can you be? Aren't you

eager to get married?"

"Yes." More than he could ever explain, but he was also eager to savor this moment. He didn't want to be pacing in a frenzy when Amelia walked through the door and took the last, final steps to becoming his wife. When she'd announce to the world and God that she wanted him as much as he wanted her.

"Well, you don't show it."

"Even so."

There was a commotion outside. Nicholas heard Lady Ruby say, "You look radiant."

And then Amelia was there, and she was all he could see. Sound died out. Temperature faded away. Even the crackling fire disappeared.

She was a vision in ivory. Everything about her etched itself in his memory and Nicholas knew he would remember her like this for the rest of their lives—glowing from within, holding a bouquet of purple heather, walking toward him like the answer to every prayer he'd ever made.

She ducked her head at his attention, but looked back up through her lashes. There was a wicked tilt to her smile that made Nicholas's heartbeat speed up. What had he done to deserve this woman? She came to stand beside him, and he took her hand.

The blacksmith stood in front of them. "Are ye ready?"

"We are," Nicholas said.

Amelia nodded.

"Then say the words," the blacksmith instructed.

Nicholas turned to Amelia. He held both her hands. "I, Nicholas Clarence Wakefield, take you, Amelia Marie Bishop, as my wife, in the name of the Father, and of the Son, and of the Holy Ghost."

She had tears in her eyes and a smile like the rising sun

when he was finished.

Then it was her turn. She took a deep breath. Nicholas squeezed her palms.

"I, Amelia Marie Bishop, take you, Nicholas Clarence Wakefield, as my husband, in the name of the Father, and of the Son, and of the Holy Ghost."

"Under the ancient rights and laws of Scotland yer now man and wife," the blacksmith bellowed.

With the clang of the anvil, Nicholas's entire life clicked into place. He'd been accepted to Lincoln's Inn. Amelia was his wife. Neither his parents or Montrose could separate them now. He was the luckiest man on earth.

Next to him, Amelia was being smothered in embraces.

"Kindly give me my wife back, you brigand." Nicholas extricated his bride from Jasper's grasp. He pulled her close, leaning down until their noses touched.

"You're my husband." She was grinning like a lunatic.

"You're my wife." God, it felt good to say.

Amelia pulled his head down. He kissed her with everything he had—every last bit of love he planned to shower her with for the rest of their lives. When he finished, they were both flushed and breathless.

"Well," Lady Ruby said, breaking the silence. "I think Jasper and I should be going."

"Going? We have to celebrate!" Jasper took a half step toward the inn's taproom.

"We have to get out of their way so they can enjoy the benefits of marriage. I wrote to Clementina and she was delighted at the idea of having us stay with her at Drumond Castle."

Jasper stared flatly at his sister. "After that mad dash from London, you expect me to spend another hundred-some odd miles in a carriage?"

"Not only do I expect." Ruby stared down her nose back

at him. "I insist."

The ensuing De Vere staring contest heated the room by another ten degrees.

"Fine," Jasper declared, relenting. "But I'm going to be terrible company."

"I expect nothing less." Lady Ruby kissed Amelia's cheeks, wishing her well. "If you need us, we'll be in Crieff."

"Thank you. For everything," Amelia said, hugging her in return.

They all walked back to the Inn, where Lady Ruby forced a grumbling Jasper into the already hitched carriage. They said their good-byes and it pulled away in a puff of road dust. Suddenly Nicholas and Amelia were alone. Married. Far away from anyone and anything that had any claim on them.

Nicholas put his lips next to Amelia's ear. "I'll race you upstairs."

Chapter Twenty

The dash up to the room left Amelia breathless and laughing. Nick was right behind her the whole way, taunting her with words and playful smacks to her backside. He caught her just inside the door, closing it with their bodies as he pressed her against the wood. Amelia was slick with wanting. From the moment he'd whispered in her ear, her body had lit up with sensation. Playfulness gave way to need as their lips joined.

They devoured each other, tugging at the offending clothing that kept their skin apart. Amelia shoved her skirts up, wrapping her legs around Nicholas's waist as he lifted her against the door. She moaned against his lips as his fingers finally brushed against her center.

"Now," she demanded.

Nicholas was taking deep, measuring breaths. "We should—"

"Now." She pulled his hair, grinding her hips against him.

Nick swore, and his hands left her to release the buttons of his trousers.

Amelia reached down, taking him in hand, guiding him

into her. Nicholas swore again, this time with his mouth pressed against the curve of her neck. Amelia moaned as he filled her. The sweet ache of it erased everything from her mind but the feel of him. She flexed her hips in, trying to take in as much of him as she could.

"God, Mia, you feel—" He lost his words as she gripped his shoulders and levered her hips away and back down again.

She bucked again. And again. He picked up her pace, holding her hips still so he could drive into her with powerful bursts that rattled the door. It wasn't enough. She needed more.

"Faster, Nick. Please," she begged.

His thrusts took a frenzied pace. Amelia clung to him, crying out her satisfaction. The ache built to impossible heights as their bodies collided, Nick's length pressing against the sensitive places inside her over and over.

Hands, thighs—her entire body tightened as sensation took over, sending her up and over the edge. She heard his shout as she came apart, the shuddering climax of his body sending hers into a second wave of ecstasy. It was almost too much to bear. Terrifying and wonderful, she relinquished all pretense of control and let it have her.

When she came back to herself, breathing hard with Nicholas's head resting on her shoulder, she felt as if she'd been unmade. "That was…"

"You're amazing," Nick said, shaking his head. "I've never…"

They were both at a loss for words.

Nick let her down, kissing her lips and forehead as her feet touched the ground again. Her knees buckled, and he caught her. She didn't protest as he picked her up and carried her to the bed. He helped her out of her clothes, and after, she watched with a surreal feeling as started removing his own.

"What?" he asked.

Amelia smiled. "I get to watch you undress whenever I want."

Nick's smile was lopsided. "You like watching me undress?"

She nodded.

He had a slight blush on his cheeks as he turned toward her. His jacket fell to the floor. He reached for the buttons of his shirt. Amelia turned on her side for a better view. As each new section of his chest was exposed, she felt a stirring response in her body. It wasn't the urgent need she'd felt up against the door, but it was no less compelling. Her fingertips traced sensual circles against her hip.

Nicholas was on the last button, his eyes locked on her hand.

Amelia let it trail down across her stomach. "Do you like watching me?"

He swallowed. "Very much."

"Then I suggest," she said, stilling the motion. "You keep removing your clothes."

Nick picked up his foot, awkwardly pulling off one of his boots. He lifted an eyebrow at her in challenge.

Amelia inched her fingers closer to the juncture of her thighs. "Other boot."

It dropped to the floor. He finished unbuttoning his shirt and let it fall on top of his jacket. She rolled onto her back, head turned on the pillow to take full advantage of the view. Her fingers dipped between her legs as he pushed his trousers free of his hips. Nicholas's manhood responded, thickening. He placed his knee on the bed.

Amelia bit her lower lip, stroking herself.

"Show me," Nick said. Amelia let her legs fall wide.

She hid nothing from him, and it was the most sensual thing he'd ever witnessed. Seeing her touch herself, her attention focused solely on him as she shifted and moaned—it was almost better than being inside her. Almost.

Moving the rest of the way onto the bed, Nick positioned himself between her spread legs. He flattened out, pressing a kiss to the inside of her thigh. Amelia watched him through lowered lids, her fingers moving faster. Nick scraped his teeth across her silky-smooth skin. She whimpered.

"So beautiful." He placed a kiss right against her sex.

Her fingers froze.

Nick had a few surprises left for her. He ran his tongue the length of her center, ending in a circling swirl over the bead of pleasure she'd been stroking.

It shocked a surprised whimper out of her.

"If you don't like it, I'll stop," he teased.

Amelia's hands tangled in his hair, pushing him back down. She was so demanding, and it drove him wild. His shy Amelia, digging her heels into his back and lifting herself to his mouth. He molded his hands over her hip bones, holding her in place while he tortured her with his tongue. Surrounded by her scent, overwhelmed by the taste of her. Nick hoped to spend an eternity with his face buried between her thighs.

His wife had different plans.

She was pulling at his hair, urging him up. "I need you."

"Right now?" He would never tire of teasing her.

Her heel thudded into his side. Nick chuckled as he crawled up her body. He took his time, stopping to lavish kisses on every inch of skin as he passed.

"Hurry," she demanded.

He pressed his lips to the space between her breasts. "No more hurrying. We have our whole lives."

Amelia actually growled at him.

He dropped a kiss on her lips. "You'll like it, I promise."

She opened her mouth to argue. Nick entered her in a smooth, single thrust. Her objection turned to a moan.

"Yes?"

"Yes," she said in a breathy sigh.

Nick withdrew, ever so slowly. She shifted her hips, bringing him back in. His own jerked in response. For a moment, they took up the frenzied pace from earlier, but Nick regained control, pulling all the way out. If he wanted to get his way, he was going to have to make a change.

Under protest, Nick flipped her on her side. He shifted behind her, pressing against the full curves of her backside.

"What are you—"

Pulling her leg up over his, he entered her again, this time from behind. He took a fistful of her hair, stretching her body out like a bowstring. His lips found the spot by her ear. "How do you want it, Mia? What do you like?"

He felt her shudder around him. From the hand in her hair or his growling tone, Nick didn't know. He intended to find out though.

Thrusting slow and deep, he spoke to her in low tones. "Tell me what you feel. Does it feel good?"

Another shudder gasp confirmed that it did. He slid his free hand around, burying his fingers in her slick curls. "Do you know what it does to me to feel how wet you are for me?"

She bowed her back even farther, resting her head against his shoulder.

Nick picked up his pace. He rocked into her with deliberate strokes, feeling her tighten around him in response. The symphony of sounds coming from Amelia almost pushed him past the point of no return right then. He needed her to come for him, needed her to grip him impossibly tight while she exploded in ecstasy.

Her cries started the telltale crescendo that Nick craved.

"Do you love me, Mia?"

"Yes. Oh, yes. I love you, Nick."

When she said his name like that, in the throes of passion, it sent a jolt of pleasure straight to his cock. "Will you come for me?"

And just like that, she fell apart around him. Nick's hips jerked in response, burying himself deep with his own release.

Amelia woke to a strawberry being placed against her lips. She kept her eyes closed, accepting the offering with a smile. A piece of cheese followed it. "Mmm. So this is what it means to have a husband."

"I'm glad you're finding matrimony to your liking."

The bed dipped beneath Nick's weight. She shifted over to make room for him. Another strawberry found its way to her lips. "Mm-hmm. I think we should live here."

"In Scotland?"

Amelia shook her head. "Here. In this inn. In this bed. Do you think they'll let us stay forever?"

Nick stretched out, putting his arms behind his head. "We can certainly ask. We might need to go back home, though, at least for a bit."

That sounded like an awful idea. Home was where Lord Montrose was, and her mother, and all the things Amelia didn't want to think about. She wanted to stay here and think about Nick's tongue between her legs. About his hand tangled in her hair while he thrust into her from behind. She reached for him, prepared to re-enact some of her favorite memories.

Her hand encountered woven cloth instead of Nick's skin. "Clothes? How could you?"

Nick's chuckle filled the room. "I doubt they would have given me any food if I'd gone down naked."

Fair point—the food was much appreciated—but he wasn't in the taproom any longer. "I think you should get naked again."

"I would like nothing more," Nick answered, kissing her shoulder. "But I suspect that would occupy us for quite some time and we have to catch the coach back to Manchester."

Amelia knew that, but she rubbed her hand over the length of him through his trousers anyway. He pulled a deep breath in through his nose, bicep flexing under the fabric of his shirt. "Surely we have a little time."

"A little, but—"

That was all she needed. Amelia moved to straddle his lap. As she did, the blankets fell away.

Nicholas's protest fell away with them. His hands came up to trace the curves of her breasts. "We have to go back eventually."

"But not yet." Amelia rocked her naked hips against his clothed ones.

"Not quite yet." Nick leaned forward, trapping her nipple between his teeth. He drew on it with his lips, spiking pleasure from her breast straight down to her sex.

Amelia gasped. "How did I get so lucky?"

Instead of answering, he did it again. Amelia writhed against him. Ripples of need rose up in her. Amelia would never tire of the way he made her feel. The way being near him made her want to do every wicked thing ever invented.

She reached between them, freeing his erection. She

stroked it in time with the pulling pressure on her nipple.

Nicholas lifted his head. "Mia. Sweet, incredible Mia. You'll be the death of me."

"Good." She lowered herself on his hardness with the same deliberate speed he'd tortured her with earlier. "Pull my hair, Nick."

His hands were there in an instant, taking a firm grip on her long curls. "Like this?"

"Yes." She rolled her hips, testing the feel of him from every angle. Finding one that made her mind go blank with pleasure, Amelia braced her hand on his chest and rocked against him, driving their bodies into a frenzy.

"God, Mia. I'm going to… I'm…" Nick grabbed her hips, trying to slow her pace.

She took them, pinning them behind his head. "My pace."

Nick groaned. She kissed him, needing to touch him every way she could. She rode him relentlessly, racing them both to a reckless finish. When Nick cried out, shuddering beneath her, she reached down between them and took herself the rest of the way.

He pushed her hair from her face and pulled her into a long kiss. "You're incredible."

"I feel incredible." She kissed him back. "You make me feel incredible."

"As a husband should."

Amelia grinned. "I'm glad you think so."

They stopped at Wakefield Manor first. It was the least likely to end well and he wanted a chance of them finishing the day on a happy note. Smithson frowned when he let them in, but he didn't try to outright refuse Amelia entry. Philip and Caroline came out of the drawing room to greet them.

"We wanted to be here to support you when you came back," Caroline said.

Philip looked significantly less charitable, but he nodded his agreement.

"Is Father…"

The slight shake of Philip's head stole his hopes. Today was not a good day, then. Well, they could break the news to his mother and worry about telling Lord Wakefield another time. Lady Wakefield was the true challenge, anyway.

"They're in the garden?"

Another nod.

Nicholas led Amelia outside where his parents were sitting in chairs, enjoying the scenery.

Lady Wakefield scowled when she saw Amelia.

He stiffened his spine. He'd known she wouldn't be gracious. "May I present Amelia Wakefield, my wife."

"So you've done it then." She didn't sound as venomous as he expected. Mostly she sounded tired.

"Amelia?" Lord Wakefield asked. "Like the neighbor girl. Plucky little thing."

His mother reached her hand out. "Arthur."

"I know you don't like her, Lavinia, but she's only a child, and I think she's good for Nicholas. She brings out his spirit. A Wakefield needs spirit. Someday, when he's a man, you'll see. That girl will be good for him."

Nicholas was shocked. Next to him, Amelia was equally spellbound.

"Did he just say that?" she whispered.

"Yes." It was a sentiment he wished Lord Wakefield had expressed years ago, but he supposed it was better late than never. Even if he wasn't in his right mind when he said it.

"Well," Lady Wakefield. "I suppose you'll be going now."

Nicholas nodded. "We will, but I'd like it if we were welcome to come back to visit."

Lady Wakefield's response was a noncommittal sniff. It hurt as much as his father's words had made him happy.

Amelia took his hand. "Come on. You can always try again later."

It was true. Nothing was set in stone, and he had Amelia. That was all he truly needed.

They were on their way out of the garden when his mother stopped them with a word.

"Easter."

Nicholas looked back.

"You shouldn't miss Easter. Caroline and Philip are bringing the boys."

It wasn't an open invitation, but it was a small triumph. "We'll be here."

Chapter Twenty-One

"Will they be home?" Nicholas asked as they crossed the field to the Bishop estate.

"They ought to be," she said. "They were only in London for my engagement nonsense."

Sure enough, the moment they stepped onto the drive, chaos broke loose.

Lord Bishop came running down the stairs with—of all people—Lord Montrose and a constable trailing behind him.

"Amelia!" her father exclaimed. "Are you all right? What the devil has been going on?"

Lord Montrose joined the fray. The imperious puffing out of his chest infuriated Amelia, but he couldn't make demands of her anymore. Let him posture all he wanted. "Arrest this man. He kidnapped my fiancée."

The constable moved toward Nicholas.

Amelia stepped between them. "Don't you dare lay a hand on my husband."

The entire driveway went silent, until Lady Bishop's shriek broke it.

"Husband?" Lady Bishop stormed down the driveway in a flurry of skirts.

"Yes, Mother," Amelia called out. She threw her arms wide, inviting any criticisms anyone wanted to throw her way. She was happy, and there was nothing anyone could do about it. "I've married Nicholas, so all your hopes and dreams are dashed."

Everyone started shouting at once. Julia made her way down the stairs and joined the fray, as did Mrs. Polk, Nora, and a few of the other household staff who had their fair share of opinions about Nicholas and Amelia's union — most of them favorable. Nicholas and Montrose started shouting at each other, with the constable keeping them separated with his outstretched hands.

Meanwhile, Lord Bishop pulled Amelia to the side. "Montrose and your mother said you'd been taken."

Amelia shook her head. The creases in his brow choked her up. He must have been so worried.

"Was it like Julia said? Did your mother lock you up?"

"Yes." She hated to tell him the truth, because of the way his face fell when she said it.

"I'm sorry," he said. "I should have done more when you told me."

"It's all right. Everything has turned out for the best."

"You're happy, then?" he asked.

"I truly am."

"Then so am I." Lord Bishop turned to the crowd in his driveway, bellowing for everyone to kindly shut the hell up. When it had been accomplished, he sent everyone back inside.

Everyone except for Montrose.

"It appears you attempted to abscond with my daughter," Lord Bishop accused.

"For her own good," Montrose argued. He looked weak

to her now, grasping at justifications for his behavior.

"Well, for your own good, kindly remove yourself from my property and see that you don't find your way back."

"You'll be receiving my breech of promise suit post haste," Embry promised.

"When you do," Nicholas interjected, "please let me know. Lord Melton, Viscount Bellamy, and the Duke of Albemarle would all like to contribute statements regarding Lord Montrose's reprehensible behavior and potentially unstable mental state."

Amelia loved him more than ever just then. Friends. She—and by extension, her family—had friends. Powerful ones. They would not be bullied by the likes of Embry.

The front door opened again, and Julia stepped out holding the pink sapphire necklace Embry had given Amelia.

"Lord Montrose. Before you go." She flung it at his chest. "I believe that belongs to you. Next time, find a woman more suited to it."

Her ex-fiancé left in an indignant huff and his constable followed him with a much more dignified apology.

That left only herself, Nicholas, Julia, and Lord Bishop in the drive.

Her father nodded. "All right. Now that's settled, I'd like to speak with Lady Bishop and Amelia in private, if you don't mind me stealing my daughter back for a moment, Wakefield."

"Amelia?" Nick looked to her, asking what she wanted.

How could she ever have doubted Nicholas would make a perfect husband for her? She kissed his cheek and nodded her assent.

"Take all the time you need," Julia said. "Nicholas and I have a great deal to catch up on."

"She looked like an angel. Her hair was up and she had this crooked little smile." Nick sat on the parlor settee, recounting his wedding to Julia. He had always taken criticism for his romantic notions, especially from the eldest Bishop daughter, but for once they were not at odds. She wanted to hear every sappy, sentimental detail as much as Nicholas was bursting to share them with someone.

"Up how?"

"Like a loose bouquet of flowers collected at her neck."

Julia sighed, flinging herself across the arm of the settee in dramatic bliss. "Was she carrying flowers?"

"Heather and thistle."

Her mouth pursed in distaste. Nicholas lobbed an embroidered pillow at her. "We were making do with what we had, and it actually looked quite lovely with the ivory."

"I suppose. Purples do suit her," Julia conceded.

"How kind of you to say so," Amelia interrupted from the doorway.

His wife looked decidedly un-distressed—calm, even. Nick gave an internal sigh of relief. He knew how much it meant for her to be in accord with her family.

"Don't let it go to your head."

"Never." Amelia turned to him with a glittering smile. "Papa would like to speak to you."

"Am I to be drawn and quartered?" Nick was only half joking. Amelia might be in accord with her parents, but Nicholas was the man who had spirited her off to the border without any word and married her without Lord Bishop's blessing.

"I think he'd like to offer you thanks and congratulations,

and since you are men, it obviously must be done over whiskey."

"Obviously," Julia echoed.

Well, that was the sort of speaking to Nicholas could get behind. He stood up. "You're all right?"

"Better than." Amelia stretched up to kiss his cheek.

Nicholas left the room with a grin on his face. He could definitely get used to being kissed by her in public.

The door to the study was open, so Nicholas let himself in. He'd only ever been in this room once, when he and the girls had snuck in to go through the desk drawers as part of an imaginary treasure hunt. It was an altogether different feeling entering it now as Amelia's husband, although he still had the lingering fear that he was going to be shouted at and told he wasn't allowed.

Instead Lord Bishop greeted him with three fingers of amber whiskey, exactly as his daughters had predicted.

"Lord Bishop."

"Nicholas. I understand congratulations are in order."

"I'm glad you feel that way," Nicholas said, clinking glasses with his father-in-law.

"Why wouldn't I? I've always thought of you as part of the family."

He'd known that, but it warmed him to have it said under these circumstances. "I know I've caused you trouble, with the lawsuit and Montrose."

Lord Bishop waved the thought away like so much dust in the air. "My daughters are happy. That means I am happy."

Nicholas smiled. It seemed he was forever smiling now. When he and Amelia had children of their own, he intended to adopt the same philosophy.

"Well, enough about the past," the older man said. "Let's talk about the future."

Dread welled up in Nicholas. This was the part where he had to admit to a man he respected that he'd married his daughter with the barest ability to provide for her.

"Mia tells me you're planning to become a barrister?"

"I am. It will take some time, but my brother has hopes of a seat in Commons for me."

Lord Bishop nodded in agreement. "I bought an estate near ours for Amelia and Montrose so the girls could still see each other. It was supposed to be a wedding gift. That will obviously go to you instead."

An estate? Nick wasn't sure he'd heard right.

"And Amelia said she means to stay in London with you while you study, so I'm sure we can find something for you close to your Inn that will please her."

"Sir, that's…"

"Then, of course, there's her bride settlement. With no sons, Amelia and Julia are each entitled to half of everything I have."

"Sir." Nicholas held up a hand. He had to slow the barrage of gifts long enough to think straight. "That's extremely generous. Too generous."

"Wakefield." Lord Bishop stared at him across the table and for the first time, Nick saw a hint of the steel that had served the man so well in business. "When my daughter is happy, I am happy."

"But—"

"If I cannot make my daughters happy, what is the point of it all?"

Apparently, there were more than a few philosophies to be gained from Lord Bishop.

Amelia was in her room—maybe for the last time. Lady Bishop was being sent to stay in a cottage they owned in Wales, far away from anything even closely resembling society. In time, Amelia hoped her parents would reconcile, but her father was not currently in the mood to be forgiving. The staff would pack up Amelia's belongings and send them to the new house once they'd seen Lady Bishop on her way, but for now Amelia was deciding what she would need in the short-term. Papa had suggested they stay with him and Julia, but Amelia had declined. If she'd learned anything over the last few days, it was that she was not a quiet lover. She didn't feel compelled to share that revelation with her father, nor did she intend to keep her hands off Nick for a moment longer than necessary.

"If you could see your face right now." Julia lounged on Amelia's bed, nosy as ever.

Amelia was going to miss that most of all. "I don't need to, thank you."

"I take it Nick is riddling you with tingly feelings."

Her face flamed pink. "He is."

"Don't be embarrassed. I'm glad. One of us ought to be having tingles."

"You'll have them, too, someday soon."

Julia rolled her eyes.

"You will," Amelia insisted. "I intend to see to it."

"Rubbish. You're going to be quite busy discovering what it's like to be a wife. You won't have time to try to achieve impossible miracles."

"Nicholas is shaping up to be a very accommodating husband. I expect I'll have plenty of time."

"I hope so." Julia's tone turned serious. "I'm still not ready to lose you, Mia."

Amelia brought the case she was sorting through with

her when she joined Julia on the bed. "You're not losing me."

"I am a little."

"Just a little, though. Did Papa tell you he gave us an estate?"

"Of course," Julia scoffed. "Who do you think picked it out?"

"I suppose you already have a room for yourself."

"My summer palace. It's already been decorated."

Amelia laughed, falling back on the pillows. "I should have known. So much for having a home of my own."

"Silly Mia. Thinking a measly marriage could set you free of me." Julia fell back with her.

Amelia wrapped her arms around her sister. "Silly me."

Nicholas arrived in the doorway and gasped. "I'm being replaced already."

"I was here first," Julia announced imperiously.

"As if I could forget." Nicholas flopped down next to Amelia.

"Do you remember these?" Amelia asked, lifting a handful of marbles out of the case.

"Of course I do."

"I knew he was in love with you the moment he gave you those," Julia said. "They were his favorite thing in all the world."

"Not quite." The look he gave Amelia was not subtle.

Julia snorted. "And I knew you were in love with him when you kept those grubby things."

Amelia blushed. "They're delightful!"

"They're not. They're ridiculous. You're both ridiculous." Julia sighed. "Someone say something nice about me so I don't suffer a crisis of confidence in the face of all this newlywed bliss."

It was exactly like when they were children, sprawled

out, talking about their dreams in the hayloft. Amelia felt overwhelmingly blessed. She turned to her sister. "We did it, Jules. I'm so happy."

Next to her, Nick grumbled. "I don't suppose I get credit for any of that."

Amelia turned back to him, threading her fingers through his. "Maybe just a little."

Acknowledgments

Thank you to my agent Rachel Brooks for snatching me out of the crowd and believing in me. Thank you to my editor Kate Brauning for making this book so much better than when I handed it to her. Thank you to Entangled Publishing for believing this story ought to be told.

Thank you to my brother, Mark, who supported me both morally and financially when I quit my self-sustaining job to pursue a career without pants. Thank you to the rest of my family for reading every book with enthusiasm and telling me they're good (and even meaning it). Thank you to Lindsay, for doing more things than I could possibly list on this page.

Thank you to the members of #RWCHAT for injecting me with sanity and a much needed laugh every Sunday afternoon. Thank you to Chelsea, Robin, and Alexis for being the best writing partners I could ever ask for.

Thank you to Sebastian, Henry, Jason, and both Jameses. You fed me. You encouraged me. And you watched me pace around with mad scientist hair without any discernible judgment.

Oh, and thank you to the lemur.